The Other Side Of The Mirror

By

Lex H Jones

Lex H. Jones

A HellBound Books Publishing LLC Book
Houston TX

A HellBound Books LLC
Publication
Copyright © 2019 by HellBound Books Publishing LLC
All Rights Reserved

Cover and art design
By Francois Vaillancourt
HellBound Books Publishing LLC

www.hellboundbookspublishing.com

Printed in the United States of America

Also by Lex H Jones

"Nick and Abe"
Full length novel
"At Peace Now"
Published as part of "The Horror Collection – Gold Edition"
"Ain't Nothing Free"
Published as part of "Dark Places Evil Faces 2"
"Foundations
Published as part of "Made in Britain"
"For One Night Only"
Published as part of "Carnival of Horror"
"AC43R0N"
Published as part of "Black Room Manuscripts Volume 3"
"Bone and Bred"
Published as part of "VS"
"Red Frost"
Published as part of "Under The Weather"
"Sonneshill"
Published as part of "Collected Easter Horror Shorts"
"Kayla"
Published as part of "Sparks"
"Yet To Come"
Published as part of "12 Days of Christmas 2016"
"A Partridge in a Pear Tree"
Published as part of "12 Days of Christmas 2017"
"Uncommon Hunger"
Published as part of "Full Moon Slaughter 2"
"Everything and Nothing"
Published as part of "Merchants of Misery"
"The Life and Times of the Moustache Beetle"
Published in "Cobweb Galaxy" comic book.

The Other Side Of The Mirror

Chapter One;
The Styx.

"She's beautiful," Detective Trent remarked as he stared down at the pale form of the young woman before him. Her blonde hair and dark clothes were soaked with dirty water, but her skin was still soft and white, her lips a pale blue giving her an even more ethereal quality. They were pouting slightly with the way the blood vessels had been swollen by the icy water.

"They always are," Detective Duggan sighed, watching Trent take one final drag on his cigarette before dropping it into the depths of the river before him. He was right, of course. They always looked beautiful when they were dead, because they weren't really people anymore. You didn't know them, know their sins, their crimes, their thoughts. The ice-cold waters of the river had baptised them, washed away the amassed sins of a life lived in the City, leaving them clean and innocent and beautiful. Always beautiful.

The river ran straight through the middle of the City, separating the rich side from the poor. To see it on a map it looked like God had drawn a thick black line through the societal plan, keeping the dogs away from their masters. Up close there wasn't much difference between one side of that line and the other, except that pimps and crack-whores were replaced with corrupt bankers and high class call-girls. Poor filth and rich filth, separated by an expanse of ebony water. You lived here long enough you learned that. If the filth from the East side made enough money to get across the river, then they joined the filth in the West side. No one ever left the City once they'd arrived. It wouldn't let them.

"Who do you think she was?" Trent asked as he looked down again at the frozen face of the dead girl.

"She can't be older than nineteen, and she's wearing a designer bracelet..." Duggan remarked, crouching next to the body. "Only one place a girl on this side of the City gets money like that, and it's the same place she'd get the bruise on her wrist."

"She's a hooker." Trent nodded.

"She was." Duggan sighed. "Now she's just another one for the morgue."

"You think she was drowned?"

"No, shot in the chest." Duggan replied, opening the young girl's sodden blouse slightly to reveal the bullet wound above her heart. The fact there was no blood or bullet hole in the blouse suggested a poor attempt to hide the wound. Someone was rushing.

"That's quite a shot to make."

"Unless you're up close, which means there's a good chance she knew the guy. Probably argued with him, pleaded and begged, and he shot her anyway."

"You think she forgot to pay her pimp?" Trent suggested.

"I don't know, seems unlikely."

"What makes you say that?"

"Look at her clothes, the jewellery. Girl doesn't make that kind of money her first year on the streets, Trent. She's experienced, been in the game awhile. Forgetting to pay her boss isn't something she'd suddenly start to do."

"Maybe she got overconfident, tried to leave town and he wouldn't let her?"

"Where would she go? Besides, classy or not she's still dressed like a tramp. She wasn't going anywhere nice tonight, just out to the streets."

"So we got a mystery on our hands, huh?"

"When you're a detective they call it a 'case', Trent."

"Hey, quit with the smart mouth, wise ass. I been on the force longer than you."

"Yeah, how could I forget that," Duggan muttered, standing up from the body. "Wait for the meat wagon to pick her up, I'm calling it a night."

Trent took his tarnished silver hip flask and knocked it back, letting its contents hit his throat like ice water. He coughed a little and then relaxed as he swallowed it down. It wasn't the body; he'd seen enough of them that nothing shocked him. Not kids, not women, nothing phased him now. It was the cold, the rain. The city never seemed to shake it off, whatever the season. Trent wasn't even certain what season it was about now. He was sure that he'd seen some Christmas lights being set up, but they put the damn things out in September now, so who can tell? Winter would bring snow instead of rain, but the cold would stay. Trent resigned himself to this and brought up the collar on his grey coat, watching his breath as it drifted away into the night before his eyes.

Duggan walked on down the banks of the Styx. The river had earned that name so long ago that no one could remember what it was actually called. It was a name that had been earned in the blood of everyone whose corpse had sank to the bottom of it. A debt paid a thousand times over, an account that would be forever in credit. Duggan could remember a body being dragged from it at least once every couple of months for as long as he'd been on the force, which was approaching two decades now. There were probably more down there, beneath the black mire that blocked any light from penetrating past three or four feet of water. Rotting bodies, food for whatever fish could survive down there, long past seeing the light and wondering if their families even knew they were gone.

The girl who'd washed up on the shore tonight wasn't even the youngest Duggan had seen. There had been two kids, each aged twelve, who had been strangled and tied together at the waist. They'd never found who did that, or why, and that haunted Duggan more than the dead faces of those damn kids. Not having an answer taunted him, he couldn't let things go. To have the Devil standing right there in front of him, holding a piece of paper with the answer written in invisible ink; it ate away at his gut. Left a burning feeling of emptiness and rage inside that nothing would quell. Carl Duggan liked answers, to leave a question without one was a pain that wouldn't die. The corpses still at the bottom of the Styx might never have their answers found: they didn't even have names anymore. Duggan didn't think about them, as that way madness lay. Tonight his focus was on the girl.

His shift was over, it was time to return home. But still his thoughts were on the latest victim of the City's cruel will. A city where the young die and no one ever lived long enough to claim Social Security. It was like some form of purgatory, with a constant turnover of its residents. The only people who stayed here past a couple years were the cops and the career criminals. Everyone else died young. No one ever left, not once the City had marked you. It was like a disease, an infection of sin that rots you from the inside out. Once it's in your soul it's going nowhere, and neither are you. You'll just take it with you, spread it wherever you go. The darkness, the soul crushing misery, the cold and the rain. Better to stay here, quarantined within the city limits. Let the darkness and the filth and the cold eat away at those who've chosen that fate—but keep it here. Where it belongs. Two halves of a dirt-covered coin separated by a river of blood.

The walk home wasn't a long one, but Carl took it slow. He liked to walk; it cleared his head, let him mull over his thoughts before he got home. Once he unlocked his front door and stepped inside, he liked to leave the city behind him. Turn the lights on, drink some coffee that didn't taste like pig crap, and sit down in a chair that wasn't forty-year-old hard plastic. An escape, a refuge, somewhere to leave the dark and the cold behind for a while. It never went completely away, of course, not with the neon sign whose pink glow taunted the gap between his bedroom curtains. It used to read 'Jesus Saves,' but now it simply said 'Save'. The sign broke years back and was never fixed. Who would bother? Not like anyone in the City wants to read that message, nor that they ever did. Hope needed light and warmth to spread, and there was precious little to be found here. Maybe in the arms of a hooker for half an hour, but even that would cost you, your cash and your soul. A heavy price to empty your sack into a stranger, but there was never a shortage of those who wanted to pay it. Everyone needs joy, wherever it's to be found, whatever the cost. Line up for eternal damnation, smile at the Devil as he takes your picture.

The third stair on the way up to Carl's apartment creaked beneath his shoe, as it did whenever he walked on it. Every time he heard that noise he contemplated telling the superintendent, but decided against it. Surly men like that don't care about creaking steps, they just want to change the light bulbs and go home. Maybe mop the floors if they're feeling adventurous. If nothing else, the creaking step would always serve to alert the cheating wife in the flat above Carl's every time her husband was on his way home. It was like a trip wire that might just give this week's lover enough time to dress and make for the fire escape. She was a toothless crack whore who'd long since lost whatever looks she might have once had, but Carl had heard she'd take it in any hole you could fit it, so perhaps that explained her popularity.

By the time his hand reached the doorknob, the thoughts of the creaking step had been forgotten, just as they did every day. Carl looked at his watch and noticed that it was past two in the morning. You get used to the night shift, adjust your eating and sleeping so that you don't always feel tired and sick. It starts to grow on you, avoiding the noise and the hustle of the daytime world. But it's easier when you live alone. Carl had lived alone since he'd moved out of home at age twenty, as soon as he graduated from the Academy. He'd never been married, not even wanted to. Women weren't something that interested him, they never had been. They were a goddamn puzzle without an answer, the kind he hated. Sexual desire wasn't even something he regularly succumbed to. If the need ever felt pressing, there was always channel ninety-three and a box of tissues, but that was rare for Carl. His mind just didn't go to those places all that often, so his body didn't either. He'd gotten used to the loneliness, the quiet, and again, it suited working the nightshift. But lately he wasn't living alone, because Jimmy had moved in.

Chapter Two;
Jimmy Galante

Carl Duggan had known Jimmy Galante since the two of them were six years old. It was one of those childhood friendships that they made crappy movies about. The kind where you can't quite remember when or how it started, but as long as you had known, you'd been friends. You could remember every detail of playing together in the backyard, tossing a ball around, pretending to be soldiers, all the usual kid stuff. But you couldn't remember the day you met, the day you introduced yourselves to each other. It's the kind of thing that comes easy as kids, after all. Making introductions to a complete stranger as an adult is a foreign concept, not something easily done even for those who are the most confident. But for kids? No problem. Just walk over, join the game, and there you have it. Friends for life.

Jimmy and Carl were inseparable from age six onwards. They would play together at home, at school, and wherever the weekends took them. To Carl, Jimmy was like the perfect friend. They liked most of the same things, and the stuff one of them liked but the other didn't was happily left alone by both of them. It wasn't until Carl got a little older that he was able to see past Jimmy's supposed perfection and start to notice the bruises on his arms and face. His dad used to hit him, there was no question. Carl didn't know why, and he never asked, as Jimmy didn't choose to mention it. If he'd wanted to talk about it then he would have. Carl never wanted to be the one to bring it up and so the subject was left alone.

After he'd first noticed the bruises, Carl would think about why Jimmy's dad might want to hit him. There was never an answer in his own ten-year old head, so the questions wouldn't die away. Carl even asked his mother once why someone would hit their child, but she didn't really give him a response. Not really the sort of thing you'd discuss with your child, he supposed. Besides, she probably didn't like Jimmy, just like everyone else. Even though Carl liked Jimmy, he always got the impression that everyone else was ignoring him. He didn't remember any of the other kids at school ever offering to play ball with him, and even Carl's mother would pay him little heed when he came around. Jimmy must have been lonely, but he always had Carl.

When Carl reached twelve, Jimmy moved away. He didn't say why, or even announce that it was happening. A few days passed by without Jimmy calling round, and it was only then that it occurred to Carl that he didn't even know where his friend lived. They'd always played at Carl's house or out in the streets to avoid Jimmy's dad, which had seemed like a smart move. After a week of not seeing his friend, Carl asked his mother what might have happened to him, and it was then that she said Jimmy had moved away, that Carl wouldn't be seeing him anymore and that he'd have to make new friends. Carl hated the idea, but he did it anyway. What choice did he have?

It wasn't until thirty years later, just two weeks ago, that Carl saw Jimmy again for the first time since they had been kids. Carl was sitting in his small apartment, listening to the rats in the walls and trying to count how many of the dirty bastards there were from the sounds of their scuttling, when there came a knock at the door. When he answered it, he saw a forty-year old man wearing eyeliner and a purple shirt, with a smile that he recognised immediately. It was Jimmy Galante.

Jimmy had always been gay, Carl had never doubted it. They'd never known each other as adolescents, when the desire for closer companionship would really kick in, but still the signs had been there. Jimmy was always more interested in Carl's mother's shoe closet than in the toy chest, for one thing. Carl didn't care, he hadn't as a kid and he didn't now. When Jimmy turned up on his doorstep, all grown up and queer as they come, he didn't care at all. He was just glad to see him.

The two had been living together for the past two weeks, getting reacquainted amidst much drinking and laughter. Carl didn't laugh much these days, living in this city didn't make it easy. It was like a strict mistress waiting to slap you across the face every time she saw a smile. Better not to laugh, not to smile, to give up on happiness. Carl wasn't gay, he'd even had his share of women, few and far between as they came, but Jimmy's sexuality wasn't an issue for him. He knew what the neighbours might think, having an obviously gay man living with Carl all of a sudden, but he didn't give a rat's ass about that either. Jimmy was probably the only friend he'd ever made that he actually missed when they'd been forced to part.

Like most of the people living on the East Side, Jimmy was out of work. Unlike most of the East Side, though, he didn't turn to crime to pay his way. He just took some workman's compensation for a while and looked for bar work. Not too many queer bars in the East Side—they were all on the West side, where people were more open. It was okay to be queer on the West Side of the river, one of the few good points of the place. People didn't care, long as you had the green. Over in the East Side it was different. Everybody hated everybody else anyway and the last thing you wanted to do was give them one more reason. Still, Jimmy had come to the City as much to meet his old friend as for work. He wasn't planning on staying indefinitely, so work could wait.

Carl worked the night shift, so he only really saw Jimmy in the hours before going to bed for the day. Jimmy warned him against night-time working, but he ignored it as he'd ignored it from the pharmacist and everyone else that had decided to give their two cents' worth. It altered your sleeping patterns, meant you'd be tired all the time, make you age prematurely. Blah goddamn blah, that's all Carl heard. What was the point working the day shift as a cop, when the slime mostly came out of the cracks at night? Other cops had families and lived outside the station house. Let them work the day shift, their focus was divided anyway. Men like Carl did the real work, the nasty stuff. The night shift was theirs.

When Carl got back from work this particular morning after finding the whore on the banks of the Styx, Jimmy was sat in the living room watching the old black and white TV set that Carl had bought years ago.

"You really need to buy some new shit," Jimmy remarked with an effeminate sigh. "You're a detective, that's gotta earn you some good dough."

"I put it away, no use spending for the sake of it," Carl shrugged as he took off his three-quarter length leather jacket and tossed it over the arm of his chair.

"See, I just think you like living in a dump. That coat you just threw over here? Four feet from the closet, Carl."

"Get off my ass, I've been at work hours," Carl replied, as he took a white bottle of pills from a drawer, popped off the cap and swallowed a single tablet without the benefit of a drink.

"Well I'm gonna clean this place up. Do something nice for you, least I can do for taking me in," Jimmy insisted.

"Knock yerself out," Carl agreed, before walking into his bedroom and closing the door.

Chapter Three;
Mirror, Mirror

The sound of his phone ringing woke Carl long before his alarm did. His eyes opened slowly, his lids refusing to break apart the dried yellow crust that had taken up residence between them. Once opened they were greeted with the pink buzzing of the sign outside his window. Inside his room, the glowing red numbers on his radio clock told him it was only a half hour before the time when his alarm went off anyway, but his body told him otherwise. No way that had been eight hours; he felt like he hadn't even slept. Maybe the health Nazis were right? Maybe sleeping during the day didn't provide the same benefits as sleeping at night? Let them worry about it, a job was a job. Carl closed his eyes for one final time and then forced himself to sit up and reach for his phone.

"Duggan," he groaned as his hand found the phone and brought it to his cheek.

"Hey, it's Glass," came the voice of the city's principal Coroner. "You awake yet?"

"No," Duggan groaned.

"Well get there fast. I've been taking a look at the hooker your boys brought in last night,"

"You matched the bullet already?"

"You kidding me? No, I found something else, something that didn't need all that much paperwork," Glass replied. "She was pregnant."

"Huh. Well that might answer a couple of questions," Carl sighed, sitting up in bed and wiping the dried yellow crust from his eyes.

"We've got some girl coming down in a couple hours to give us a positive ID on the vic. You might want to come along, ask her a few questions."

"I'm on the way."

Carl hung up the phone and wearily shuffled his way into the bathroom. It was a miserable effort, having to search your entire body for enough strength just to put one foot in front of the other. Like walking the last few feet of a hundred-mile run, except that Carl hadn't been running anywhere. He'd been asleep for eight hours, so why was he so tired? Maybe he'd go see a Doctor, or Kenny the pharmacist, and pick up some sleeping pills. The strong kind, not the crap they advertise on TV.

There'd be time for that later, for now Carl had to get ready for his shift. His feet managed to find the bathroom despite their complete lack of energy or motivation, and he was now stood before the mirror that hung above the sink. It was an old mirror, the kind that seemed to be going rusty at the edges, and just wouldn't come clean. Carl wondered how the hell glass could go rusty, but still refused to buy a new one. That didn't stop him thinking about it every night when he was forced to look in it. He'd bought just about every cleaning product he could think of to bring the damn thing clean, even that spray they advertised incessantly on the tube. The one where the annoying prick shouts far too loud and enthusiastically for someone who's talking about a cleaning product.

Carl hated staring in this mirror, and it wasn't anything to do with the dirt. He hated looking at the man who stared back at him; the lonely, miserable old bastard who was doomed to die alone in the worst side of a bad city. If he lived long enough to retire, he still wouldn't leave, Carl knew it in his bones. He had the disease, the infection that came with living here. No use spreading it, just stay right here in the quarantine zone, with the rest of the walking damned. The mirror in the bathroom was worse than the only other mirror in Carl's apartment, because it showed the truth. At the start of the day, this mirror was the first he looked into. It showed him as he was, before shaving, before cleaning up and making himself feel halfway human. This mirror was absolute truth, and Carl hated it.

The full-length mirror in the corner of the living room was hardly used, but in much better condition than this one. It had been Carl's mother's, and despite how out-of-place it looked here, he couldn't bear to part with it. Jimmy had pointed out the mirror almost as soon as he had arrived. Said it belonged in a mansion house somewhere, with wooden banisters and family portraits. Not here, in a dirty apartment whose hollow walls were filled with rats, half of its only bedroom illuminated by neon pink. Jimmy had been relieved that he got to sleep on the couch, as he knew that trying to sleep with the company of the incessant pink buzzing would be impossible for him.

Washing and dressing took as much effort for Carl as making his way to the bathroom had done. Still, the splash of cold water on his face served to sharpen him somewhat, although it did nothing to remove the weight from his eyes. Keeping them open was a chore, but it would be easier once he'd passed by Stu's Coffee Pot. It always was. Stu ran one of those little vending carts, the kind that usually sold ice cream or hot dogs. For some reason he'd decided coffee was an untapped market in this respect. Get people the hell away from one of those faceless brands where every outlet is the same before they needed to take out a goddamn bank loan just to drink. Stu served old fashioned coffee, the kind that Carl liked. Black or with milk, sugar or none at all. That's it. No mocha latte chocolate sprinkles or any of that pretentious art-student shit. Just coffee with the options of milk and sugar. The way God would have intended had he created coffee. Maybe he did, and just forgot to put it in the Bible.

Carl didn't see Jimmy as he left the apartment, so he assumed he'd gone out for the night. Wasn't much of a gay scene on the East side, but Jimmy was no doubt desperate to prove this theory wrong. Let him have his fun. If anyone caused him grief then they'd hear from Carl, and the threat of that alone was enough to deter most of the city's scumbags. Carl had something of a reputation for being excessive in the use of force with regard to people who pissed him off. He wasn't a bad cop, he just had a temper. Maybe that was due to the lack of sleep, he wondered. Or maybe he was just an irritable asshole. Either one was possible, each no more or less likely than the other.

Stu, the coffee vendor, was standing proudly on the street, the steam from his coffee rising above his cart to join the night sky above it. The smell greeted Carl first, fresh ground coffee beans, the kind that tasted the way coffee should taste.

"Evening, Detective Duggan," Stu smiled, already pouring a black coffee, no sugar, as Carl walked over.

"Stu," Carl nodded, handing him the correct change for the coffee.

"Got a case tonight?"

"Yesterday we pulled a dead girl out of the river. Tonight I'm gonna try and find out who she is. Got to act quick though, before City Hall decides they don't give a crap."

"Still riding your asses every time you investigate something like this, huh?" Stu asked with a sigh.

"They don't like having cops over this side of the river, period. Far as they're concerned, no one over here deserves police assistance one way or the other," Carl remarked as he blew the steam from his coffee. "Maybe they're right, maybe this place is beyond any hope of redemption. But that girl was young, and now she'll never get any older. Someone should know why, should know her damn name at least."

"Amen," Stu nodded.

"Take care of yourself, Stu," Carl nodded before continuing his walk to the station.

"Same time tomorrow?" Stu called over.

"You know it," Carl replied without turning around.

Chapter Four;
Smoke-Coloured Soul

Doctor Glass ran the city morgue. As the Chief Coroner on the East side of the city, any corpses that turned up found their way into one of his drawers. He didn't like to leave his morgue much, preferring to send one of his staff out to the crime scenes themselves. Once the bodies arrived in his domain, then he would usually take over. Or not, if he was high, which had become more frequent of late. The police knew about his habit, but there were few people with his qualifications on the East side, so they let him be. What other choice did they have? Allow a smaller sin to slip by unnoticed so larger ones can be discovered. Pay a dime and get back a dollar. Selling your soul by degrees is less noticeable, after all.

"Evening, Glass," Carl remarked as he entered the morgue, putting his hands in pockets to shield them from the cold that was necessary in such a place, but no less discomforting.

"Detective Duggan," Glass nodded, looking over the rim of his narrow spectacles.

Glass was wearing a white apron which was covered with spots of blood and dirt, but not as much as Carl had seen it lathered in before. There were smears along the waistline from where he had wiped his hands at some point. Carl was slightly uneasy at the thought of this, that you could so easily wipe away the blood of another human being like it was any other crap you'd put your hands in. Comes with the job, Carl supposed. If Glass saw the bodies lying in his drawers as anything close to human, he couldn't cut them open so casually with his scalpel. To him they were a puzzle, a Rubik's cube, and it was his job to make all the sides match. Nothing more, nothing less. Any deeper connection with them paved the way to madness.

On the cold steel table in front of Glass was a body, mostly covered by a white sheet. Only the head and feet were showing, and Carl wondered what it looked like underneath the cover. He assumed that Glass must have cut into it, partly at least, to discover the pregnancy. From the face, Carl recognised the body as that of the young woman he had seen pulled from the river the previous night. Her lips were even paler now, her blonde hair dry and clean, but her face was still as ashen. She'd never have any colour in those soft cheeks again. No more smiles, no more frowns, never a laugh or cry to be uttered from her pouting lips.

"Poor gal," Carl muttered out loud in conclusion to his own thoughts.

"Forensics are matching the bullet to a gun right now, for what it's worth," Glass shrugged. "I don't need to tell you that most of the shitheads in this city buy guns from the same two or three runners, so matching it to an individual owner is practically impossible. Might have traded hands five times since it was last fired."

"I'll work with what we have."

"Her pimp is the first port of call, I assume?" Glass suggested.

"Seems like a logical start."

"If it was Dice, I want you to kill him," came a new voice in the room.

From beneath the green-lit 'Exit' sign, Carl watched as a slender, female figure walked towards him. She was wearing a long red dress that clung to her every curve, her arms covered by black lace gloves and her face painted with dark eye makeup and deep red lipstick. Her blonde hair hung down loose over her shoulders and around her neck was a necklace centred with a diamond larger than any that ever existed in the stores on the East side. The heels of the woman's shoes echoed in the morgue as she approached.

"You're the Detective?" She asked, taking a long drag from her cigarette.

"That's right," Carl nodded.

The blonde nodded and blew the smoke out between her pursed lips, letting it curl softly around itself as it rose up towards the ceiling. It moved slowly, dancing in the air as it reluctantly left the touch of those deep red lips. Carl watched the exhalation with a mesmerised feeling of wonder, as though he were observing a fragile, smoke-grey soul rising from its host and reaching up for the Heavens.

"Felicity," the blonde said suddenly, offering her hand to Carl. "Felicity DuBois."

"Carl Duggan," Carl nodded, shaking her black-gloved hand gently. "I'm assuming you're related to the deceased?"

"She was my sister," Felicity nodded. "Amber."

"And you're in the same business as Amber was?"

"No," Felicity said firmly. "She was a prostitute. I work for Diamond Experience."

"That's an Escort Agency on the West side," said Carl. "Which means that you *are* in the same business as your sister."

"It's not the same," Felicity said again, her blue eyes growing narrow.

"You wear fancier clothes and leave calling cards...but you're still a hooker," Carl remarked.

Felicity slapped him hard across the face and scowled at him without saying a word. Carl touched his cheek where she had hit him and then said; "Alright, I probably earned that."

"You shouldn't judge what you don't understand," Felicity replied.

"What I don't understand is how a West side escort could have a sister that worked the streets over here on the East."

"Are you here to discuss our family feuds and history or arrest the bastard that did this to her?" Felicity hissed.

"When you walked in, you said the name Dice. Who's that? I'm guessing it's some pimp that gave himself a fancy nickname, but I find it hard to distinguish between one of those pricks and all the others."

"I thought everyone knew Dice. He owns the Three Lions Casino over the river."

"I don't go over the river much, Miss DuBois," Carl informed her. "So you're telling me this guy's not a pimp?"

"He also owns one of the larger agencies, the same one that I work for. I suppose in your eyes that makes him a pimp," Felicity said with a scowl, before taking another drag from her cigarette.

"What makes you think he's a murderer, and why would he come over here and kill an East Side hooker?"

"Dice has a reputation for abusing his girls."

"And Amber was one of his girls?"

"She used to be, before she quit and came over this side of the river. Amber was always one of his highest earners."

"Then why quit? Was he hurting her?" Carl asked.

"No, she wasn't happy with some of the things Dice wanted her to incorporate into her services."

"Like what?"

"Let's just say that some of Dice's richer clients were fond of the idea of two sisters that looked alike."

"And you were okay with that idea?" Asked Carl, raising an eyebrow.

"No, of course not. I was going to discuss it diplomatically with Dice, try to reach some sort of agreement. I could live with slapping my little sister round the ass a few times if that gets them off, hell knows I had to do it enough once Mom ran out on us...but anything more than that was a definite 'no'. Before I got chance to talk it over with him, though, Amber made a run for it, came over to the West side."

"And I'll take a guess that Dice was pissed off."

"Just a little," Felicity nodded nervously, her hand shaking slightly as she took another drag from her cigarette, the ash dangling from the end in a desperate attempt to avoid the pull of gravity. "Amber had clients booked through the month. If they were let down, they'd make sure Dice knew about it, and their friends. That was bad for business, and Dice is always thinking about the business."

"Why didn't Amber at least try and discuss this with him?"

"She was scared of him. All the girls are, but Amber was new to the agency. She hadn't learned how to charm him, how to play things to her advantage. She just freaked and ran, like she always has. Even when we were kids, if something scared her, she'd just run away."

"Do you know where your sister was staying whilst she was over here?" Carl asked.

"She called me and gave me an address, but I never went there."

"I'm gonna need that information, I want to see her home."

Chapter Five;
Ninety-Seven Percent Effective

The Home from Home Hotel was probably the most poorly named place in the entire East Side, unless your home was a rat-infested crap-hole with dirty sheets, rotting wallpaper and lights that decided whether or not they'd work on the toss of a coin. Carl looked down at the sheets that covered the bed in Room 402, studying them for details that others might fail to notice. They were creased in a way that revealed they'd been slept in recently, but it wasn't clear by how many people. Carl didn't know if this was where Amber would bring her clients or not, however that wasn't really very relevant given that her clients weren't currently suspects. He hadn't ruled out the possibility altogether, but since hookers were some of the only forms of entertainment on the East side, it was a rarity for them to be killed by their own clientele.

"I can't believe she lived here," Felicity said with a sad sigh, standing in the doorway of the room, not wanting to step foot inside. If she stayed where she was, perhaps the room wasn't real. Perhaps her sister had never come here, had never died and ended up washed down the Styx.

"I've seen girls on this side of the city that lived in worse," Carl remarked.

"You trying to make me feel guilty?" Felicity scoffed.

"Why would I do that?" Carl asked with a tone of genuine surprise at the comment.

"I got out, okay? I was raised in crap, told that all I would ever have was crap, and I moved past it. I got out, took my sister with me. She came back to it, but I didn't want to. Even if it meant leaving her alone here."

"You can't go home again," Carl said quietly with an understanding nod. "Look, Miss DuBois, I get that you don't like me. You think I'm an asshole, probably think all men are, which is fair enough, given the kind of men you're used to. You evidently raised your sister from a young age, which means your dad wasn't around any longer than your mom was. At a guess I'd say he left first. Now your sister is dead and I'm not the soft-hearted and gentle cop you might have hoped for, but for what it's worth, I'm not judging you, okay? You've had a hard life and you've had to make hard choices, I get that. Sometimes they take you down roads you don't want to walk down, and sometimes you get so far down them that you can't head back. Sometimes you don't even want to head back. None of that changes the fact that, whatever you think of me, whatever I think of you, I am going to find out who killed your sister and they are going to spend the rest of their goddamn lives in jail."

Felicity looked at the floor for a moment as though she were slightly ashamed, or embarrassed—Carl couldn't tell which. Then she looked up at him through her long black eyelashes and quietly said; "Thank you."

"Just doing my job, Miss DuBois," Carl nodded as he stood up from where he had been crouched. "I'm fairly certain that she didn't die in here. No blood anywhere, no signs of struggle, and anyone could tell that this place hasn't been cleaned in years. Whoever killed her, they didn't do it here."

"Dice wouldn't know where she was staying. He must have found her on the streets," Felicity suggested. "If it was him."

"Of course it was him, who else would have..."

"All due respect, I know that finding someone to blame makes this kind of loss a lot easier. You can turn your loss into hate and direct it at a single target. Easier to deal with, less frustrating. But we have no evidence to really suspect Dice over anybody else at this point. He had motive, but that's about it. If we go looking for evidence purely to support the theory that he did it, we're likely to miss a bunch of stuff that says otherwise."

"Easier to be objective when you don't know the victim, huh?" Felicity said with a sigh, opening her expensive snakeskin purse and taking a pack of cigarettes from inside.

"Exactly," Carl nodded. "You want it to be Dice because you have your own reasons for hating him."

"Who else would kill her? She didn't even have friends, how could anyone have known her well enough to want her dead?"

"Was she an addict?" Carl asked as he started to look through some of the drawers in the bedside cabinets. He chuckled to himself when he came across a Bible. Like anyone in this shit hole had use for false hope and words that lost their meaning before the last millennium.

"She wasn't into drugs," Felicity said defensively.

"Not necessarily drugs. Gambling, maybe? Drink? Anything she'd owe someone for and have forgotten to pay up."

"If she was, it can only have been since she came over the river. Dice doesn't let his girls drink or do drugs. Says it makes them ugly, which I guess it does. He'd doesn't even know that I smoke. He'd slap the crap out of me if he did."

"When did she move here?"

"About a month ago,"

"Not really long enough to build up any serious debts, unless she was incredibly stupid."

"She was the smart one of the two of us. She wasn't an idiot," Felicity insisted, again with the defensive tone.

"I appreciate that you want to look out for your little sister and honour her name, but at some point you have to be honest with me, alright? If she was a Meth-head who was a complete fuckwit, then I need to know because it might help with this. Painting her as a saint is next to useless."

"She wasn't a saint," Felicity scowled. "But she wasn't an idiot either. She wouldn't run up a debt that she couldn't pay off. She knew the risks, especially over here."

"I think you're right," Carl nodded as he found something in one of the drawers. "She knew the game, she wasn't a fool."

Carl lifted a small box from the drawer and opened it, sliding out a strip of plastic which contained seven raised plastic bubbles, inside of these were small yellow tablets. Three of them had been removed, the foil at the back of the bubble already broken. Underneath each of the tablets was a letter, in the sequence; "M, T, W, T, F, S, S"

"Birth control pills, marked for each day of the week," Carl explained, although he had the feeling that Felicity already knew.

"She knew what she was doing," Felicity reiterated. "Lot of guys won't wear their gloves with an escort...but she wouldn't risk..."

"I assume Glass told you?" Carl asked as his eyes met Felicity's.

"She was pregnant," Felicity nodded.

"Her pills didn't work. Why wouldn't they work?"

"Those things are only like ninety-seven percent effective anyway," Felicity informed him.

"Has she slept with enough guys for the statistics to come into play?" Carl enquired. "I guess you did say she was a high earner."

"Not through numbers, she was quite exclusive. She had a small rotation of clients who liked...specialist stuff. She was young enough that the schoolgirl outfits didn't look tired, you know? Guys like to think they're fucking a virgin, taking their innocence and all that messed up shit," said Felicity, taking a long inhalation from her cigarette and blowing the smoke back into the room, letting it join the rest of the filth in the air.

"She's only been here a month, even if she saw a different guy every night, the odds of the pill not working..." Carl mused. "We can't rule it out, but something seems off. Maybe she was sick, doesn't it stop working if you get sick?"

"Yeah, it can do," Felicity nodded. "What does this have to do with anything anyway?"

"I dunno, maybe nothing," Carl shrugged. "Do you think she told anyone she was pregnant? Like Dice, maybe?"

"She always ran away when she got in trouble...didn't even look where she was running sometimes," Felicity said quietly, her eyes glazing over as she stared off into the emptiness of memory.

"You think she'd run back to Dice if she got into this kind of trouble? Not the best older brother figure to have, but if he was all she had..."

"If she was pregnant, then even if she went back to him, she'd lose her entire client list... no-one wants to fuck a schoolgirl with a kid... he killed her! The bastard killed her!" Said Felicity, holding her hands to her face.

"Look, it's late and I have work to do," said Carl. "Why don't you find somewhere to stay tonight and I'll call you when I know more. You should get some sleep."

"Why do I get the feeling you're not going to be following your own advice?" Asked Felicity, handing Carl a black card with her number written in pink, next to which was a picture of a kiss imprinted in red lipstick.

"You sure Amber was the smart one?" Carl smiled.

Chapter Six;
Hard Eight

The Steel Gate Bridge had been constructed in the late fifties, replacing the old iron one that had rusted away to nothingness, almost as though nature had wanted it gone. The bridge crossed the river and linked the West side of the city with the East. Like every other man-made construction in the surrounding area, it was a cold monstrosity built entirely for necessity and with no time taken to make the thing look even slightly presentable. It was dark and heavy, the old, dirty steel barely even reflecting the gloomy streetlights that ran along its sides. The bridge was about two hundred feet from one end to the other, easy to walk across and barely used by traffic. Truth be told it was barely used by anyone. Not much call to move from one side of the city to the other, except through desperation. Like Amber. Poor, dead Amber. Washed clean by the Styx, like so many others.

Carl stood at the East-side of the bridge and felt the cold air fill his lungs. He put his hands in his pockets to try and stop the wind biting at the flesh of his fingers, but it did no good. Wind was so damn cold it went through everything, straight down to the bone. Across the other side of the bridge, Carl could see bright lights, yellow and pink and blue, luminous and tacky as holy Hell. The neon lights that led the way to the cesspool of corpulent excess and hedonism that was the West side of the city. Crime with a more expensive price-tag, that's all that could be found there. You wear a suit to work and think that makes your enterprise legit, but people still suffer for you to take home your paycheque. Nothing legit about that—not as far as Carl was concerned.

He often wondered if the entire City had secretly died and gone South for its afterlife. A kingdom where one's wage was measured in the number of innocent souls it cost; the more the better. Take a few girls and turn them into whores for a few bucks a night, you're a pimp in the East side. Take a whole school full of girls and call it an agency, charge a few hundred a night, you're a businessman in the West side. Same crime, different price tag. Demons bartering for a better life with the souls of those they've damned along with themselves. He who has the most wins. Nothing more, nothing less. Welcome to the City.

With a prolonged sigh, Carl stepped forward and began to walk along the bridge to the West side of the city. He hated going over there, hated it more every time he had to. The East was a shit-hole, he knew that and wouldn't deny it to anyone. But it was home, shit-hole or otherwise. At least people were honest about what they did, who they were. They didn't hide behind expensive clubs and drive cars that were worth more than a cop's annual paycheque. You knew who the good guys were, few as they might be. In the West you couldn't trust anyone you met. The friendlier they seemed, the nicer they came across, the more of an asshole they'd turn out to be when the mask dropped.

Knowing that this was what you were stepping into was worse when you didn't have a choice. Carl needed to speak with Dice, and on no day of the week was he likely to be found in the East side. That meant Carl going to him, however painful. That also put the ball in Dice's court, meeting him on his own turf this way, but it couldn't be helped. It was a conversation that had been destined since the night the latest dead girl washed up from the Styx. One more pair of lifeless eyes staring up at whoever would find them, begging for an answer to the mystery of their death. Carl had been the one to find her, so the answers were his to find. For that he'd step into the West side a hundred nights in a row if he had to.

The Styx lay beneath his feet, cold, dark and foreboding as he crossed the bridge, carried along by the same icy wind that bit through the skin and down to the bone. Carl glanced over the side of the handrail and looked down into the black waters below. The way the moonlight reflected off the surface of the moving water, it gave the appearance of thousands of ghosts being swept along in the undercurrent. Lost souls, taken to whatever fate the Styx had in store for them at the end of its flow. No Ferryman for them, just the dark and the wet and the current. There was no dignity in death, not in the City. Just blackness and cold.

With one final step against black steel, Carl now found himself facing the luminous, oppressive presence that was the West side. The neon lights bore into the flesh and the soul, their silent voices whispering you to come and find what they had to offer. Women, drugs, games of chance, pornography, whatever you could want was to be found inside the buildings these lights hung from. Sell your soul one step at a time, carve it into little chunks and serve it up on a cheap platter to the demons waiting behind each counter and bar. Carl felt himself shudder as the light shone upon him. He didn't belong here and he knew it. The touts for the strip clubs he walked by tried to convince him otherwise as they made their play to tempt him inside, but he didn't even give them a response. Don't get into any conversation that might end with you or the other guy breaking some bones. Sound advice, a good way to live. Conflict had its place, but entering into it without good cause was pointless.

The Three Lions Casino was easy enough to find, even for someone who didn't know the geography of this side of the City. Two enormous spotlights shone into the sky like calling cards for those willing to come and throw away their money, drawing them in from miles around. Once in view of the place, it was impossible to mistake for any other casino. To start with there were three enormous statues of lions outside, made of what looked like solid gold, but could easily be stone and paint. The building itself was made out to be an old English castle, with a great big Union Jack made from red white and blue light bulbs centring the front. Elegance and cheap excess combined into one with such little effort; the soul of the West side given form.

The outward appearance of the Three Lions was a theme that continued through the interior. Old English was the order of the day, with suits of armour, more Union Jack flags, and portraits of the kings and queens that had ruled England through the ages decorating the walls. Strange theme for a Casino, but Dice was the man to thank for that. He wasn't actually the least bit English, but he'd studied in Oxford for a year during college. When he returned, he'd picked up this phoney accent and a taste for all things British. It had stuck this long, and now it made him money from idiots who failed to realise that they never won anything from the slot machines or card tables. Let them pay, everyone here had money to waste after all. Carl entered the casino and was greeted by a woman wearing a short black dress, her name tag itself a Union Jack with the name 'Amy' inscribed on it.

"Good evening, Sir!" She smiled over-enthusiastically, earning Carl's instant contempt.

Friendliness without genuine meaning was worse than being rude. At least rudeness was honest.

"I'm here to see Dice," Carl replied without the use of a smile.

"Do you have an appointment with him?" Amy enquired.

"How's this?" Carl asked, reaching into his coat and taking out his police badge.

"Not good enough, I'm afraid," Amy shook her head, her smile dropping and revealing the condescending expression that she had probably held on her inside face since the moment of his arrival.
"This any better?" Carl asked, moving his coat back and revealing the gun holstered at his shoulder.

"Security!" Amy screamed, at which point a large black man dressed in a tuxedo ran over to stand between her and Carl.

"I need to see Dice," Carl said without flinching, staring up at the man who was at least a foot taller than him. "Police business."

"He's not available tonight," the large man said with a snarl.

"I'm sure he can make some time," Carl insisted.

"You're done. Go bother someone else," the large man replied, putting a hand on Carl's shoulder as he moved to forcibly eject him from the club.

The first blow hit the large man in the stomach before he even saw it coming. It was so hard and fast that he doubled over in pain, every square inch of air being forcibly ejected from his lungs as his ribs pressed against them. Violence wasn't Carl's first choice of action in any situation, but knowing how to use it was an inevitable learning curve in the City. This ape was bigger than him, sure, but he probably relied on that size far too much. Knowing where to hit and how to hit it was worth more than how hard the blow actually was. Carl knew both, as the ape would now attest in his efforts to re-inflate his lungs. It was a painful task that he would never complete, as being hunched over in the way that he was, meant his head was perfectly placed for Carl to drive it down into his raised knee. Carl felt the bones in the man's nose break against his leg, and the wet seep of the blood that instantly flowed from it. He let the man drop to floor where he remained curled in the foetal position, struggling to breathe even more so than before as his nostrils began filling with blood and broken bone. Carl wiped the worst of the warm wetness from his leg and looked back up at the horrified Amy, then repeated, "I'd like to see Mr Dice, please."

The girl didn't hesitate and instead took Carl into the main Casino hall, keeping several feet in front of him and almost tripping over her own heels in an effort to do so. Carl was led to a large table on which a game of Craps was being played by one gambler whilst a small crowd, mostly made up of loose-looking women, stood and watched. The rules of the game were beyond Carl, but he wasn't particularly interested. Gambling had never been a hobby of his, so why bother to learn? As he watched the player toss the dice down the long green-carpeted table, he noticed how eagerly the women at his side clutched his sleeve, fondling him like slaves at a Harem. Was it the fact that he was evidently winning the game, or did he have some other source of attraction that Carl wasn't yet aware of? The guy himself wasn't bad looking, but he wasn't a head-turned either. He had one gold tooth which looked stupid on a white guy with long hair, particularly one wearing a blue suit with a pink shirt.

"That's Mr Dice," Amy said nervously as she nodded towards the man playing the game. "Please don't tell him it was me who brought you to him, or I'll lose my job."

"If I asked you to suck my dick to keep that secret, what would you say?" Carl enquired.

"I'd ask if you had a hotel room nearby," Amy said with a nervous smile.

"Get the fuck out of here," Carl sighed, turning his attention away from the young girl and back to the gambler, who was evidently just the man he had been looking for. He moved through the small crowd until he had a spot on the edge of the table, from which he was only several feet away from Dice himself. Once more the dice were thrown to the sounds of cheering and words of praise, at which point Carl chipped in, "What kind of dumbass plays at his own Casino? Gotta know you can't win for long, right?"

"You can always win here, my friend. Loosest games in town," Dice smiled, ever the professional. He reached into his pocket and took out a red playing chip, then tossed it over to Carl. "Here, play a few games on me."

"I'm not much of a gambler. I prefer paying money knowing that I'm guaranteed to get something in return," Carl replied, tossing the chip back.

"Then what are you doing in a casino?" Dice asked, his fake British accent cutting into Carl's eardrums in a way that made him want to punch a man for the second time this evening.

"I need to talk with you, as it happens. You got a minute?"

"I think there's a fair few ladies here who have that privilege before you, mate," Dice smiled, putting his arms around the girls to his left and right. "Maybe another time, eh?"

"If I can avoid coming to this shit-hole again, I will do. So indulge me," Carl said with a forced smile, taking his badge from his coat.

"Oh, what the fuck..." Dice sighed. "Who let him in here?"

"You want to do this here in front of all your friends, or in private?"

"How about not at all? I think that's a better option, don't you?" Dice chuckled but didn't even raise a smile from the stone-faced Carl. At the sight of this he sighed and conceded, "All right, let's make a game of it. If you can roll a hard eight, we'll go to my office and talk about whatever you want, mate."

"What's a hard eight?"

"Two fours on two dice. One roll."

"Fine," Carl nodded, walking around to the table and taking the two dice in his hand.

He stood just beside Dice, and shook the small red die in his hands, before tossing them across the table. They each hit the wood at the end and then bounced back to a stop, one landing with the number three faced up, the other the number five.

"Ooh, that's an easy eight. Almost, but not..." Dice started, but stopped short when he saw the barrel of the gun now pressed against his forehead.

"I got eight bullets in here," Carl said with a low grin. "And if I pull this trigger they're gonna hit you hard. That's my hard eight. Get it? I can be a fucking smart-ass too. Now take me to your office."

Chapter Seven;
Damaged Goods

"So to what do I owe the pleasure of this visit?" Dice asked as he sat down at the desk in his office.

Carl looked around and was surprised at the room in which he now found himself. He had expected something overly lavish like the rest of the casino, filled with faux British memorabilia and furnishings. A desk that cost more than some people's living rooms, perhaps, or a lamp embedded with actual diamonds. Instead Dice's office turned out to be rather simple. A nice leather chair, a desk and a wall full of television screens showing the scenes in the casino below. Carl assumed that Dice had his own security room full of the same, but evidently he liked to keep his own greedy eye on how much money he was stealing from the idiots downstairs. The sight of these screens put a different focus on the seemingly simplistic room, as it was now obvious to Carl that Dice needed little else in the room when his attention would be solely fixed on the moving black and white images.

"Amber DuBois," Carl said with a shallow tone.

"What about her?" Dice asked.

"One of your girls, right? In the agency you run?"

"She was, until she ran away. Lord knows what she's doing with herself now."

"Not much of anything. She's dead."

"What?"

"You heard me. Did you know she was pregnant?"

"She was? Oh shit, that's—wait, you think I did this?" Dice asked, looking up at Carl, who remained standing before him with his hands in the pockets of his long leather jacket.

"You telling me you didn't?"

"Kill a pregnant girl? No, I fucking didn't!" Dice protested.

"Forgive me for the accusation, what with you being such a fine and upstanding citizen and all," Carl scowled.

"Look, there's a difference between getting rich by any means and murder! Especially a pregnant nineteen year old,"

"You beat your girls. That's why she ran," Carl explained, taking a walk around to the side of Dice's desk. "Maybe one day you lost your temper more than usual, reached for your gun..."

"She was shot?" Dice asked.

"That's right."

"Well, here you are then..." said Dice, unlocking his desk drawer. Carl saw that he was about to take a gun from inside, so instantly drew his own. Dice raised his hands suddenly and cried, "Whoa whoa, hold on big man... I'm just going to pass it to you."

"Do it slowly," Carl warned him, keeping his gun fixed on Dice's forehead.

"You're a bloody gun nut, like all you Yanks," Dice protested in his phoney English accent. He passed the gun to Carl, revealing it to be a customised Glock with a silver polish. On the handle was engraved the symbol of a playing card Spade.

"Nice gun," Carl remarked.

"Take it to your CSI boys if you want. They'll tell you it hasn't been fired recently, and that the bullets don't match the one you probably found in Amber."

"Maybe you got another gun you're not telling me about."

"I have that one out of necessity. I certainly don't want any more of the bloody things. You'll notice that one was locked in my desk drawer, to which only I have the key. I don't even carry it on my person."

"Seems an expensive gun to have purely for necessity."

"Everything I have is expensive. This suit probably cost more than your annual wage."

"Be a shame to bleed all over it then, wouldn't it?" Carl asked, putting his thumb to the hammer of his gun.

"Hey, hey, cool it... I told you it wasn't me that killed her, all right? I swear," Dice protested, his hands raised in submission.

"Okay," Carl shrugged, re-holstering his gun at his shoulder.

"You believe me?" Dice asked, the surprise evident in his tone.

"Yup," Carl nodded.

"Mind if I ask why?"

"Because in my experience, the guilty guys don't usually wet themselves under pressure," Carl remarked.

Dice glanced down and saw the wet patch around his groin and then rolled his eyes, "For fuck's sake."

"Yeah, classy bunch, you English guys," Carl smirked.

"Can I go now? I need to get cleaned up and back down to the casino floor. My boys will start worrying."

"I already had a nice chat with one of them. If the others have seen him, they won't be in any rush to make my acquaintance.

"Always violence with you lot on the East side, isn't it?" Dice sighed.

"Did you know that Amber had come over to my side of the river?" Carl enquired, perching on the edge of the desk as Dice hopelessly tried to clean his suit with a handkerchief.

"I assumed as much, but it's not like I went looking for her," Dice replied, tossing the handkerchief in a waste paper basket and opening a cupboard in the corner of the room. Carl reached for his gun once more, but Dice raised a hand and said, "I'm getting some spare pants, alright?

"In England they call them trousers," Carl smirked.

"Do you mind if I use the bathroom next to this office? Sink and toilet, no window, no gun cabinet," Dice assured him.

"Go ahead. I'm getting sick of breathing in piss anyway."

Dice walked into the small bathroom, leaving the door open behind him so that he could continue talking to Carl as he washed and changed.

"I heard that Amber was one of your higher earners. Why didn't you chase after her when she made a run for it?" Carl asked.

"Damaged goods, mate," Dice called back from the bathroom. "No one on my client list is going to hire a girl that's worked on your side of the City."

"Fair point," Carl nodded. "And you weren't a little ticked off at all?"

"Course I was, lot of money to be lost. But that doesn't mean I'd shoot a pregnant girl!" Dice said sincerely, re-entering the office as he fastened a new orange shirt, his trousers already changed.

"So when she left, you made no effort to find out where she went?"

"Can't say that I did, no. Why would I? Like I said, she wasn't worth it anymore. Bringing her back would be pointless, so I just let her run."
"How kind of you."

"Look, I'm not a fucking saint, all right? Never said that I was."

"Lucky you. Then you won't be getting a visit from His Holiness," Carl said with a sinister smile.

"You bloody haven't..." said Dice, the blood draining from his face as his eyes widened beyond their normal measure.

"Relax, you think I'm the sort of guy that would get Pope involved in police business? The further he stays away, the better," Carl assured him. "Once that guy steps in, I get a clock on how long I have to speak with my suspects. I don't like feeling rushed."

"Oh, thank Christ," Dice breathed an audible sigh of relief, his entire body letting go of the tension that had just frozen it.

"Amber was found on the banks of the Styx. Girl like that, we assumed at first that she'd been killed on your side of the river. Now we know otherwise, and if you had nothing to do with it, then it makes sense that she was killed in the West side."

"I said that I wasn't the kind of guy who could kill a pregnant girl... but you have plenty of arseholes over there that would," Dice reminded him, somewhat unnecessarily. "I'm assuming she found work? Only one type of work a girl like that can do. Perhaps her new pimp found out she was up the duff and didn't take too kindly to it."

"That was actually my next train of thought."

"Sure it was, Detective," Dice smiled.

"Don't get smart. I think you're innocent in this but I'm damn sure I could think of about another ten reasons from tonight alone that would warrant me hauling your ass to the station."

"You could, but you won't. That's not the way things work and you know it," Dice said with a confident grin, revealing once more the tacky golden tooth on the side of his mouth.

"I have jurisdiction over the entire city, Dice."

"Technically yes, but you won't take me because it's a waste of time. I have friends that sign your boss's paycheque. I wouldn't even get to trial and you know it. That's why you threatened me in a purely 'off the record' way when you entered. You knew that the threat of anything legal was meaningless."

"True enough, so what's to stop me blowing out the back of your skull right now?"

"Look, I have a date with three lovely ladies tonight, two of them related. I really don't want to turn up with any wounds, visible or otherwise, that might impede the evening's enjoyment," Dice explained. "So if I make it worth your while, how about you leave without laying a hand on me?"

"What have you got?" Carl asked, folding his arms.

"I know the names of all the pimps in your shite-hole half of the city. I know which ones would specialise in providing younger girls like Amber. There's only two of them, actually, as most of your clientele over there prefer dirty old hags, for some reason. Anyway, one of those is still serving time, so that just leaves Big Dog."

"Big Dog?" Carl asked with a sigh. "That's what he fucking calls himself?"

"The man's an idiot, what do you want?" Dice shrugged. "I thought a man like you would know all the players in your half of the city?"

"I work homicide, not prostitution. If one of them turns up dead it becomes my business, otherwise not so much."

"In that case you'll be interested to know that Big Dog can usually be found near the bus station. Trolling for new employees, as it happens. Runaways, emancipated kids, that sort of thing. Good business strategy, I have to say."

"I'll let myself out," Carl nodded, taking his leave of Dice before he wavered his agreement and broke the prick's face.

Chapter Eight;
One-Way Ticket

The City Bus Station was the centre of new visitors into the city and could be found in the East side. There was a reason for that, of course, which was that no one who was new to the city got to go straight to the West. That was a privilege you had to earn. Desecrate enough of your morals, sell enough of your body and soul and you just might win that golden ticket. But to start with you came here, into the dirt and grime. Off the bus and away from the land of the bright and the living, into darkness and desolation. No one ever bought a return fare because they knew that once in the City, they wouldn't be leaving. A one-way ticket to the worst place you'd ever go.

The bus depot was adjacent to the old train station, but it was decades since a train had actually rattled along those tracks. Most people that came here couldn't afford the fare on a train, and the lack of business had caused one service after another to be withdrawn. Now the worn out old husk of the train station had become a den for drug addicts and the homeless, dirty and cold, but at least it was shelter. Now and again someone would find a corpse on the tracks, usually one of the addicts tripping over his own feet and cracking his head open on the rails. Anywhere else and they would have blocked the whole place off, but here the authorities simply didn't give a crap. Let them shelter there, let them die there. At least it stopped them from being anywhere in sight.

Carl sat on a bench that at some point in the past was painted green, but now covered in so much graffiti that its colour was virtually invisible. It wasn't the good kind of graffiti either, the kind that almost resembled art. This was just the dumbass idiots writing their name and random gangster words in an attempt to justify the importance of their own existence. Juvenile morons shouting at the world because they knew no one was listening. Above the bench was a sign that displayed the number of the buses that would stop here when their appointed time arrived. Strangely enough, the buses were always on time in the City, as they didn't have to compete with any other traffic. No one wanted to come here, after all, and those that did never left. Little coming in, nothing going out. Empty roads, buses running smoothly.

Several buses came and went as Carl sat there on that bench, wondering when the sky would give it up and let the rain fall. He wasn't waiting for a bus, but rather the right person getting off one of them. A girl, aged between fifteen and twenty, clearly naïve and vulnerable, desperate for help from someone. The kind that would draw scum like Big Dog to her like a moth to a flame. Carl assumed that the pimp or at least some of his cronies were in the station already, but he couldn't act until he was sure. If he gave away his game too early by making a move on the wrong person, the whole thing would blow up. He'd promised Felicity that he would find the man responsible for killing her sister, and the Dog could be him.

The number 50 bus pulled up at the stop where Carl was sat, and its four passengers descended from the steps. There was a middle-aged couple that looked miserable and downtrodden, a single man with a dog, and then just what Carl had been waiting for; a young girl, barely seventeen from his estimation, her hair died a cheap purple and the rucksack on her back, worn and old. She wore a denim skirt with torn fishnets and unlaced boots that were seemingly too big for her, the way they rode up and down her ankles as she walked.

Either this one had run away from home or she'd never had one to begin with, Carl mused.

Perfect.

Sure enough, as the girl stepped off the bus and looked around, a figure from the other side of the station put down the newspaper he had been reading and made his way towards her. As he came closer, Carl saw that he was a black guy wearing a dark grey suit, gold-rimmed sunglasses covering his eyes and gold beads adorning his long dreadlocks. On his belt buckle were golden letters which, when illuminated in the headlights of a parked bus, spelled the words "Big Dog". Carl congratulated himself on the shortest time it had ever taken him to decide that someone was an asshole.

"Gotcha," Carl smiled as the pimp approached the purple-haired young girl.

"Can I help you, sweetheart? You look a little lost," Big Dog said gently as he put his arm around the young girl.

"Um, I'm okay... I just need to find a place to stay tonight," the girl replied with a nervous smile.

"Well, I might be able to..."

Big Dog didn't get a change to finish his sentence before a strong arm locked itself around his neck, at which point he found himself forcibly dragged away by an unshaven man much larger than himself. As Carl easily moved the pimp away from the girl, he called back, "Find a motel."

"Yo, what the fuck is this?" Big Dog asked as Carl tossed him onto a bench.

"Big Dog?" Carl enquired.

"That's right, who wants to know?"

"My name's Duggan," Carl informed him, opening his coat and taking out his badge.

"Aw come on man, I'm paid up for this month. I ain't got no more to give you blue boys."

"I don't want your damn money, you shit. I want you to tell me about a girl," Carl growled.

"Why didn't you say so, big guy? I got lotsa girls, blonde ones, brunettes, redheads. I even got chicks with dicks if that's your thing."

"I want a blonde." said Carl.

"Blondes we got," Big Dog nodded, straightening his coat as he sat himself more comfortably on the bench.

"I have one in mind, actually. Amber DuBois."

"Ah, she don't work for me no more."

"Why not?"

"We had a disagreement. Bitch got pregnant on me."

"So where is she now?" Carl asked, feeling his hand reach for his gun.

"What's it matter, man? You can't use her no more. But I got a ton of blondes, sure you can find one that..."

"Where. Is. She. Now?" Carl repeated, drawing his gun and pointing it directly at Big Dog's crotch, a shot made all the easier by the way in which the pimp insisted on sitting with his legs wide open. A statement of pride gone horribly wrong very quickly.

"Jesus Christ!" Big Dog exclaimed. "What's it to you?"

"Answer the damn question."

"Like I said, we had a disagreement. She wouldn't ice the damn kid, so she was no use to me."

"She wouldn't get an abortion, so you killed her?"

"I didn't say I killed her, man. You putting damn words in my mouth."

Carl felt his cell vibrate, so he took it from his pocket and answered it, keeping his gun trained on Big Dog. He muttered a few words and then replaced the phone. "Give me your gun," he instructed.

"I ain't packing."

"Don't bullshit me, Dog. Take it out, slowly."

Big Dog could never claim to be the most intelligent businessman in the city, but he was smart enough to know when he was beaten. This wasn't an overweight cop that he could hope to outrun, nor one of the skinny young ones that he could bribe. This was the real deal, the kind that would beat the living shit out of him if he even attempted to draw his gun for any purpose other than to hand it over. Wasn't even worth the attempt, he decided, passively handing the revolver to Carl.

"Well what do you know..." Carl remarked, popping the chamber to the side and studying the bullet he removed. "Same calibre."

"Same calibre as what?" Big Dog asked nervously.

"The bullet my CSI guys have been studying. The one they took out of Amber. Bunch of nerds don't know what the outside of that lab looks like, but they have their uses."

"All right, all right, I killed her. But look, man, I just hired that bitch. Got a lot of clients lined up, big people, powerful people. She was booked solid for months, skank didn't tell me she was pregnant. You know what these people were gonna do to me?"

"Worse than this?" Carl asked, firing a single shot straight into Big Dog's testicles.

The gunshot echoed throughout the bus depot and a few heads turned, but not nearly enough to cause a scene. It was hardly an unfamiliar sound in the station, after all. Two guys having a disagreement and one of them gets shot. Who gives a shit? No one that was in the vicinity to hear it, that much was certain. Big Dog screamed, then fell from the bench and rolled on the floor. He lay hunched into a ball and sobbing as he clutched at what remained of his genitals, the blood pouring out onto the wet ground below him.

"What the fuck man, what the fuck..." He sobbed.

"I know how this works, Dog," Carl explained, crouching over the figure. "You go to jail, guy like you makes a name for himself. The big Pimp with the big dick, the man everyone wants to work for. You make friends, and prison becomes an easy ride for you. I didn't want that, it's not close to what you deserve. So I took away your—let's call it your tactical advantage. I hear that in lockup, with all those tough guys, it's either fuck or be fucked. What I just did leaves you with only one of those options, doesn't it? From Big Dog to someone's bitch. Not quite justice, but close enough that I'll sleep happy tonight. I'll send some blue boys round to pick you up."

Carl stood up and holstered his gun, then turned and walked away from the scene.

"You gonna call me an ambulance?" Big Dog cried after him.

"I will if I remember the number. Never had to call it myself."

Chapter Nine;
Endless Cycle of Shit

"You've solved a case haven't you?" Jimmy smiled as Carl walked into the apartment. Carl was surprised to find him still awake at this hour, but then Jimmy was something of a night owl himself.

"What makes you say that?" Carl asked.

"You have that look, like you're somewhere close to happy because you've solved a problem, but not quite because there's always another one right behind it."

"Case got wrapped up tonight. Guy got what he deserved, a young girl can rest in peace. Good night's work, I guess," Carl shrugged, taking his white bottle of pills from the kitchen cabinet and popping one into his mouth.

"When do you eat?" Jimmy asked.

"What the fuck kind of question is that?"

"I just never see you eat. Coffee and pills, that's all I see go into your mouth."

"Everything you say sounds fucking queer."

"Homophobe," Jimmy scowled. "Seriously, I'm gonna cook you something."

"Don't be cooking something just before I go to sleep, it rests heavy."

"Fine, then I'm making you a sandwich."

"Christ, it's like living with a woman."

"You wish," Jimmy scoffed as he joined Carl in the kitchen area and began preparing a sandwich. Baloney, lettuce, some cheese and wholemeal bread.

"Since when do I have that much sandwich stuff?" Carl asked as he watched Jimmy prepare the snack.

"Since I did some shopping for you. You were getting all 'Mother Hubbard' in here."

"Christ, Jimmy, you turned my fridge queer," Carl sighed, glancing at the low-fat products inside the fridge.

"There's a great fresh produce store near here, you know. Bet you've walked past it a thousand times and never been in."

"You do the shopping, I'll solve the cases," Carl agreed, taking a bite from his sandwich and giving a satisfied nod.

"It's like we're a married couple in the fifties."

Carl still had a mouth full of sandwich when the phone started to ring. Jimmy glanced at him but made no move to answer the phone. Lazy shit, Carl thought. My house so I got to answer the damn phone. After taking a moment to flip Jimmy the bird, Carl swallowed the last of the sandwich and lifted the phone to his ear.

"Duggan, that you?" asked Detective Trent, his voice as damn miserable as ever.

"My shift's ending, Trent. This better be good."

"Oh it is, I promise. Course if you're not interested we could always talk about the pimp motherfucker we just found with his balls blown off. Says it was a cop that did it."

"And does anyone at the station give a shit?"

"What do you think, Carl?"

"Okay, so let's talk about the reason you called me," Carl sighed.

"You remember Judge White? Fat bastard with the stubby hands?"

"The hands that were in the pockets of every drug lord on the West side you mean?"

"The very same," Trent replied.

"What about him?"

"He's dead."

"I'm shocked. And I should give a damn why?"

"Get this. He died in court, in the middle of a trial. They think he's been poisoned."

"Guy like that gotta have had an endless list of enemies."

"Damn straight, which is why we want you on it. You'll cut through 'em faster than most."

"All right, I'll look into it tomorrow," Carl agreed.

"You ain't gonna start tonight?"

"It's four a.m., Trent. My shift is over, and he's not gonna get any more dead between now and then, is he?"

"Guess not."

"Then good night."

Carl replaced the handset and took the rest of his sandwich into the living room. He sat down in his armchair and relaxed, before switching on his old black and white television. The first channel to illuminate the screen didn't grab his attention, so he reached for the remote and idly flicked through them before he found an old horror movie, which he decided to leave on.

"I was surprised to discover that thing actually has a remote," Jimmy gasped in mock amazement. "I thought it was a relic from times past when you actually had to get off your ass to change channel."

"It's not that old, it's just cheap," Carl said defensively.

"I'm gonna buy you a new TV. I got a little money saved, I think it'd be nice. I know how you hate being given gifts, so consider it a gift for both of us."

"What would be a better gift would be you shutting up whilst I watch this."

"Oh come, you must have seen this like a thousand times already."

"Yeah, well I can't remember how it goes. Seen so many of these old ones that they all blend together."

"That's because they're all the same. Movies from back then weren't big on originality, especially the horrors. They found a formula and flogged it to death. You can interchange the werewolf for a vampire or a mummy or a robot and get basically the same film."

"Better than the crap you like to watch."

"You don't even know what I like to watch!" Jimmy protested.

"It'll be crap, whatever it is. Cooking shows or musical theatre or something,"

"Why do you do that?" Jimmy asked, resting his head on his fist as he stared at Carl.

"Do what?"

"Make all the gay jokes. We both know you're not a homophobe, so why feel the need?"

"I like the cheap shots. If you were black I'd be going for the race stuff, and God help you if you were in a wheelchair."

"I think it's because your dad hated gays so much. You get it drilled into you that it's okay to call us names and stuff cause we're not really people or something."

"My dad was okay. Didn't hate gays like your dad did."

"Maybe not, but stuff like that still gets imprinted on your brain. It becomes a habit whether you know it or not."

"Does it offend you?" Carl asked, sounding almost thoughtful.

"Nah, because I know you don't mean it."

"Then quit with the damn psych analysis and let me watch this... fag!"

"Oooh, haven't heard that one in awhile," Jimmy teased. "So what's this new case? That's what the call was, right?"

"Yeah. Some fat ass judge got poisoned or something. Died in the middle of a trial. Guy had a lot of enemies."

"Guessing that a judge makes those anyway, right? Sends so many bad guys to prison, or worse?"

"True, but White had more than most. He was as dirty as they come, turned a blind eye to anything for the right price. No loyalty in him either. The same guys he'd bail out one week, he'd send down the next 'cause someone paid him more."

"Well I may not be the smartass detective, but I'm gonna assume that makes your job harder, right? Long list of suspects?"

"Yeah, but you start at the closest. Friends and family are the usual suspects when a rich guy buys the farm. They stand to gain the most. If you rule out the friends, then you move onto the enemies. That's the way things work."

"God, you're pessimistic."

"Welcome to the City. It's just an endless cycle of shit. You bury one corpse and another floats down the river."

"Speaking of which, you going to call that woman? What was her name, Felicity? I think she'd wanna know that you found her sister's killer."

"Yeah, I guess so," Carl sighed, taking the card that Felicity had given him from his coat pocket.

"You'd have completely forgotten about that, wouldn't you?"

"I guess I figure that once the bad guy's caught, my job's done. I don't always think about the families. Someone else tends to take care of that stuff."

"That's cold, for you to wrap it up so simply in your own head," Jimmy remarked.

"Yeah, I guess it is."

"Lot of shit has happened to you since I last saw you, huh Carl?" Jimmy said with a sad smile.

"I don't know beans about what's happened to you either."

"Nothing interesting. Worked some clubs, broke some hearts, wore some fabulous clothes. The usual."

"Living the gay dream, huh?"

"Amen to that."

"You think it's too late to call her? Probably is, right?" Carl asked as he turned the card over and over in his hand.

"She won't be asleep. I bet she hasn't slept properly since this started."

Carl nodded and picked up the phone, then dialled the number as he read it from the card. The line rang at the other end four times, and then a soft feminine voice answered. Carl sighed and then spoke, "Miss DuBois? Hey, it's Detective Duggan. I, uh, I got some news for you..."

Chapter Ten;
Everyone Hated His Fat Ass

Judge Gerald White was a rich man, by anyone's estimation. He had a huge house, a luxury car, took more vacations a year than most people had in a decade, and a wife that was twenty years younger than him. He could regularly be seen in the high-class casinos, drinking expensive drinks and talking to expensive call girls. His wife knew about his nocturnal activities, of course, as had the first five women he'd married. White wasn't the least bit ashamed of his ways, so made no effort to hide them. As far as he was concerned, his wealth was like a can of whitewash that could be liberally applied to anything that he did. His wives had always tolerated it, for fear of going back to the nothing they'd all originated from. Get treated like crap and have a fancy lifestyle or go back to the gutters. Good old-fashioned family values.

"What makes you think it was poison?" Carl asked Dr. Glass as he looked down at the large body on the slab before him.

"He suddenly stopped breathing, grabbed his chest and hunched over," Glass replied, his breath leaving his mouth in a visible cloud owing to the usual cold of the morgue.

"Well you're the doctor here, but that sounds like a heart attack."

"True, and when I cut him open I'm sure that I'll be able to confirm it," Glass nodded.

"Then where does the poison theory come from?"

"Two things; firstly he had a heart attack with no real history of heart trouble. That always strikes me as suspicious. Call me paranoid if you must."

"Makes sense, so what's the second reason you suspect poison?"

"The same reason he's been laying here on my slab for a full day and night and I haven't so much as touched him," Glass said with a tone of clear frustration. "His damn wife got an injunction. Don't know what kind of fancy legal shit she pulled to block an autopsy, but with the money this fat ass left her, getting the best lawyers wouldn't be a problem. Hell, this guy was a judge, right? She probably used some of his old friends."

"So she doesn't want you to cut open the body? Sounds like she has something to hide."

"See? I could be a detective."

"That's common sense, Glass, but you're right. If her husband died suddenly, you'd think she'd want to know why." Carl agreed.

"Unless she already knows.

"You think she poisoned him?"

"Without knowing which poison it *was*—which I can't tell until I get inside the fat prick—I can't tell what delivery system was used. Was it injected, did he swallow it, eat it, breathe it, was it in his bathwater? Once I know that, I can narrow down who would have been able to give it to him. If it was in his food, I'd say the wife. But his wife wasn't in court with him that day. So if it was in the water he drank at the trial, for instance, then it had to be someone else."

"You're smarter than you look, Glass."

"Hey, I'm a doctor."

"Please, you can get a doctorate for turning up at the college doors these days!"

"Yeah, well I turned up early!" Glass retorted with a smile.

"So this injunction, it can't last forever, right? I mean the law's the law, they can only delay something like this, not prevent it altogether."

"They don't need to prevent it altogether. Some poisons exit the body after a couple days, alive or dead, leaving no trace of themselves. Once that happens we can't prove shit."

"Damn, that bitch is clever," Carl cursed.

"She must have hated his fat ass."

"Everyone hated his fat ass, but there's a line between hating him and killing him."

"Evidently she chose to cross it."

"Why now? What changed? This guy's always been a bastard, he must have really pissed her off," Carl mused. "I'm gonna go talk with the wife. See what I can scare out of her. If I sweet talk her enough I might just get her to drop that injunction."

"Hurry it up, will you? It's freaking me out staring at a corpse this long without cutting into it."

"You're one strange sonnovabitch, Glass."

Chapter Eleven;
Broken Heart

Carl found himself in the West side of the city for the second time in a week, much to his dismay. His record was four visits, back when he was investigating a child-porn ring that turned out to be the work of his own commanding officer. That wasn't a record he was particularly inclined to beat. In fact he'd be glad to never again come close to equalling it. The West side left a bad taste in your mouth, like a lump of tobacco wrapped in taffy. Seems all right to start with, and you think you might be onto something good. But the longer it's inside you, the more you start to become aware that something just isn't right. By the time you realise what it is the taste is there to stay, and nothing is ever going to take it away.

His second trip over the bridge this week took him to the residential apartments on the northern edge of the city. Away from the hustle and bustle so that the rich folk could have their quiet, but close enough so that the bright lights were never out of reach. You could still leave your fancy home to get drugs or an escort or both, and be back within the hour. Depravity on tap, just the way the West-side folks liked it. The apartment building in front of which Carl stood was the most luxurious and exclusive in the city, hence the somewhat overstated name of "Diamond Heights". Carl had barely set foot onto the red carpet which led to the door before the surly doorman accosted him.

"I'm not sure that this is where you live, Sir," he said, trying to be polite but his voice evidently carrying a thinly veiled threat. Whatever the words that actually came from his square jaw, the meaning was the same; you don't look rich, so fuck off.

"I'm here to see a friend," Carl smiled, resisting the urge to break the big guy's teeth.

"You have a name for this friend?"

"I have several, depending on the situation. If we're being formal I call her Fei Ling White," Carl remarked.

"Oh, excuse me, Sir. You're one of Mrs. White's friends..." The doorman nodded. "I didn't know she was expecting company so soon, all things considered."

"I don't think she wants to be alone," Carl shrugged, satisfied that his ploy had worked. Let the big fuck think he was ploughing the spoilt bitch. If it got him in the door then why the hell not?

"Go on through, Sir. Shall I call upstairs for you?"

"I'll take care of it. She knows I'm coming," Carl smiled, slipping the doorman a twenty as he shook hands with him. It probably wasn't necessary, the idiot already seemed to trust Carl's story. But the twenty bucks was the icing on the cake. A few dollars to keep his mouth shut, the same as all the tramp's lovers probably gave. And if not, then this meant he'd like Carl the most. Either case a winner.

Once in the hallway, Carl nodded at the desk attendant and walked straight to the elevator. He didn't have time for small talk, and he knew that too much of it would give him away. Not just the fact that he wasn't one of Mrs. White's lovers, but the fact that he didn't belong here. Period. His clothes weren't designer labelled and didn't cost more than some people's cars. His after-shave wasn't endorsed by some prick celebrity, and he wasn't wearing any products in his hair. At first glance he could pass as someone with the "roughing it" look, perhaps his lady-friend liked that. But any prolonged time in his presence would break the ruse, and he wasn't prepared to chance it.

The elevator had fourteen floors to travel past before it reached the top floor where Mrs. White could be found. Carl was annoying himself trying to place the music that was coming through the hidden speakers, and eventually he resigned himself to the fact that he didn't give a shit. At the back of the elevator was a large mirror that covered the entire wall, the sight of which caused Carl's eyes to roll. What kind of vein jackass checks himself out in an elevator? Hookers on their way up to their clients probably. Like anyone cares how pretty your hair and makeup is. They're gonna fuck you, not put your headshot in a photo frame on the mantle. Once your face is pressed against a pillow, who cares how nice your hair was when you walked in?

The elevator music was interrupted by the automated speaker announcing that the elevator had reached the fifteenth floor. Carl still hadn't figured out what song had been playing, and now he knew that it was gonna bug the crap out of him all night. With a frustrated sigh he departed the elevator and made his way to the first of the only two apartments that were on the top floor. Together they were big enough to leave no room for any other residences. Carl wouldn't have minded this in most circumstances. People's money was theirs to spend how they liked. If that means a home bigger than most people's, then whose business was it? That didn't apply to the late Judge White, though, because Carl knew too much about where his money came from. After taking a moment to straighten himself up a little, Carl knocked on the door of the apartment 202.

"Mrs. White?" He asked as he came face to face with the woman who answered. She was a Taiwanese woman in her early thirties, slim and attractive. Carl had done his digging, he knew that she used to be White's favourite call girl before he promised her a better life. Just like he had done for all his previous wives. Still, she cheated on him as much as he had her, so perhaps they deserved each other.

"Who wants to know?" She asked sharply, folding her arms.

"My name is Detective Carl Duggan. I want to talk to you about your husband."

"My husband is dead, Detective."

"Why do you think I'm here?"

"All right, come in. Let's get this over with," Mrs. White sighed, stepping to one side to let Carl into her home.

She offered Carl a seat on the luxurious red leather couch and then poured herself a glass of red wine, taking a bottle of imported beer from the large fridge and bringing it over to Carl. As she walked, Carl noticed how well her figure fit the short black dress she was wearing; how the shape of her hips pressed against it, the fabric rose ever so slightly above the middle of her thigh, and how her breasts held tightly in perfect shape at the front. Carl allowed himself to be impressed by her appearance, but at the same time wasn't stupid enough to be sucked in by it. She'd been expecting a cop at some point, that much was obvious from her reaction when he arrived. That she would expect a male cop was an easy guess as there were no female cops in the City, and the fact that she would dress in an appropriate way to distract him was to be expected for a woman with her past. She knew how to play people, and no mistake.

"I hope this stuff is all right, it's what my husband used to drink," Mrs. White remarked as she opened the beer bottle with her teeth and preceded to pass the bottle to Carl.

"Looks nicer than the crap I usually buy," Carl admitted.

"So, let's be honest here, Detective... Duggan was it?" She asked, sitting down on the couch opposite the armchair where Carl had seated himself.

"That's right."

"What's your first name?" She asked, sipping her wine and leaning back on the couch. At the same point she crossed her legs so that her already short dress rose even more, revealing the perfectly toned flesh of her upper thighs.

"Carl."

"Can I call you Carl? Or would you prefer Detective?" She smiled with an expression that made the blood-flow in Carl's veins change its destination slightly. Not enough for her to win him over though. He admitted to himself that he'd plough this woman until she cried, and then put it to bed. Carl had been manipulated by better than her in the past and he'd learned from it.

"Carl is fine," he nodded.

"So, Carl... my husband is dead, and you think I might be involved. That's why you're here?"

"Yup," Carl replied casually with a sip from his beer. That one was obvious, sweetheart, he thought to himself. Don't go patting yourself on the back just yet.

"Why would you think that?"

"Everyone knows the guy cheated on you with near enough every woman he met. That's gotta sting after he takes you into his life the way he did."

"I was hardly a saint in our marriage either, Carl. It wouldn't really be fair of me to judge him harshly for his wandering eye, would it?"

"True, but in my experience that kind of logic never really matters to beautiful women like you. They can cheat on their husbands as much as they like, but as soon as he does it to them then he's the worst bastard on the face of the earth."

"That's rather sexist," Mrs. White said defensively.

"Yeah it is," Carl agreed. "It's also true."

"You're right, it probably is," Mrs. White shrugged. "Beautiful women can be bitches, especially the rich ones. It's what society forces us to be. Let the world know it if they don't already. We'll wrong you a thousand different ways, and you'll always come back. But cross us once and you'll be served with divorce papers."

"Didn't find any of those in your dead husband's pockets," Carl commented.

"It was in process."

"Uh huh. And His Holiness was your divorce lawyer, I assume?"

"What is that supposed to mean?"

"You got a computer?" Carl asked, taking a USB stick from his coat pocket.

"There's a laptop in the bedroom."

"Would you mind?"

"Go ahead," Mrs. White nodded, setting down her wine glass and leading Carl into the bedroom.

Carl couldn't help but notice that the bedroom was the size of his entire apartment, but he wouldn't let himself be bitter over it. He'd rather live in a small apartment that he'd paid for honestly. Not much reason to have a luxury bed if your guilt won't allow you any sleep. Carl was still holding his beer, not being overly eager to let it go to waste. It was the best he'd ever tasted, but he'd carry that admission to his grave. He watched as Mrs. White leaned into a low drawer and removed a shiny black laptop, which she then placed on the vanity unit. As the machine booted up, she walked back around to where Carl stood at the end of the four-poster bed and stood before him.

"What is it you have to show me on that memory stick, Detective?" She asked, her breath soft against Carl's neck as she stood directly in front of him.

"What happened to calling me by my first name? Have I pissed you off now?" Carl asked with a chuckle.

"No, I just like calling you by your title. It's more... authoritative. Big, strong police officer in my bedroom, asking me questions..."

"You like that, huh?"

"Oh yes. It never would have worked with my husband. He was so... soft. Not like you."

"I see," Carl nodded, repressing the smile that so badly wanted to force him into fits of laughter. If this dumb bitch actually thought he was going to fall for this then she really was an idiot.

"Would you like me to be a cooperative suspect... or not?"

"I always preferred not..." Carl remarked, reaching down to Mrs. White's wrists and holding them behind her back. She gasped softly and then there was the sound of a soft metallic click. Mrs. White looked over her shoulder to see that Carl had now handcuffed her hands around the bedpost at her back. She smiled at the sight of this and bit her bottom lip, and then turned back to Carl.

"Well I'm going to have to cooperate now, aren't I?" She said in mock submission.

"That's the idea," Carl smiled, before walking straight past her to the laptop. "Hope this thing doesn't want a password."

"Oh you are fucking kidding me!" She hissed.

"What? You thought I'd actually forget why I was here and end up banging you? Sorry, sweetheart, I've resisted hotter than you in my time."

"Yeah, like hell you have."

"See, that's the problem with spending years listening to a fat old shit telling you that you're the most beautiful woman in the world. At some point you start believing it. You're hot, sure, but I've seen just as hot on late-night porn. They have a whole channel for skanky Asian chicks. You might want to consider signing up since your husband isn't here to buy you pretty things anymore," Carl suggested as he plugged in the memory stick and loaded up the files that were stored on it.

"You're a prick, Duggan!"

"So I've heard," Carl shrugged without turning to face her. "Ah, here we go. See, I knew I'd be coming here to see you so I pulled your bank records. I see here a twenty-thousand dollar transfer to an account in the name of Zebediah Goldman. Now, I know that's a false name and I know who uses it. Remember I made that crack about you hiring His Holiness as your divorce lawyer? You should have remembered it, it was a good joke. Cause from what I see here, you've evidently paid him for something."

"If you know who he is then you know what he does, which means you know why I paid him," Mrs. White hissed again, her tone one of frustration as she had now given up trying to force her freedom from the handcuffs.

"Yeah, but I want to hear you say it."

"I didn't have my husband killed," she said firmly.

"See, now this says otherwise," said Carl, tapping a finger against the bank records displayed on the screen of the laptop.

"I know... but I didn't. I wanted him dead, but it never went down that way. He had this heart attack before Pope did his job."

"You're saying this wasn't what you paid for?"

"No, this was just a heart attack."

"Drop the injunction," Carl said suddenly.

"What?"

"Let us autopsy your husband. If you're telling the truth you got nothing to worry about."

"You'd still arrest me for putting the hit out on him to start with," Mrs. White protested.

"I hit a few keys here and I have no evidence that you did any such thing," Carl informed her, pointing at the laptop.

"Why would you do that?"

"Because I don't give a flying crap about your husband, Mrs. White. I just want to know how he died. If it wasn't you then I don't care that you also wanted him dead. I don't really see that you're a threat to society so why waste my time and yours putting a case against you?"

"Come over here and I'll thank you properly for that," Mrs. White smiled, licking her lips.

"Sorry, busy night ahead," Carl replied. "So what's it gonna be? You gonna let us do the autopsy?"

"Hand me the phone and I'll call my lawyer right away. I only got that thing because I didn't want you cutting into him."

"Why would you want to stop that?" Asked Carl, taking the phone from the bedside table.

"I know that he wasn't murdered, so an autopsy isn't necessary. If it's not necessary then I would rather you didn't cut him open. Let him be buried without scars all over him."

"That's an Asian thing, right? That your ghost walks in the next world with the same wounds it carried in this one? So you don't want him to have any wounds that aren't necessary?"

"Yes," Mrs. White nodded.

"But you were going to have a bullet put in his head."

"Which I had made peace with myself for. Now that it wasn't necessary, there's no need to cause him any further harm, in this world or the next one."

"That almost sounds like respect for your husband, Mrs. White."

"You can love someone and hate them at the same time, Carl."

"Not in my experience."

"Then you've never been married," she smiled.

"Tell me your lawyer's number and I'll dial for you."

"You're not going to take off these handcuffs?"

"I will when you've dropped the injunction."

Mrs. White gave Carl the number and he dialled, then held the phone to Mrs. White's ear. To his surprise the phone was answered quickly, which was impressive since it had just passed midnight. Carl assumed that Mrs. White had a direct number for one of her more expensive lawyers, possibly even his home number. She was probably sucking his dick, after all. With the instruction given to lift the injunction, the call was ended.

"Please don't leave more scars than you have to," she requested.

"I'll ask my guy to do his best," Carl nodded, reaching to unfasten the handcuffs.

"You couldn't leave them on just a little longer?" Mrs. White teased as Carl unfastened the cuffs.

"Christ, you don't give up do you?"

"I haven't had a man in days. I get frustrated easily," she smiled seductively, rubbing her wrists now that Carl had freed them.

Carl walked over to the bedside cabinet and rooted around in the drawers until he found what he was looking for. What he knew would be in there. With a satisfied nod, he took the red plastic dildo from the drawer and tossed it onto the bed beside Mrs. White.

"Knock yourself out," he suggested as he took back his memory stick and walked towards the door.

"Where are you going now?" Mrs. White called after him, sounding genuinely disappointed that he was actually leaving.

"I gotta go to church," he replied as he left.

Chapter Twelve
His Holiness

Saint Michael's Church was the only holy building in the entire West side. There were a few rescue missions run by various churches in the East, but most of the churches had long since abandoned the City. Little hope was to be had there, divine or otherwise, so the messages never got through. The Catholics were still clinging on for dear life though, and St Michael's was the last bastion of anything even slightly divine on either side of the Styx.

Carl entered quietly, closing the large door behind him and trying to stifle the echo of his footfalls on the aisle. The church was dark, lit mostly by the candles along its walls and at the altar. It was also empty, save for the lone figure seated on one of the pews facing the altar, his back to Carl. The man was seated beneath the shadow of a large statue of Christ on the cross, his head hung in prayer. He was completely bald, the only hair on his face the small black goatee around his lips and chin. On the back of his head was a tattoo of the Jewish Star of David, inside each segment of which was a single number. Carl also knew that the man had further tattoos, one on each hand, which were Hebrew symbols for 'Hope' and 'Mercy', respectively.

"Hello, Charles." Carl said quietly as he sat in the pew directly behind the bald man.

"If you're planning to draw your gun, then I would request you not to. If not out of respect for me, then for him," the bald man asked, nodding towards the statue of Christ.

"Alright, I'll keep her holstered," Carl agreed. "But only because I'm pretty sure I could take you without it."

"Last time was a fluke, and you didn't stop me."

"I don't call three ribs and that scar on your face a fluke," Carl smirked.

"I admit, you're better than anyone who's ever tried to stop me before. But if you recall the climax of our previous altercation, I still made my target."

"Yeah, 'cause I gave up on getting in your way. After I found out what my commanding officer was involved in, I didn't want to protect him anymore. He deserved your bullet and about a hundred more."

"Yes he did," the bald man nodded. "So perhaps you'd be kind enough to tell me why you've sought me out tonight?"

"You didn't take much finding. Only one place to find Charles Pope at this time of night."

Carl had only met Pope the once before, but he knew him by reputation long before that. He was easily the best hit-man money could buy, not just in the City but quite probably in the whole country. He was also what you might call 'complicated'. The tattoos that decorated Pope's flesh didn't match his name or his faith, and few people knew why. Carl knew, of course. It was his job to know.

Pope's father hadn't even been ten years old when the Germans invaded Poland. He'd been taken to a concentration camp with his entire family, and was the only one to leave, four years later. He grew up fast, but a part of him never left that place. For as long as he lived, he slept in the attic of every home he had, jumping out of his damn skin every time there had been a knock at the door. He'd wash himself in the bathtub or with a washcloth. Never a shower. He wouldn't even set foot in a bathroom that had a shower in it.

Even when he married and had a kid, Zebediah Goldman couldn't leave his demons behind him. He called his son Charles and changed his surname to Pope. Bit overkill perhaps but Goldman thought no such thing. On the day he figured Charles was old enough to understand, he started to teach him Catholicism. He didn't want his son to be Jewish, didn't want anyone to know where he was from. The Nazis were long gone, but Zebediah never felt safe. As far as he was concerned, it would happen again. Someone else would decide they hated Jews and the whole fucking mess would start over. Not again, not to his son. So he gave him a Catholic name, told him to shave his head and never grow a long beard, never read the Torah and learn the Bible instead. Keep safe, hide where you're from.

Charles never really understood his father's obsession with hiding his origins, but he didn't have to. His respect for his father was enough that he honoured the wishes without the need for understanding them. But he wouldn't allow himself to forget who he really was, where his origins really lie. When his father died, Charles had the tattoos done. The star of his people, the numbers in each segment making up the same number that was marked on his father's right wrist. A memory in black ink, a sign that would firmly state the words 'never again', hidden in a code all their own.

Zebediah had worried that he might pass his fear onto his son, but in actually he hadn't. The fear that he had felt had turned into hate in Charles' hands. Hate for anyone who abused their power, who thought their wealth, status and authority should allow them to flaunt the laws of morality and decency. Men like the Nazis. Men like Judge White. Choosing his profession was easy when it came with the prospect of removing just such men. 'Never again'. Not if Charles could help it in some small way.

"So what would you like to ask me about, Detective Duggan?" Pope asked without turning around.

"Judge White."

"Corrupt, rich bastard who abused his power and position of trust."

"That's the one. You know he's dead, right?"

"I didn't know that."

"Right. See, I actually knew that you weren't aware of it yet. That's why you're here. You were going to go and kill him tonight, weren't you? That's why you're here praying, like you always do before a hit."

"I wasn't aware that you knew so much of my methods."

"I know you always kill them fast, painless. Death with mercy, that's your thing. You want them dead, but you don't want them to suffer. I also know that it was White's wife who hired you, and her own faith might have given her reason to request that you didn't leave too many wounds on him."

"How did Judge White die?"

"At the moment we're thinking he was poisoned. Had what looks like a heart attack during a trial. Which might be nothing giving the fact he wasn't exactly healthy, but he has no history of heart problems so I'm treating is as foul play. Until I'm proven wrong, at least."

"And you don't believe I had anything to do with this?" asked Pope, turning to look Carl right in the eyes. "No, I don't," Carl replied firmly. "Poisoning isn't your thing. Too messy, too prolonged."

"Then why are you here?" asked Pope, reaching into the inner pocket of his floor-length black coat. As he did so, Carl tensed and prepared himself to reach for his weapon. Pope saw him do this and stopped, opening his coat so that Carl could see the phone he was taking out. As he did so, he remarked; "You can relax. I would never attack you in here."

"Can't ever be too careful," Carl shrugged "You catching up on some work e-mails?"

"I'm transferring my fee for White's murder back to the sender. I won't be earning it now."

"You're a strange kind of murderer," Carl said with a weary sigh, shaking his head slightly.

"I'm not a murderer," Pope said quietly.

"Right, you're an Angel of Death and Mercy or whatever. Except that you're not. The way I see it, we each become our own monsters, Pope. Kids who get smacked around become violent wife beaters. Kids who get molested turn into paedophiles or rapists. And you? Well, you've marked out an entire set of people and decided by your own authority that they deserve to die. Sound familiar?" Carl remarked. "Like I said, we become what we feared."

"And what are you going to become, Detective?" Pope asked with narrowed eyes.

Carl met Pope's stare but didn't have an answer to the question. Instead he simply looked around at his surroundings and commented, "You know, this is quite a nice church."

"You're not a religious man, are you?"

"Can't say as I am."

"Why is that?"

"I've never seen anything that would make me believe in a God that could love us the way he's supposed to."

"Do you live your life the way your parents want you to? To the letter?" Asked Pope.

"No, but what does that have to do with..."

"And do they come your home all the time to interfere with your life?" Pope continued.

"No, but then they're both dead, so..."

"My point is that God lets us make our own mistakes, so that we might learn from them."

"And that's what you're doing, huh? Correcting our mistakes?"

"Some decades ago, it was decided by the law makers that we would allow most evil, sinful men to continue to live, whatever their crime. Since then, the world has become increasingly more horrid and depraved. I would therefore cite the decision as a mistake, wouldn't you?"

"I got enough on you to put you away for the rest of your life. You know that, right?" Carl asked.

"Yes. But I also know that you won't."

"True," Carl nodded. "Mainly because putting you with the prison population isn't smart, no matter how much it might help the overcrowding situation."

"That's not the reason you're going to leave the church without arresting me."

"Then what is, smart guy?"

"Because you know that I'm right, and you'd rather have me out there than not," Pope said with a soft curve of his lips. "If you wanted to arrest me, you would have done it two years ago when you broke three of my ribs and cut my face open with the butt of your gun. I was down, you had me... and you let me go."

"Let's talk about why I'm here tonight, shall we?" said Carl.

"As you will."

"I know that you don't associate with the other guns-for-hire, but you know their patterns, how they work.

Can you think of anyone that might be hired to poison a guy?"

"It could just be the wife herself." Pope suggested.

"I've spoken with her, and I don't think that it was."

"She could be lying to you, Detective. I know that it seems unlikely she would kill him herself after hiring me to do the job for her, but trust me when I say that I have seen such things before. For someone as rich as the Whites, money would be irrelevant. Quite simply she wanted him dead. If she saw an opportunity to achieve this goal herself, say by slipping something into his drink, then she'd take it."

"I agree with your logic, and she could certainly afford to lose twenty grand… but I usually know when someone is lying to me. I didn't get that vibe from her."

"Are you ever wrong about such things?"

"Yeah, but I'm fairly confident this time. She's letting us do the autopsy, which might just prove her guilt if she did kill him. I called my guy before I came to find you, he's cutting into the fat shit even now."

"When you know which poison was used, contact me on this number," said Pope, handing Carl a small black card, similar in size to the one that Felicity had given to him. "and I shall endeavour to find out which assassin would use it in their work."

"Thanks," Carl nodded, standing up to take his leave of the church.

"Before you go, which gun are you carrying now?"

"You wanna get out the tape-measures or something?" Carl sneered.

"Your weapon bulks out your jacket more than it used to, so I know you have changed it. You used to carry a revolver, from my recollection of the wooden handle hitting my cheek."

"Yeah, I upgraded to a Colt. Bigger clip, have to carry less in my pockets."

"Do you still have the revolver?"

"Yeah, I keep it hidden in my apartment. Why?"

"I wanted to buy it from you, if you're interested."

"Buy my old gun? Why would you want to do that?"

"As a souvenir of the only man who has ever gotten close enough to pistol-whip me," Pope smiled.

"I'll think about it," Carl replied. "Good night, Pope."

"Take care, Detective Duggan. God is with you."

"Yeah. Sure he is."

Chapter Thirteen;
Homophobic Bastard

"**C**arl, where the hell have you been?" Trent yelled down the phone, the spit leaving his mouth with such violence that Carl could almost hear it land against the receiver. "Couldn't get hold of you at all last night."

"Been working the White case, had to go West."

"Jesus Christ, Carl, what did you go and do that for?"

"Chief wants the answers to who killed the fat shit, and we're not gonna find them on this side of the fence, Trent. No-one on the East side could get close to White and we all know it."

"None of the West side blue boys saw you, did they?" Trent sighed.

"Don't worry, Trent, you won't have to explain why some real cops dared to set foot in that crap-hole. Would hate to think the bribes they send you to keep your nose out might get cut back."

"I don't take any bribes, Carl."

"Yeah, like spit you don't," Carl said under his breath. Out loud he said "Relax, no cops saw me. I got some answers and left as soon as was practical. Got Glass looking over the corpse right now."

"His wife dropped the restraining order?"

"I persuaded her that it was in her best interests."

"You didn't hit her, did you?"

"Jesus Christ, Trent, I don't hit women!" Carl snapped.
"You hit everyone, Carl, it's what you do."

"I find it hard to believe you're checking up on me, so I can only assume you want something. What is it?"

"We got a dead guy that needs a look-over. Killed in his own home, looks like."

"So what's wrong with your eyes?"

"You left me with all the paperwork from the dead hooker and the pimp you shot in the 'nads, remember? I ain't having more piled on my desk, so this one's yours."

"Fine. What and where?"

"East Side this time. Fifth Street Apartments. There's some blue boys on scene, they'll talk you through it."

Carl sighed as he replaced his phone in his inside pocket. The shit in the City had swelled in the last few weeks, flowing up and out of the drains with increased frequency. Three deaths in as many weeks, each one random and not even remotely connected to each other, which was actually worse. If there was a serial killer it could still be judged as one thing to be dealt with, but random meant there was no greater reason. No singularity of cause that could be cleaned away. Random meant things were just bad everywhere. A dead girl floats ashore on the banks of the Styx. A fat old judge gets poisoned in the courtroom. And now a guy gets killed in his own apartment. One of the worst ways to go, by any standards. Home should be safe, the last refuge against the world's evil. Not here, though. Not in the City. Home was just one more place you were likely to find the shit creeping under the doors.

Stu, the Coffee vendor, had already prepared Carl's beverage as the Detective walked towards his stall. Carl didn't stop to talk tonight, though, as he wanted to get to the crime scene. Trent had said that the blue boys were already there, which meant he was on a clock. Cops had a way of messing up crime scenes, whether they'd intentionally been bribed to do it or just because they were goddamn retards. A footprint here, fingerprints, loose hairs messing up the place. Carl could no longer remember the amount of times a case had pointed to a cop who just happened to be at the crime scene. It wouldn't have surprised Carl if some of them had actually been the guilty party in some cases, but the truth was simply that they'd left their mark over the crime scene and messed up the actual forensics.

The coffee in Carl's Styrofoam cup had just about run empty when he reached the Fifth Street Apartment building. There was a homeless man seated on the stairs of the derelict building next door, his hands tucked under his own armpits to stave off the cold. As Carl tossed the coffee cup into an already-overloaded trash can, the homeless man remarked, "You should recycle that, man."

Carl contemplated whether or not to tell the homeless man to go fuck himself, but decided against it. The guy clearly had enough to deal with as it was. This wasn't a city you wanted to be homeless in, West or East. You wouldn't get any sympathy, even if you were holding a starving baby in your arms. People on the East side had no spare change to give to you, people on the West had it but wouldn't part with it. Either way, you were getting nothing.

Sure enough, Carl found two cops loitering in the hallway outside the apartment in which the crime scene could be found. One of them was actually leaning against the door, and Carl cursed under his breath at the prospect of how many fingerprints this prick might have eradicated already. Evidently they knew Carl by reputation, however, as they promptly moved aside and let him onto the scene as soon as he arrived. The two cops waited in the hallway whilst Carl was left alone in the apartment. He looked around at the room first, before taking in the body itself. This was always his way, know the person before you jumped to any conclusions. If you took in the body and just the body, you'd never be able to see anything but a corpse. Carl needed to see more than that, the puzzle always demanded it. See the person they were before, where they lived, what they liked. It might give answers, it might not, but at least it made them seem human. No corpse is ever just a corpse. It's someone's son or daughter, someone's best friend, someone's wife or husband. Carl knew it was impossible for men like Glass to see things this way, but not for him.

The apartment was a large single room, with the bed in the far corner and the kitchen near the entrance. There was a separate bathroom, but everything else was in the same room. Carl instantly noticed how clean everything was, taking care not to touch anything but having no real need to either. His eyes glanced over the extensive CD collection, the DVDs that were stacked in genre rather than alphabetical order, the contents of the fridge that had been left open by one of the idiot cops who'd helped himself to a beer. The doors to the wardrobe were open as well, although Carl wasn't sure if they had been that way before the cops arrived. He convinced himself as he glanced through the various items of clothing that were hung inside the wardrobe that taking a dead man's clothes was a step too far, even for the most corrupt cops in the force.

Finally, Carl walked over to the bed and looked down at the motionless figure that lay there. It was a man in his early thirties, slim built and naked, laying face down on the bed. The side of his face was covered in the pool of blood that had stained the sheets beneath it. Some of the blood had ran over the side of the bed and formed a sticky puddle on the hardwood floor beneath. From where he lay, Carl could see that the young man had a bullet hole in the middle of his back. A soft sigh left Carl's lips as his gaze momentarily met the dead man's own, and then he took out his phone.

"You fucking prick," he snapped as Trent answered.

"What the hell is wrong with you?"

"Paperwork my ass, you've already seen the body, haven't you? Or the cops told you about it before you called me."

"What is that supposed to..."

"The dead guy's gay and you knew it. That's why you didn't want to take the case, you just couldn't force yourself to give a shit."

"So I don't like queers, so what?"

"You're the most homophobic bastard I ever met, Trent. You disowned your own son, for Christ's sake. Even when he got sick you couldn't force yourself to see past it!"

"I fail to see what this has to do with..."

"It wouldn't take a genius to figure out this guy's lifestyle. I hadn't even finished looking at his CD collection before it hit me. Once you heard, however that might've been, you decided that you honestly didn't give a crap how he died, so put it on me instead. Like I don't have enough to deal with right now!"

"All right, look. I don't like gays, I admit. That's why I asked you in on this one. I ain't gonna bring my A-game to the table for a queer and we both know it. If I took the case and you found out that I'd half-assed it, you'd be even more pissed," Trent explained.

"I'll take care of it. Get Glass to call me when he's done cutting into White," Carl snapped with a frustrated sigh.

"Thanks Carl, I appreciate..."

Carl didn't give Trent the chance to finish his sentence before he hung up the phone. People had their prejudices, especially in somewhere like the City. Everyone had more problems than they could deal with. The kind of problems that led most people to a bottle of pills or the edge of a bridge. Those kind of problems build an anger in you, an anger that either becomes self destructive or turns itself into hate. The second option is easier, find someone to hate and put it all on them. Blacks, gays, women, whatever you want. It's all their fault; your life sucks because of them. You're not a failure, not a worthless sack of crap. It's all because of the immigrants, the Democrats, the fill-in-the-blanks. Carl understood that, and he knew that it was no different for the cops, which was why he surprised himself at how he railed off as Trent. It was because of Jimmy, Carl knew that without giving the matter much thought. He'd always felt guilty for the crap Jimmy had been forced to put up with. Jimmy was white, American, physically able and intelligent. No different from Carl, except for his sexuality. One tiny difference that made a huge change in the way people treated him. Collectively, the world is a fucking child and always has been.

"Detective Duggan?" Came a soft, nervous voice from the doorway. It belonged to CSI Reeve, a bookish little guy who was probably the best in the East side. Like Carl, he was far too qualified and skilled to stay on this side of the river, but his sense of duty to the worse-off in the City stopped him from moving. Carl liked him, and always had. There were few people on the force that he respected, but Reeve was one of them.

"Hey, Reeve. How's it going?"

"I'm here, to, uh... that is, if you..." Reeve answered sheepishly, still as nervous around men like Carl as he had been when they met five years ago. Carl reminded him of the jocks that used to kick the crap out of him at school, and no amount of pleasantries from Carl would change that. He was a big guy and Reeve wasn't. Sometimes it was that simple, no thirty-dollar-an-hour therapist needed. Just nature at work.

"Yeah, I'm done. Come on in, kid, do your thing," Carl nodded.

"You find anything?" Reeve asked.

"No evidence of forced entry, no signs of struggle. Whoever did this didn't break his way in here, he was invited. Can't see that the guy was forcibly undressed, either, which says to me they were having sex when he was shot in the back."

"Looks like it was intentional... not accidental," Reeve remarked as he carefully studied the bullet wound.

"What do you mean?"
"Well, gun play is pretty common in sex these days," Reeve remarked. "Not that I've ever..."

"Reeve," Carl said with a tone of slight frustration.

"Sorry. Anyway, playing with loaded guns, pretend rape, that sort of thing, it's quite a big scene right now. It's quite common for people to get shot accidentally, that kind of thing. But it's rare for that to result in a killshot. This was right over the back of the heart. Which means either it was intended, or they were being very risky. And when the barrel is aimed at the heat, it's not the kind of mistake you can correct, you know?" Reeve explained. "But my professional opinion? I highly doubt the gun just accidentally went off."

"So from that, you think the murderer was on top of him?" Carl asked.

"That's right. Once we get this guy to the crime lab we can look for bruises and pressure marks on his back, estimate the guy's weight and height. That's good, because from what I see here they were sensible. Attacker had his gloves on, you know? No DNA for us to search for."

"Whatever else I might say about you guys, you're fucking good," Carl chuckled.

"What do you say about us?"

"You know, just that you're a bunch of nerds who should get out more," Carl shrugged.

"Oh... well that's probably true," Reeve smiled.

"Wouldn't have it any other way, Reeve," Carl assured him, patting the CSI on the back as he left. "Give me a shout when you have something more. I'm taking this case."

Chapter Fourteen;
Clearing the Air

The Ninth Street Police Station was the only station house on the East Side. There used to be another close to the bus depo, but it got so corrupt that it collapsed in on itself about ten years back. That's the thing about corruption in any sort of department, private or public; it's like a cancer. It can only go so far before it eats itself. A few guys taking bribes, dealing under the table, the department can still limp onwards doing what it does. But if every single person in the damn place is doing things they shouldn't, it breaks apart and the whole sorry mess falls like a house of cards. When that finally happened to the other station, City Hall couldn't honestly give a rat's ass, so they never made an effort to set up a new precinct. They didn't want cops on the East Side anyway; saw it as a waste of time and money. Let it burn, let everybody die.

Carl was one of the few officers in the East Side's only remaining precinct that wasn't corrupt. Sure he broke the rules now and then, but breaking the bones of dealers and pimps when a caution would suffice is hardly the same as corruption. He was still doing his job, after all—just doing it a little too enthusiastically. Near enough everyone else on the force has their hands in the shit somehow, even if it was just taking a few dollars here and there to look the other way. Detective Trent fell under that category, Carl was sorry to say. There were a good few shit-heads who never had to hear their Miranda Rights because they happened to have enough copies of Mr. Lincoln in their pockets to choose an alternative. Mr. Lincoln now spent a lot of time in Trent's wallet and he seemed quite happy there.

It was rare that Carl came to the station, he had little use for it. He had his own office, being a high-ranking Detective, but it was rarely utilised. His superiors, such as they were, knew better than to ask him to do paperwork, so the cleanup to his cases was usually delegated. With that in mind there was never really any reason for Carl to come down to Ninth Street, but right now he wanted to speak with Trent. Corrupt or otherwise, the two were friends and had even been partners a long time ago. That was before Carl decided that he worked better alone and took the solo shift instead. He had always been better on his own, of course, but his superiors had hoped that sticking him with Trent might cool his temper a little. The reality was different though. Trent took the bribes whilst Carl beat the crap out of people. Not much better a situation, so it was agreed that Carl could work alone.

His failings aside, Trent was a real cop. The kind who worked when it got dark, ate and drank as a necessity to keep on moving, and didn't really take any pleasure from anything. Small family, not many friends outside of work, and a sex-life that cost you each time you wanted to indulge in it. The glamorous life of law-enforcement in the City. Not many could stand it, hence the corruption setting in so easily. Trent liked the extra money the kickbacks brought him, but he was far from the worst. The dealers and pimps that he chose to ignore would never have been in prison more than a couple weeks anyway. The revolving-door prison system of a liberal, loved-up, fuck-hole society would have seen to that nicely.

"Hey, Trent," Carl called over to the older Detective as he stood outside the door to his own office.

"What are you doing down here? Didn't know you remember the way?" Trent called back.

"Smartass. Can I speak to you a second? My office?"

"Sure, two minutes," Trent responded, returning his attention to the officer with whom he had been speaking.

Carl entered his own office whilst he waited for Trent, admiring the dust-covered desk and the filing cabinets which he hadn't opened in months, if not years. His black-leather chair creaked as he sat down in it, reluctantly giving up its long-standing emptiness. At the back of his desk were two wooden drawers, neither one of them locked, which Carl decided to root through. They were mostly empty save for the usual random crap to be found in abandoned drawers; a notebook that wasn't even taken out of the plastic wrapper, a box of chewed pens, and an apple or orange that now resembled a lump of coal. The only item in the drawers which Carl found to be even remotely interesting was an old photograph of him and Jimmy, probably the only one from when they were kids. They were sat in a small boat holding up a fish the size of a small cat. Carl smiled to himself as he looked at the old photograph, and then grew frustrated when he couldn't remember who'd taken it. Surely it must have been his dad that took him fishing, but why would he have taken Jimmy as well, when he so clearly hated Carl being anywhere near him?

"What's up then, you miserable bastard?" Trent sighed as he entered the office, interrupting Carl's train of thought.

"Look, I was an ass when we spoke on the phone last night, I'm sorry," Carl conceded.

"So you don't think I'm a homophobic bastard?"

"Of course you are, but everyone's got their prejudices, right? Not for me to judge you on them, I guess," Carl shrugged.

"Then why'd you get so pissed off? If you know how I feel about gay guys then why throw a hissy fit when I don't wanna take a case that involves one of them?"

"I got this friend who's gay, alright? A close friend, probably the closest I ever had. Now I ain't gonna go marching in any parades for him or any of that bullshit, but I do kinda feel bad that I haven't been there for much of his life. I know he must've been through a lot of crap, taken his lumps more than once. And if I'd been there for at least some of it, I would've been able to stick up for him, I guess. Defend him from..."

"Guys like me?" Trent asked.

"Yeah," Carl nodded. "That guy on the bed wasn't Jimmy and you're not one of the assholes who probably kicked Jimmy around at some point, but I just got this guilt, I suppose. Always have done with that kid, even his own dad hated him."

"Don't go where I think you're gonna go, Carl," Trent warned.

"We're not talking about you and Lewis, alright? Your business with your kid is your own," Carl assured him. "I'm just saying, I shouldn't be passing my guilt over Jimmy's shit-hole of a life onto you."

"Okay, well I appreciate that, but it's weird coming from you. I don't know what you want me to do with that?"

"Just take the damn apology and get out of my office," Carl smiled.

"All right, apology accepted," Trent smiled. "Now when you leave, make sure you slam the door behind you, all right? If you don't leave looking pissed off then people will think we actually had a polite conversation in here. That wouldn't be good for either of our reps."

"Shit, you're right," Trent nodded, walking to the door and opening it, before shouting, "And fuck your goddamn proposals too, Duggan, you fucking prick! I don't want nothing to do with it, so suck my goddamn balls!"

With that, Trent slammed the office door and stormed off through the station. Carl watched him go and smiled to himself, chuckling softly.

"Nicely done, Trent. Nicely done."

Chapter Fifteen;
Moby Dick

"**I**'ve got him, Duggan! He's on my boat, his guts cut open!" Doctor Glass giggled down the phone.

"Come again?" Carl asked with a simultaneous rub of his sinuses.

"The white whale! His secrets are mine now!"

"Pretend for a moment that we don't all speak 'crazy' and explain to me what you mean," Carl said with a weary sigh.

"Judge White. He's a big fat guy and his name's White. So I compared him to Moby Dick? Get it?"

"You're high, aren't you Glass?" Carl asked with a second sigh.

"A little."

"Jesus Christ, Glass! Don't you remember what the DA said?"

"She said a lot of things."

"The most important of which being the fact that we can only keep your licence if you agreed to stay clean whilst on the job. You wanna get doped up in your own time, then that's your business. You start coming into the lab high as a kite again and we're gonna lose our only coroner."

"I was at home!" Glass said defensively. "But they called me in to say the injunction had been dropped and I couldn't wait to get started. There's a clock on poisons, you know. I told you that."

"You actually sounded lucid there so I'm going to assume you're on your way down. You clear-headed enough to keep at it? Don't want you crashing on me."

"Caffeine is a wonderful creation," Glass giggled. "Hey, it's not even that late yet, what're you doing up anyway?"

"I had an early meeting with Trent, and why the hell are you calling me if you thought I was gonna be asleep?

"I got a message to let you know as soon as I'd gotten some info on Moby Dick."

"I'm assuming that you do have some info?"

"Oh yes, like you wouldn't believe," Glass giggled again.

"Glass, I swear to God if you're calling to tell me he had a small dick..."

"No, of course not. I mean he did, but that's not what this is about," Glass assured him. "See, you wanted me to figure out which poison he'd been dosed with, right?"

"That's right. Once you knew the kind, you'd be able to tell the delivery method."

"Bingo. Except I hit a snag."

"Which was?"

"He hasn't been poisoned."

"What?"

"No poison in his system whatsoever," Glass reiterated.

"Did you cut him open in time? Could it have just left his system already?" Carl suggested.

"Nah, there'd have been some sign after this short a period, even if it was just trace damage in his veins. This guy didn't die from being poisoned, I'm sure of it."

"Do you know what did kill him?"

"Heart attack."

"Did he have a history of heart problems?" Asked Carl.

"Not yet. But I mean, he was probably heading towards them with his lifestyle. But he didn't get there naturally." Glass said, his voice barely stifling another giggle. Carl could tell from the increasing clarity of Glass's words that whatever crap he'd taken was wearing off, which could only be a good thing. Nothing more annoying than speaking to an addict in the middle of a high, especially when you had no other choice.

"What are you saying, Glass? I don't have time for riddles," Carl said firmly.

"I looked into what medication he was on, in case he might have had a bad reaction to any of it. Apparently, he was taking a prescription calcium supplement. Strong ones, but they wouldn't induce a heart attack. But when I cut into his heart, it showed signs of strain. The kind that'd be caused by nonsteroidal anti-inflammatory drugs. Again, nothing illegal, just prescription stuff. But if you didn't know you were taking them, and took them with too great a frequency?" Glass made an 'explosion' gesture with his hands to illustrate the effect on a man's heart.

"So you're saying that for two weeks at least he hasn't been taking the pills that he thought he was? Why would he switch to something else he didn't even need to take?"

"Well it's not me with the Detective badge, but I'd say that as far as Moby was concerned, he was taking his pills as normal. Only he wasn't."

"Someone switched them," Carl nodded.

"I doubt he'd do it himself." Glass shrugged. "Seems a very slow, lazy suicide."

"Which brings us right back to his wife," Carl said with a frustrated exhalation.

Chapter Sixteen;
History Lesson

To his self-confessed delight, Carl found that Jimmy had left him some dinner in the fridge before heading out to God-knows-where this evening. It was just a few slices of Pizza that needed warming, but Carl was glad of it. Left to his own devices, he wouldn't have eaten. One more night of pills and coffee to keep him going. His pills always went down better after having eaten something, the warning stating this was on the label on the bottle but Carl had never read it. If you spend time reading the warning labels on medicine, you'll find that the possible risks are worse than the condition that you are taking them for. Better to just swallow them and not worry about it. It was only through Jimmy's insistence that he eat something first that he'd actually noticed the lack of nausea accompanying the small white tablets.

The microwave pinged at the conclusion of its efforts, and Carl almost burned his hands in his eagerness to get the plate from inside. It smelt good, the combination of hot cheese and three kinds of meat wafting into his dry, cracked nostrils. To have the apartment filled with the smell of anything other than damp was a blessing. Still in a rush to head out to work, Carl just leaned against the kitchen counter whilst he ate. From this perspective he noticed the changes in his apartment that he had neglected to take note of earlier in the day.

"Son of a bitch! He cleaned!" Carl remarked to the empty room.

There were no discarded food wrappers on the floor, no half-drank cups of coffee left lying around on the surfaces. The dust that had long since laid down its roots on the window sills and surfaces was gone, replaced by a soft shimmer and the light smell of lemon. Carl smiled to himself, for a moment enjoying what it might have been like to have gotten married. An old-fashioned view, to be sure, but Carl was an old fashioned guy. In his head, the women did the cleaning and their husbands punched guys out for not telling what they knew. The world had changed, but not for the better. Independence was one thing, but it seemed like no-one was happy anymore. Freedom to do whatever you want, when you wanted to do it, brought as much misery as complete confinement. Having no purpose defined for you let some soar to the heavens, but it also meant that some would have no purpose. Period. The City was the perfect example of the latter option.

Funny thing was it hadn't always been this way. When it had been constructed at the turn of the nineteenth century, the City had been a vibrant new ground of hope and opportunity. Factories on the East side, in which goods were manufactured to be shipped out to every state in the country. And on the West the finest entertainment an honest buck could buy. Movies, theatres, dance stages and concert halls. The people of the City worked hard and played hard, who could blame them. The cops didn't have much to do, of course, but everyone knew their names.

The bullet that killed the dream wasn't even fired from the Great Depression. It came a couple of decades later, when the people buying the goods that funded the city decided they'd rather get them a couple of bucks cheaper from overseas. The major sources of industry in the City dried up, and hundreds of blue-collar guys went out of work. Some moved away, some didn't, and the city started to run low on funds with so much social security being paid out all of a sudden. A crippled local government and a vacuous hole in the economy is like a steaming great pile of shit that attracts flies with nice suits. Nice suits paid for through illegitimate means, of course.

Fortunately, or unfortunately depending on who you asked, the Mob never actually moved into the City. It would have been the perfect place for them to set up shop, but they left it alone. Instead, the void was filled by otherwise legitimate businessmen who now turned their heads to less morally-acceptable enterprises. Theatres became strip clubs, concert halls became massage parlours, and the manufacturing industry became the drug industry. Big business became crime, but the kind of crime that wears nice clothes and an expensive haircut so never gets arrested. The guys raking in the cash lived in the West, getting richer and fatter off the guys doing the leg work in the East, who all the while got poorer and sicker. The city followed suit with its people—the West growing so grand and opulent that it looked like it might collapse in on itself with having no foundation whatsoever, and the East giving way to decay and ruin. Only a few honest workers survived on either side, running coffee shops and DIY stores. The general rule is that if you make more than ten bucks and hour in the City, you're not making it honestly.

Ironically, since the corruption set in like a cancer, the cops that had actually been needed more than ever became increasingly useless. Most of them grew tired of arresting the same guys over and over, only to see them set back on the streets after slipping a few Lincolns in the pocket of the judge or the jury. Working your hardest every day to keep the streets clean seemed a goddamn waste of time when the same filth was just poured back out of the trash cans the following morning.

Some of the cops quit and moved away before the City took hold of them with its disease, others stayed on the job but placed themselves neatly in the pockets of the guys in suits. A very small number did their job well and with little or no corruption. That's the best you could hope for in the City—the lightest shade of grey.

Chapter Seventeen;
Queen Bea

His hands tucked firmly into the pockets of his long leather jacket, Carl ignored the cold night air and set off into the city. He was full of warm food and that seemed to help, but the air was biting. The kind of cold that felt like a thousand tiny demons scratching at your face with every step you took, invisible and silent but there all the same. Every now and then one of them would successfully breach your clothes with their claws, causing a shudder down the length of your spine. Carl was just coming close to acclimatising to the cold night when speckles of white started to fall around him, landing on his head and resting against his dark hair, the air too cold to let them melt.

"Wonderful," Carl muttered as the snow grew heavier.

Turning up the collar on his jacket he walked on, over towards the Steel Gate bridge. The dark black metal of the bridge was covered with a soft blanket of white, and Carl slipped twice as he made his way across it. He couldn't remember if it had snowed the previous year, but he supposed that it had done. The City was always cold, even in summer, so snow in the winter months made sense. Carl hated snow, mostly because it reminded him of everything it wasn't, and everything it should be. Anywhere else and a snowfall would be a source of happiness. School closures, kids sledding, preparations for Christmas. Not in the City. Here it was just one more thing to kill the homeless souls and the young girls selling themselves so that they could eat. Here the snow just meant that a cold night just got colder. Nothing more, nothing less.

Half way across the bridge, Carl's shoes lost their fragile grip on the ice-sheathed steel, causing him to fall forwards and hit the floor hard. His hands stopped him from smashing his face against the cold metal, but the frigid air enhanced the stabbing pain through his bones at the moment of impact. Carl swore through gritted teeth, obscenities leaving his lips in a cloud of frozen air. He was about to push himself back up when he noticed that he could see the Styx flowing by beneath him, visible through the steel-grated floor against his face. Staring down into the water, its frozen ghosts reflecting the moonlight, Carl thought he could make out a face staring back at him. His eyes struggled to focus against the dark water, the image broken as it was through the criss-crossed lines of black metal. When finally the image cleared, it was unmistakable.

"Amber?" Carl said aloud.

The ghostly face stared back up at him from below the bridge, somehow remaining in one place as though the dead girl was treading water. The image said nothing but her eyes bore into Carl's soul, sending a shiver down his spine that had nothing to do with the snow which had slowly begun to rest there. As Carl met the gaze of the phantom, a look of sadness passed over her, before the image faded back to the nothingness from which it had come. The cold snapping him back to reality, Carl pushed himself up and furiously rubbed his hands together, desperate to avoid the onset of frostbite that might now be a risk given the length of time he had left his hands pressed against the ice-cold metal of the bridge.

Carl Duggan didn't believe in ghosts, which is why he knew that what he had just seen was anything but. As a matter of fact, he knew exactly where the image of Amber had originated from, and that troubled him all the more. This wasn't the first time he'd seen such an image, after all. Ten years ago Carl had been working a missing person's case where a young bride disappeared the day after her wedding. Her ex-con former boyfriend was arrested and convicted on lousy evidence, much of which Carl himself had dug up. The guy had been obsessed with her, and never really got over it. His house had a wall on which every inch was covered with photographs of the girl. Not surprisingly, he was first on the list of obvious suspects when she suddenly disappeared. Carl thought the matter was put to bed, but for days after the conviction he would see the young girl staring at him. On a park bench, in his bedroom, anywhere he went alone when his mind would relax.

His mind was the source of the visions, there was nothing supernatural about them. When he let it wander, Carl's mind would tell him things that it might have missed during periods of conscious thought. That nagging doubt he'd always felt regarding the ex-boyfriend's guilt turned into a vision of the dead girl's ghost looking at him, trying to tell him that she couldn't rest. Not yet. Not until the real killer was found. So Carl went over the case again, ignoring everyone who told him to leave it be, and found some things that he might otherwise have missed. Like the fact that the dead girl's new husband was deeply in gambling debt until he married a naive little rich girl. Like the fact that his alibi wasn't worth shit when the witnesses were cross-analysed. Like the fact that the Chief of Police had bought a new car the week before the ex-boyfriend' trial. The case was reopened, the husband was convicted, and the dead girl went away. More accurately, Carl's mind stopped bugging him to keep looking.

The knowledge that this was the way his mind worked troubled Carl all the more at the sight of Amber staring up at him. He'd caught her killer, even shot him in the nuts as a final insult. The guy had confessed to everything, and not even under any threat or forced admission. He had been casual, brutally honest, cavalier. Big Dog had killed her—there was no doubt about it. So why was Carl's mind forcing Amber to haunt him? What had he missed? Why couldn't she rest yet? With a long sigh, Carl leaned against the edge of the bridge and closed his eyes.

"I got him," he whispered to the waters below, "I got him for you, kid...what do you want from me?"

Finally he turned from the dark water and continued his walk across the bridge. Carl had just crossed to the other side of the City when his cell phone rang, vibrating against his chest on the inside of his jacket. He cursed the damn thing for ringing, as he now had to take his hands from his moderately-warm pockets and introduce them to the cold air once more. Just after he'd regained the feeling in them, too. Damn cell phone. Damn snow.

"Duggan," Carl answered, the words leaving his mouth in a cloud of grey, frozen breath.

"Hey, Duggan, it's Trent. I got something for you."

"Is it a pair of gloves?" asked Carl, his fingers already tensing up as the freezing air caused his skin to stretch tightly across the bones of his hand.

"What? No."

"Then hurry it up," Carl insisted, keeping his other hand firmly inside his pocket, as though he could generate enough warmth in this one to compensate for that being lost in the hand clutching the phone.

"I felt kinda bad about landing that dead guy on you, so I did some digging. Trying to help you out a little, you know? Anyway, turns out our fairy was called Danny Delane. He worked for a club called the Hive, over on the West Side. Don't know much else, but if you're heading that way anyway then maybe you might wanna call in?"

"So you're gift for me was the fact that I now have to go to a gay bar?" Asked Carl.

"Um, yeah..."

"You're a fucking saint, Trent," Carl sighed.

"Yeah well, don't do anything I wouldn't do," Trent chuckled.

"I'll try and keep focus."

Carl replaced his phone and eagerly thrust his cold hand back into the waiting pocket. To his immediate relief he found that some of the warmth generated earlier had remained in the lining. With a final shudder against the cold, Carl increased his pace and ventured towards the nightclub district. Fei Ling White would wait, after all. As far as she was concerned she was no longer a suspect, so she wouldn't be running off anywhere soon. Whatever she had to say about the pills her husband had been taking in place of his usual meds, she'd say it just the same an hour or so later. The club-goers in the Hive, however, needed to be spoken with as a matter of urgency. People in locations like that had notoriously fickle memories, Carl knew that from experience. The longer he left it to ask about suspicious goings on, the less likely it was that any information he got would be accurate.

The Hive nightclub could be found on the main-street, illuminated by a glowing sign in the shape of a honey pot. Carl wondered if it symbolised something somehow, but decided that he'd rather not know, given the choice. The bouncer on the door of the club was a skinny black guy with white lipstick, wearing a cheap blonde wig. The doorway in which he was stood was sheltered, but he was still visibly shivering. Despite this he managed to smile at Carl as he approached, commenting in a decidedly feminine voice, "Now let me guess... you're either here to drag your son out of a gay bar, or you're a cop."

"What makes you think I'm not just a paying customer?" Carl asked.

"Oh please, honey, you're not fooling anyone," the bouncer laughed, gesturing his right hand as though he was pushing Carl away. "You're so straight-laced I'm surprised your shoes stay on."

"That's a good one, I haven't heard that before," Carl chuckled, taking out his badge. "Look, I need to speak to some of your regulars, people who come here often."

"Oh God, is someone in trouble?" The bouncer asked, putting his slender hands to his face.

"Did you know a guy called Danny Delane?"

"You mean Queen Bea? Oh he's not been caught dealing again, has he? After the last time he swore that..."

"He's dead," Carl interrupted.

"He's...are you sure?"

"Last I saw him, he had a bullet hole straight through his chest. That usually means I'm pretty sure."

"Oh God... Oh Shit, Danny..." Said the bouncer, his hands shaking as he brought them to his face once more.

"Look, I'm sorry..." Carl sighed, feeling a little guilty at his brazenness. "I'm used to this stuff, you're obviously not. I just need to talk to someone who was here the last time he worked."

"Well he was on a couple of nights ago, but then he had two days off, so we haven't missed him or anything."

"Do you know what he was planning on doing with his nights off? Anything that might get him into trouble?"

"Well we all just assumed he'd be spending them with the new friend he made. His latest little drone."

"You wanna explain that?" asked Carl.

"Sorry. Danny was a drag act, called himself Queen Bea. Wore a yellow and black dress, had a wig like a beehive, you get it?"

"I think I understand the joke. Go on..."

"Well every night after his performance he picks out someone from the audience, someone who catches his eye, and takes them home with him. Real rock and roll, that was Danny. He calls them his Drones, like with the worker bees that dote on their queen?"

"Still getting the joke, kid. Keep it relevant," Carl insisted.

"That's about it. He left with his latest drone and we weren't expecting him back until tomorrow," said the bouncer. "I can't believe he's...I mean, it doesn't feel real, you know?"

"It never does at first. If this guy was your friend, then when it hits you, you need to be at home, somewhere safe where you can relax and grieve."

"Not sure my boss would approve of my just going home," the bouncer smiled, trying to sound jovial but wiping a visible tear from his eye.

"He has a problem then tell him to speak with me," Carl insisted. "Look, right now the guy Danny left with is my prime suspect. Do you know anything about him?"

"He wasn't a regular, I'm pretty sure of that," the bouncer replied, shaking his head. "I didn't catch his face, but from his build, I'd say that I've never seen him before. And I see everyone that comes in here, obviously. They left together but I didn't get the best look at him, I'm afraid."

"Anything you remember at all would be helpful."

"Well he was quite a big guy, butch looking. Not as butch as you, of course, but then you're the real deal, not just a queen acting macho," the bouncer explained. "Dark hair, didn't really see what he was wearing. Sorry, I know that's probably useless."

"You never know, it's often surprising what turns out to be useful and what doesn't," Carl remarked. "Look, I know how things work in clubs over on this side of the City…everyone knows everyone but they don't *know* anything. I could go in there and speak with every single person and get nothing better than what you've told me. Am I right?"

"I dare say so," the bouncer sighed.

"You've been really co-operative so far and I'm grateful, but if there's anything else that you can tell me…"

"Alright, look…I can let you in on something but if my boss fires me, you have to promise me that you'll kick his ass."

"I'll do what I can," Carl assured him.

"Look behind your left shoulder and upwards, but don't make it obvious," The bouncer instructed.

Carl nodded and then glanced at his boot, pretending the lace was untied and crouching down to address it. As he did so, he glanced up in the direction that the bouncer had suggested, and noticed the camera hidden behind the traffic lights just outside the club entrance.

"You guys making cheap videos or something?" Carl asked as he stood back up.

"Videos? Yes. Cheap? No."

"Ah," Carl nodded. "So… stop me if I'm wrong here... you video people coming and going from this club, and bribe the ones who might not be so open about their sexuality to the general public?"

"Wow, smart and rugged."

"Being smart is my job. The ruggedness is a bonus," Carl remarked. "So your boss makes a lot of money from bribery, huh?"

"Yeah, but trying to bring it down on him is pointless. You'll never make it stick, not with the lawyers he has."

"I ain't interested in that."

"Good, 'cause that's not why I pointed it out to you. I thought you might want to have a look at the tapes and see who Danny left with. Big Pauly…that's my boss... his office is upstairs. He'll let you have a look if you pay him."

"You're a smart one, kid," Carl smiled as he opened the door to enter the club. "You ever think about joining the force?"

"As much as I'd like the uniform, I think my place is here."

"Whatever makes you happy," Carl shrugged.

"Look, one more thing. You should know that Danny was a good guy. He wasn't all that nice, bit of a bitch like the rest of the performers, but he was still a good guy. Decent, honest… whoever killed him probably knew that. Took advantage of it to get close to him."

"You're probably right," Carl nodded as he stepped inside the club. "Thanks for the help, kid."

"Just remember, if Big Pauly fires me, you kick his ass," The bouncer called after him.

"I'll try, but I think it kinda depends on how big 'Big Pauly' actually is," Carl called back.

Chapter Eighteen;
Big Pauly

"What the hell? Where's the rest of you?" Carl asked with a raised eyebrow as he looked down at the dark-haired midget sat in what seemed to be a ridiculously large leather chair.

"Smart guy, huh? Go ahead, try another, I heard all of 'em," Big Pauly smiled back with a simultaneous raising of his middle finger.

"Alright, I'll try and think of a good one before I leave," Carl shrugged, walking around the impressive office above the nightclub, whilst also taking note of the view of the city that could be seen from the large window. Even from above, the yellow and pink lights made it look tacky and oppressive. No real darkness, nowhere to hide. Everything right out in the open for the world to see and indulge in. No shame, no regrets.

"I look forward to hearing it. Now what do you want?" asked Pauly, taking a drag from the cigar stub he held in his tiny hand, adorning which were several golden rings Carl assumed to be custom made. They didn't make genuine sovereign rings in children's sizes, after all.

"I hear you're the guy to see if I want to watch a video?"

"You want some gay porn, go to the store across the street," Pauly replied.

"Not what I meant, Pauly, but thanks for the information. I'm looking for someone who came to your club two nights ago. He left with one of your performers, Queen Bea, otherwise known as Danny Delane,"

"Danny's due in work tomorrow, you can ask him yourself who he left with," Pauly shrugged.

"My name's Detective Carl Duggan. Danny's dead, Pauly. He was found murdered in his own room. The guy he left with is the last person I can guarantee saw him alive."

"Danny, you idiot," Pauly sighed to himself.

"Something you want to tell me?"

"Only that leaving with an audience member was nothing new for Danny. Different one every night. He was a man-whore, and not a kind one. After he'd had them once he'd give them the royal brush off. They tried to so much as speak with him again and he'd turn into the most venomous queen you ever met."

"So there could be an endless line of guys that hated him?"

"Hated him? Yeah, definitely. But guys that would murder him? No chance. The guys downstairs don't have that kinda inclination, you know?"

"You assume they couldn't be murderers because they're queer?" Carl asked with a doubtful raising of his left eyebrow. "You know how fucking stupid that sounds? Don't have to be straight to pull a trigger, Pauly."

"That's now what I meant, dickwad. You spoken with the guys downstairs? Queeny bitches, the lot of 'em. Worst they'd do is talk shit about him for the rest of time. Violence just ain't in 'em, not any of my regulars."

"You know your customers, then?"

"Why wouldn't I?"

"Well I don't get the impression that you're gay yourself, which means this is purely a business enterprise for you. Gay guys have a lot of disposable income, so you set up a place where they can come and piss it away into your pocket."

"All true," Pauly chuckled, tossing the remains of his cigar into the metal waste bin at his side. "But I'm not some homophobic bastard that sits up in his office all day and night. They got a sense for these things, you know. If they get the idea that the guy running the place is a queer-hater, they take their business elsewhere. So I go down to the club floor every night, talk to a few of 'em, give out cakes at birthdays, that sort of thing. Let 'em know that I don't give two shits where they stick their dick."

"How very modern of you."

"Never understood why some straight guys don't like 'em, you know? Just cuts down the field for the rest of us and seeing as how gay guys are almost always pretty boys, it just makes things even easier!"

"It occurs to me that you don't sound too upset about Danny's death," Carl remarked.

"What can I say? I didn't like the guy," Pauly shrugged. "That's not a crime is it, Detective?"

"Not last time I checked," Carl replied. "Why didn't you like him?"

"He was a tool. Thought he was too good for this place. Always talking about how he was going places, and would leave us all in his dust, that kind of thing. Never did it of course, he wasn't any more talented then your average drag act. Still, he thought he was better than me, better than this club, and delighted in telling everybody that."

"Then why not just fire him?"

"Tool or otherwise, he was a money maker. Like I said, he had a reputation for going off with guys at the first meet. We'd get a lot of guys in here hoping to be his next 'drone'. I won't miss the guy, but I'll miss the line of idiots throwing money to get near him."

"Which brings us back to why I'm here. Let me see the tapes."

"Not going to happen, sorry. I have to respect the privacy of my clientele."

"Then why have the camera in the first place?"

"Security."

"The security of your pension fund, you mean?" asked Carl.

"I have no idea what you're..."

"Cut the crap, Pauly," Carl snapped, walking over to the seated midget and staring down at him. "You keep those tapes to blackmail people who aren't quite as 'out' as they might be. I know it, you know it, so let's not dance around the fucking bush, alright?"

"Okay, I make a little from extortion. So do you, you're a cop. You gotta be on the take."

"Show me the tapes, Pauly," Carl growled, refusing to acknowledge the insult he'd just been dealt. That a cop's reputation was worth so little in the City grated on him, and Pauly wore his patience down to nothing just by mentioning it.

"I get paid a lot of money to get those tapes out from where they're kept, Detective. I don't really see you offering to pay up, so they're staying where they are."

"This is the last time I'm gonna ask you nicely, Pauly."

"Then I'll say this one more time, in the event that you didn't hear me all the way up there," Pauly replied, leaning forward in his chair so he was looking directly into Carl's face as he stared at him. "Not. Going. To. Happen."

Carl didn't say another word but grabbed hold of Big Pauly by his left ankle, then proceeded to drag him from his chair and across the office towards the large window.

Pauly struggled and cried out, but it was more than useless. A normal sized man would have been ill-equipped to break Carl's grip when he was pissed off and not only was Pauly far from normal-sized, but Carl was very pissed off. He lifted Pauly from the ground with one hand and opened the large window with the other, at which point he dangled the flailing midget outside, leaving him staring down at the street far below.

"You're a goddamn psycho!" He screamed, his voice sounding high pitched and almost comical.

"And you're a moron if you think wiggling around like that is actually a smart move right now."

"Let me go!"

"Again, not a smart thing to suggest," Carl remarked casually.

"You're not gonna let me drop, you tall streak of piss!"

"Maybe not intentionally," Carl agreed. "Hey, did you know I used to box? Not professionally, of course, but just to keep in shape. Station had its own gym in those days, of course. Not quite sure where the money came from, but still. Had me a trainer and everything, I developed quite a right hook."

"What the fuck does this have to do with anything?" Pauly screamed, desperately twisting and turning in Carl's grip, trying in vain to find something on the wall in front of him that he might cling on to.

"I'm telling a story. Don't interrupt, it's rude. So anyway, only thing was my trainer always told me I used to overdo it on the right. Relied on it too much, both for defence and attack. Messed up some of the muscles in my arm something fierce. Nothing to worry about, of course, but I had to stop with the heavy weight lifting. You know why?"

"Alright, why?" Pauly screamed.

"'Cause now and again, if I was holding something heavy, my arm would just seize up and I couldn't keep my grip on it. Kinda dangerous when you're holding a barbell or something."

"Jesus Christ, let me up!" Pauly cried, his panic suddenly increased by Carl's revelation.

"Are you going to share your toys with me?"
"Yes, you can watch the tape, just let me in!"

"Thank you," Carl smiled, dragging Pauly back in and letting him drop somewhat gracelessly back into his leather chair.

"Christ in Hades, you this friendly with all your witnesses?" asked Pauly, straightening his suit in an effort to regain some dignity.

"Depends how cooperative they are. So... videotapes?"

"You know how much money you're losing me here?"

Pauly walked over to a large black filing cabinet and input a code into the key pad which was affixed to a drawer at the bottom. Carl wondered if the entire thing had been custom made, as such a security device would usually be placed at the top of the cabinet. It wasn't as though a custom filing cabinet would break the bank of a man like Pauly, of course. He could afford a dozen of them in a week and still put away enough money to buy half the buildings on the other side of the City. The value of someone's life in the City was frequently judged by their bank balance, and in Pauly's case he was high up on the list. None of that mattered to Carl, of course. To him, Pauly was just one more person who knew something he wanted to learn. One more piece of the puzzle, even if it was just a small one.

"Tell you what," Carl suggested. "Show me the tape without giving me further reason to hang your little ass out that window, and I'll let you keep it for your collection."

"You're not going to arrest me for admitting to blackmail?" Pauly asked, turning from the open drawer through which he was currently searching.

"The paperwork for blackmail cases is hassle I don't need, Pauly. The way I see it, you're a businessman, right? And a smart one at that. You ain't gonna be blackmailing any guys that don't have money to spend. And in this City, the guys with money like that aren't the guys I care about protecting."

"So I'm not going to have to bribe a load of cops to keep this quiet?"

"Nope."

"I like you, Detective. I'm almost willing to forget the whole window thing. And, you know, the fact that you're a goddamn prick."

"You're making me blush, Pauly."

"Here's the tape," said Pauly, closing the drawer and handing the black tape to Carl.

"You got a TV in here?"

Big Pauly set up the small portable TV at the back of his office and pushed the videotape into the VCR that was connected to it. It loaded up immediately, revealing a surprisingly high-quality picture of the street outside the club. The date and time in the bottom-left corner of the black-and-white image showed that it had been taken two nights previously. Carl nodded at Pauly to confirm that they were viewing the correct tape, and then Pauly proceeded to fast-forward the tape until the time showed 9 p.m.

"That's about the time Danny left for the night," Pauly explained, tapping the screen where the clock was. "He was the early slot—we get into the more raunchy performers later on, that's how it works."

"Picture's pretty good," Carl remarked.

"I know, the camera's state of the art. Just can't figure out how to hook the damn thing up to record on CD rather than tape."

"And hiring a technician would mean there was one more person you needed to bribe," Carl smirked.

"Hey, it ain't easy making money on this side of the Styx, you know."

"Tell that to the people on my side who can't afford a loaf of bread, Pauly. Sure you'd have a long discussion about how tough things are."

"My heart bleeds. Wait, here we go..."

Pauly paused the tape at the point where a slender white guy left the club with another white male of much larger frame. The man was tall and broad, his denim jacket stretched across his shoulders. Carl narrowed his eyes as he estimated the man's measurements, deciding that they must be just slightly less than his own stature. The man's face, however—the most relevant part of the picture—was obscured. This wasn't due to the angle of the camera or the usual hindrances faced with surveillance equipment, but rather the fact that the man's face was covered with a dark-coloured opera mask, not unlike those worn at Masked Balls.

"What the hell's he wearing?"

"I'd say it's an Opera Mask, Detective."

"I can see that, Tiny, what I mean is why is he wearing it?"

"What am I? A guru on queer fashion? They wear all kinds of things. Some guys come in wearing fireman's helmets or dressed as sailors. This guy obviously has his taste set in a more classic period."

"Or he's deliberately hiding his face."

"Always gotta be something suspicious with guys like you, hasn't it?" Pauly sighed.

"If he was wearing a full Period costume then I'd buy your theory, but the fact that he's wearing a denim jacket with that mask puts it to bed. Gay guys tend to be kind of particular about their fashion, right?"

"You can't use a stereotype to reinforce your theory!" Pauly objected.

"True, but no one in their right mind can think that combination looks good. He's wearing that mask for a reason, but Delane obviously didn't pick up on it."

"He wasn't the smartest kid when it came to things like that. Thought he was in control of every situation, always the guy on top."

"Not this time," Carl said with a soft exhalation. "That guy would only hide his face if he knew the camera was there, which means it's likely to be someone you've blackmailed before."

"I remember the guys I've gotten money from before and even with the mask I can see that's not any of them."

"You sure?"

"Hey, if someone I messed with is pissed at me, you don't think I'd let you know exactly who it was?"

"Fair point," Carl nodded. "So maybe he didn't know the camera was there, but just didn't want to be seen at all."

"Newbie, gotta be," Pauly nodded. "Insecure about his sexuality, didn't want to risk being recognised. We got a lot like that, but they usually just change their hair or something. Wearing a mask is extreme, but smart, I guess."

"All of which means this little trip here was damn useless," Carl said with a frustrated sigh, standing up and banging his hand against the side of the black filing cabinet.

"You need a partner," Pauly suggested.

"What?"

"All that stuff you just went through out loud, it wouldn't have happened if you didn't have me here to bounce it off. You need someone to talk with for stuff like this."

"I work better alone."

"You might think that, but clearly it ain't true."

"Well, I'll be sure to take your suggestions regarding police work under advisement, Pauly," Carl nodded, irritated at the fact that Pauly was right. Police work was easier when you had someone to discuss ideas with. Unfortunately, Carl had precious few people he could trust with his cases anymore, so that left talking out of the question. Just him and his thoughts, for better or worse.

"So now you're gonna leave me in peace?" Pauly asked, his tone filled with fragile hope.

"You don't have anything else that I need, so I'll let you get back to whatever it is you do all night," Carl assured him.

Pauly smiled and opened his desk drawer, taking out a small dark-brown box and opening it so that it was facing Carl. Inside were two-dozen perfectly-rolled cigars of the finest quality.

"Just to show there are no hard feelings," Pauly smiled.

"Cubans?"

"The very best. Hundred bucks a piece."

"Legal?" Carl enquired.

"Not in the slightest."

"Which is exactly how much I care right about now," Carl shrugged, taking a cigar and letting Pauly light it for him with his solid gold lighter. He took a satisfied puff and then asked, "What's with the making nice now? Considering how our conversation started this evening?"

"Bygones," Pauly smiled, placing a cigar in the corner of his own mouth. "The way I see it, you're probably one of the few cops left in the city who's not in someone's pocket. Plus you're a crazy bastard and strong as a goddamn ox. Ass-wipe or otherwise, I'd rather have you as a friend than an enemy."

"Words to live by," Carl agreed as he took his leave of Pauly's office, the cigar providing some warmth as he ventured back out into the arctic cold.

Chapter Nineteen;
The Witch Is Dead

Carl felt sick. The black, nauseating bile that he always experienced when he spent too long on the West side had started to build to a crescendo in his stomach. It was like water put on to boil, and now it had started to bubble towards the top of the pan. He wanted to go home, to get away from the lights and the noise and the goddamn feeling of dirty underneath his skin. But he couldn't, not yet. Glass, high as a kite or otherwise, had a point when Carl spoke to him. If Judge White's pills had been switched, the obvious culprit was his wife, Fei Ling. Carl hadn't gotten the impression she was lying, but there was no question that she was a manipulative bitch. She'd probably pulled the wool over the eyes of men smarter than Carl in her time. That didn't stop the Detective from cursing himself for being such an idiot, but still it provided some comfort.

The Diamond Heights apartment building reared up before him once again, mocking him with its decadence. A red carpet led to the door, on either side of which was a row of gold-painted bollards linked by dark velvet ropes. Stood at the door was a large doorman, different to the one Carl had seen before and not quite as well dressed. His jacket seemed a size too big, his tie was in an awkward knot, and his shoes didn't match the smart black suit in any way imaginable. Carl assumed that the guy had received some form of bribe from one of the call girls that invariably arrived earlier in the evening and had taken himself temporarily off duty to enjoy it. His rushed appearance could be explained by the hurried way in which he redressed himself after getting his rocks off. Given the size of the guy, Carl felt sorry for the girl.

"Evening," Carl remarked. "Brisk tonight, huh? They don't give you a scarf?"

"What do you want?"

"Friendly," Carl commented. "I'm here to see Mrs. White, top floor."

"Mrs. White is busy. She has other guests this evening and is not to be disturbed."

"She won't mind, we're old friends."

"Then call her on the phone when you get home. She ain't sucking your dick tonight. Now beat it."

"Look...this has not been a good night for me. I'm cold, I'm tired, and I fucking hate everything in a five mile radius around me right now. The sooner you let me go talk to Mrs. White, the sooner I'm gone and we're all happy."

"Like I said, Mrs. White is not available this evening. You retarded or something? Go home."

Carl didn't ask again, but the right-hook to the doorman's jaw seemed to settle the matter. He went down hard and smashed his temple against one of the gold-painted bollards, dragging the red velvet ropes down on top of him in an awkward pile. Two fingers to the left side of his neck confirmed to Carl that the guy was still alive, leaving him to enter the apartment building without further hassle. As he entered the lobby, however, he cursed under his breath at the sight of the reception desk. If the attendant had seen what had just occurred then they'd surely have called security, which would make things that much harder. Carl's relief at seeing an empty reception desk didn't last long, however, as a nagging feeling began to creep its way up his neck.

The desk shouldn't be empty, not in a hotel like this. The arrogant, self-important pricks who lived here would expect to be greeted each and every time they entered. They couldn't bear the thought of sitting on their asses before someone kissed them. The thought of carrying their own bags was enough to give most of them convulsions, for one thing. An empty desk was not an option, so why was it unattended now? As the thoughts on this matter ran through his head, a sound slowly began to reach Carl's ears; it was the monotonous, droning sound of a phone that had been lifted from the receiver and left there. The kind of sound that remained lingering in the ears long after it had actually stopped.

Carl followed the sound to the reception desk, where he found the phone rested on its side. Slumped forwards on the desk was the receptionist, her blonde hair stuck together in clumps from the sticky red blood that had pooled against it. Walking around the side of the desk, Carl gently lifted the girl to an upright position, so that he could confirm what he already knew—there was a fresh bullet hole in her forehead, still dripping slightly. Her eyes were wide open, staring in horror at whoever was the last person she would ever see. With a gentle movement, Carl closed her eyelids and then rested the girl's head back against the desk, sideways this time as though she were sleeping. He knew that he had just messed up a crime scene, but he didn't really care. Let her have some dignity, it was the last gift anyone would give to her.

Instinctively, Carl drew his gun as he walked towards the elevator. Stairs were probably safer in this instance, less chance of exploding. He knew that of course, but he wasn't about to exhaust himself before even coming across the killer. As the elevator doors opened before him, Carl raised his gun, gripping it tightly and pointing it inside the car. The only person he found there was the corpse of the doorman he had spoken to on his previous visit, his limp form slumped in the corner. His jacket, shirt and tie were removed, and he too had a bullet hole in his head. Carl held the elevator door open and glanced back at the "doorman" he had been knocked unconscious, assuring himself that the impostor was still in dreamland. Satisfied that he wouldn't be coming after him in the immediate future, Carl entered the elevator and pressed for the top floor.

The numbers on the right-hand wall next to the doors lit up one by one, circled by a red ring of electric light. Eight, nine, ten. As the number "fourteen" lit up, Carl raised his gun once more, so that it was ready to immediately discharge into the chest of anyone stupid enough to be waiting for him on the next and final floor. The doors opened onto an empty hallway, but Carl still moved quickly and quietly through it. Only three doors were present; the two apartments that could be found on this floor and the fire exit. The latter door was closed, but that didn't mean it hadn't been used recently. Those things were heavy, they'd close themselves even if the escapee didn't take the time to cover his tracks. Carl looked at the fire escape and then back towards Mrs. White's apartment. He was about to move towards the fire door when he heard the sound of something breaking into Mrs. White's room. A vase, a lamp, it didn't matter. Someone was in there, and the woman hadn't seemed like the clumsy type.

Keeping close to the wall, Carl approached the door to apartment 202, slowly turning the handle as quietly as he could. With a silent count of three, he then swung the door open wide and entered, gun first. The sound of the door banging back against the wall was immediately followed by the noise of someone scuffling and tripping across the floor in a desperate effort to get away. Carl turned sharply and saw a small figure to his right, at which he instantly aimed his weapon.

"Not another step," he warned.

The figure froze and raised its hands, standing upright now keeping perfectly still. Carl could now see that it was a girl, young and skinny with hair died a cheap purple. The girl was dressed in a pirate costume; white shirt, black shorts and striped knee-socks, with a black waistcoat and a black bandanna. Her face was painted like a skull in luminous pink makeup, but Carl still recognised her; it was the girl he'd rescued from Big Dog at the bus station.

"Please... I... I didn't know what they... what they were going to do... I just..."

"What are you on?" Carl demanded.

"I'm not, I..."

"Heroin?" Carl asked, noticing the way the girl shook despite the pleasant temperature of the room.

"They said... they said they'd give me another hit... all I had to do was come along, and..."

"Who said?"

"Zack... he's... he's my friend, he took me in and..."

"Captain Zack," Carl said through gritted teeth. "Where is he?"

"He's left... they all left, I was supposed to... supposed to clean up, before..."

"Clean up what?" Carl said, suddenly reminding himself whose apartment he was stood inside. "Where's Fei Ling White?"

"I didn't... it wasn't me, I swear. I didn't know what they were..."

"Where is she?" Carl demanded, grabbing the girl by the shoulders and shaking her furiously.

"The bedroom! She's in the bedroom!" The girl sobbed, dropping to her knees and crying as Carl let go of her.

He left the girl where she was and kicked open the door to the bedroom. Carl knew what he would find inside, of course, but he wasn't sure exactly how it would present itself. Sure enough, Fei Ling White lay dead on her luxury bed, the blood drained from the open wound on her throat. She was sat up in her bed with the gaping smile across her neck, her arms tied to the bedposts at either side of her. Hung on the wall above her was a black flag on which was adorned a white skull and crossbones.

"Shit," Carl muttered to himself.

'Captain' Zack Taylor and his Jolly Rogers were the most prominent gang on the West Side. Their activities consisted of dressing like pirates, decorating their faces and clothes with neon paint, and driving around the city doing whatever they pleased. Robberies, murders, whatever took the mood of their leader that particular evening. At last count there were about fifty of them, but it was hard to be sure. More joined all the time, for the ride, for the high. Zack himself was the kind of criminal Carl hated more than any other. When not "in costume", Zack was an investment banker. The kind who made enough money in a week to buy himself out of trouble for a whole year. He was untouchable and a hedonist. Dangerous combination, and the kind that attracts others of like-mind.

Entering a residence like Diamond Heights would have been hard work even for Captain Zack, Carl thought to himself. Especially considering the fact that his chosen victim for the evening was on the very top floor. Lot of effort to go through for a random killing.

So that left the likelihood that it wasn't random. With that thought settled, Carl returned to the living room and found the purple-haired girl still sobbing to herself. He reached down and pulled her up by her arm, then held her tightly to stare directly into her dark-rimmed eyes.

"Why did they kill her? What was she to Zack?"

"I don't know, I swear," she sobbed. "This was the first time I've come along with them... I only signed up a day ago, I..."

"Wanted free drugs, yeah I got that part," Carl said impatiently. "They must have said something, I know Captain Zack. He likes to brag. What did he say about Mrs. White?"

"I don't know, I wasn't listening to that... I kept asking him for a hit, I..."

"You didn't get it, did you?" asked Carl.

"He said he'd give it to me after I cleaned up... wiped away their boot prints, cleaned up the stuff they'd broken..."

"Goddamn, you're even more of an idiot than you look," Carl sighed. "There's a dead body tied to the bed with a pirate flag hung above it in that bedroom! How were you gonna clean that up?"

"I... he didn't say, he..."

"He's playing you, you moron! Set the new girl some stupid task, promise her drugs, let her take the rap as she's the only one still present when the cops arrive!"

"Why would he do that?" The girl sobbed hysterically, the realisation of her situation dawning on her at last.

"Because he's a fucking tool, that's why! Jesus, you honestly thought a guy who dresses like a pirate and shoots people was someone you could trust?"

"I just... I needed a hit... he said he would... he said..."

"Tell me what they said about Mrs. White, kid," Carl said with a sigh, unable to stay angry at the girl who seemed more pathetic with each passing moment.

"Before they left...just before he told me to clean up... he said 'that's as close as the bastard's going to get'. That's all I remember, I swear."

"Alright, I believe you," Carl nodded. "I need to get some blue boys down here, preferably from my side of the river. You might wanna get out of here before they arrive."

Carl walked towards the door and opened it, then stopped as he heard the girl call after him, "Please help me... I don't know anyone here... I... I don't know where to go..."

Carl had better things to do than help a heroin addict. This case just took a nose dive into the insane, and his attention couldn't be distracted. But the girl looked barely seventeen, if that. The only thing she had to go back to was Zack. If she turned up alive, he'd probably kill her for the fun of it. Probably rape her first, knowing his M.O. Carl asked himself if he could live with that, and immediately turned back towards the girl when the answer bludgeoned the inside of his chest like a sledgehammer of guilt.

"Come on," Carl said softly, taking his leather jacket and wrapping it around the girl's shoulders. "Let's get you somewhere safe."

Chapter Twenty;
Skye

The Seven Saints was the only hospital on the West side of the Styx and was undoubtedly the last place that many of the City's unfortunates would see the inside of. It was a good hospital with good doctors, but doctors who had to manage with far less than a hospital should. What kept the hospital good and pure was the same thing that kept it poor and ill-equipped—lack of funding. The two hospitals on the other side of the river were owned by private investors, which kept them clean, well-staffed and very, very corrupt. Poorer patients might suddenly die in their beds if a rich guy needed an organ transplant, for instance. Write it up as 'medical complications' and nobody sues. Medicine's complicated, you can't be suspicious when you don't understand the science to begin with. Lots of loopholes through which more money could be made by those that already had more than enough.

Carl had left the young, purple-haired girl in the care of the doctors at Seven Saints on the previous night. By the time they'd walked from Diamond Heights to the Steel Gate Bridge, the girl had collapsed from sheer exhaustion. Carl had lifted her into his arms, still wrapped in his coat, and carried her the rest of the way. His arms ached and the cold bit into his flesh through his grey shirt, but he ignored both. Neither was relevant enough to put the girl down, to let her succumb to whatever crap Taylor had given her. Carl wasn't an idiot, he knew that the girl was probably an addict long before she arrived at the City, but Taylor and his band of Pirate dickwads hadn't helped her. New to the City, alone and afraid, and they immediately set upon her, feeding off her addiction. That's how the City works; if it sees a weakness in you, then you'd better expect to have a knife stuck in it and twisted.

As he walked in the direction of the hospital, Carl glanced at his watch and noticed that it was a few minutes before five. He looked at the shops on the sides of the street, the few that weren't either boarded up or long-since boarded up and knew that they would be closing soon. This quickened his pace somewhat as he crossed the street, almost tripping on a loose piece of pavement as he made his way to "Street Vibes" clothing store.

"You need to get her some clothes," Jimmy had told him when they had spoken the previous night.

"Why?" Carl had asked.

"Because she's scared and homeless and dressed like a pirate! Jesus, Carl, even you're not that dense! She's gonna need some stuff—help her out."

"I wouldn't know what to get."

"How old is she?" Jimmy asked.

"I dunno, about seventeen maybe?"

"And what is she? What's her style?"

"How the fuck should I know? You're the fashion guru."

"You assume that because I'm gay?" Jimmy asked with an outraged folding of his arms.

"I assume that because you have more shoes than I have socks. I'm running out of room in my damn closet."

"We're not discussing my shoe collection," Jimmy had reminded him. "What did the girl look like?"

"Purple hair, a piercing in her nose, I think... maybe a tattoo on her right arm, thought I saw it though the shirt but that could have been a bruise."

"Relax, I figured it out at 'purple hair'. You want to get some rock-chick type stuff. Nothing that looks too fancy or expensive, just some jeans, loose T-shirts, stuff with bands on them. Any bands; if you haven't heard of 'em that's probably good. If no one's heard of them then that's even better. Now if she hasn't heard of them you're golden."

"Why would someone want to wear a shirt with a band on they haven't heard of?"

"It's kids, they think it's all cool and nonconformist, or whatever."

"Sounds fucking retarded," Carl remarked.

The store owner was just about to close the steel shutters over his window when Carl ran over to him.

"Hey, wait a second," he called.

"Sorry pal, you'll have to come back tomorrow."

"I need some clothes, it's kind of an emergency," Carl explained. "I'll pay you double whatever it costs."

"You serious? I only sell clothes, you know. No drugs or anything."

"Just open the damn shutter, will you?" Carl asked, catching his breath after the mad dash across the street.

The inside of the store was like a nightmare for Carl. He remembered clothes stores being organised in garment type and size. Not in here, where you'd find shirts and pants and belts on the same damn wrack. Who the hell had organised this place? How was anyone supposed to find what they needed? Carl decided to forgive the organisation of the place, however, when he noticed the prices on the plastic tags. For a shop like this to stay in business on the East side, the prices would have to be competitive, and they certainly were. Carl was self-admittedly ignorant about the cost of modern clothing, but he'd heard horror stories about jeans going for over a hundred bucks, so was glad to find some for less than thirty.

"Not sure those would fit you, big guy," the shop tender remarked as he stood impatiently at the cash register, tapping a chewed ball-point pen against the counter.

"Funny," Carl smirked.

"Your daughter?" The shop tender asked.

"Not exactly."

"You old dog, good on you!"

"I'm a cop and I'm carrying a gun right now, smartass. You might wanna consider that before you say anything else," Carl informed him.

"Hey, we all got urges, buddy," said the tender, raising his arms in a defensive gesture. "You know her size, I take it?"

"I got a rough idea," Carl replied, his Detective skills having come in use at estimating the girl's height and measurements. "You got any shirts with bands on them or anything?"

"Over there," the tender remarked, pointing at a small rack in the corner of the shop.

"Who the hell are F.T.O?" Carl muttered, lifting a black T-shirt which bore a design featuring the band name and a sketch of an octopus-like creature.

"How should I know?" The tender shrugged.

"Nothing like knowing your own business," Carl muttered as he took the shirt and three others, then walked over to the counter.

The clothes were folded and placed in a large brown paper bag, and after Carl had made his feelings known regarding the fact that the shirts had each cost more than the jeans, he left the store and continued his walk to the hospital. There was a dirty white covering of snow lingering on the ground from the previous evening's fall, causing Carl's footfalls to make an audible crunch with every step. The sky was filled with thick cloud promising more to come, but for the moment it was holding itself at bay. Carl was glad of this, as he didn't relish the though of another night walking through freezing snow.

The doors to the hospital were automated but didn't open when Carl approached. A small paper note in the corner of the glass revealed that they were out of order, so Carl stepped to one side and opened the left door by hand. Upon entering he walked over to the desk attendant who was dressed in a thick sweater and gloves, owing to the cold temperature of the hallways. Any funds to heat the hospital were used to keep the occupied rooms at a comfortable temperature; there wasn't enough to keep the staff areas warm as well. Not that any of them complained, that wasn't the type of person you would find in these old, crumbling walls. Each and every one of them, from the administration staff to the doctors knew that they could do the same job for ten times the pay across the Styx, but at the expense of their soul. Not a price any of them were willing to pay, regardless of how shiny and tempting the gold might look. Carl hated how the few good people of the City were so neglected and downtrodden but could not remember a time when it had been any different. Sin brought comforts, decency brought pain.

"Hello there," The wrapped-up receptionist smiled with a shiver.

"Hi. I'm looking for a young girl, I brought her in yesterday?" Carl enquired.

"Oh, of course, I remember. She's in room twelve, just down the hall and to your left,"

Carl thanked the woman and walked quickly down the hall, the brown paper bag tucked under his arm. The number twelve was written on the door in thick black ink, the metal numbers that were formerly stuck there having long since fallen away and been lost. Carl knocked twice and then opened the door gently. The room was lit by a single lamp at the bedside, and the purple-haired girl was laying facing away from him as he entered.

"Hey," Carl said quietly.

"Hm?" The girl muttered, having been almost asleep when Carl entered. She turned and saw him, then smiled. "Hey! It's you!"

"Yeah. I wasn't sure if you'd..."

"Remember you? Of course I do, you saved me! Twice!"

"Twice?"

"The bus station. That was you, right?"

"Yeah."

"Then thank you twice," the girl smiled, sitting up in her white bed and brushing her long hair from her face. Carl looked at her in the light of the old lamp, the style of which didn't really match the room decor and noticed for the first time how pretty she was. That was partly due to the fact that she looked much better than she had the night before, her pale skin no longer covered in bright pink makeup and her eyes no longer glassed-over.

"They put you on some meds?" Carl asked.

"Yeah, something to clean the crap out of my blood." The girl smiled, lifting her arm and revealing the drip line attached there.

"You feeling any better?"

"Yeah, actually. I think a lot of that is having a good night's sleep for the first time in months, you know?"

"Where have you been sleeping?" Carl asked.

"Bus stations, parks, anywhere I can get really. But I never sleep properly, I can't. Last night was different, I guess. For the first time in years I felt, well, safe."

"I'm glad you're feeling better," Carl smiled, feeling somewhat awkward, given that the situation was far removed from his area of expertise. Unable to think of anything to immediately say to the young girl, he took the paper bag from under his arm and passed it to her. "This is for you."

"For me?" she asked with a look of surprise.

"Yeah," he shrugged. "I didn't think you'd want to be wearing that pirate costume or whatever, so..."

"You bought me clothes?" The girl laughed, smiling so broadly that her lips almost touched her ears.

"Sorry if they're crap, I don't really..."

"You are the greatest guy I've ever met. Ever," she beamed, taking out the clothes and looking at each item in turn.

"Well... glad you like 'em," Carl smiled again, hating himself for the fact that he was visibly blushing.

"You didn't have to do this, you know. Any of it."

"Yeah I did. You needed help and I was there. That's kinda my job, I'm a cop."

"What's your name?" asked the girl. "You might have told me, but I don't think I was in any state to remember."

"Detective Duggan... Carl."

"I'm Skye."

"Okay, Skye, well, I actually need to ask you a few questions. Don't think that's the only reason I came here, but..."

"You gotta do your job, I get it. And don't worry, you couldn't do anything now that would change my opinion of you," she smiled. "You're my hero."

"Don't put that on me, I'm just a guy who..."

"You're my hero and I'll always think that no matter what you say, so just shut up and take it, okay?"

"Um… okay," Carl replied, not really knowing what else to say. "So do you feel up to answering some questions?"

"Sure."

"Thank you," Carl nodded, grabbing a chair from the corner of the room and pulling it over, taking a seat next to the bed where Skye sat. He took out his notebook and then asked, "So how did you meet Taylor?"

"Who's that?"

"Captain Zack, sorry. Guessing the asshole didn't tell you his name."

"Oh right. Well I was sleeping at the bus station and his boys came in. Shot a few of the homeless guys, scared 'em off, then said I should come with them. They gave me a hit and I don't really remember much after that. God, it must have been some strong stuff, I've never felt anything like that."

"Nothing but the best from that prick," Carl nodded. "So where did they take you?"

"This club... like a basement, but lots of graffiti everywhere in that neon paint. I was sat getting pawed at by some of the guys in his gang, whilst he spoke on the phone about some gig."

"What gig?"

"I don't remember, I was kind of out of it, you know?"

"Anything at all, Skye. Please, this is important," Carl insisted.

"He called the guy Boss, said he'd 'take care of the loose ends,' and 'clean up the mess'. Then we went off to that Asian woman's house. God they... they killed her, didn't they?"

"Yeah, they did. Don't worry I'm not going to charge you with anything."

"But I was there, I was part of it!"

"No you weren't, not as far as I'm concerned. And if anyone asks, you weren't even there, you understand?" Carl said firmly.

"Why do you keep helping me?" asked Skye, tilting her head to one side and looking right into Carl's eyes.

"Because you're as much as a victim here as Mrs. White was. This City has a habit of mixing up the bad guys from the good. I don't."

"I'm not a good person. I've done some shit that..."

"We all have," Carl interrupted her. "But what I see now is a frightened young girl making whatever choices she has to in order to survive. You got hooked on drugs, ran away from home and everything since then has been a clusterfuck, right?"

"Yeah..." The girl nodded.

"You're not the first and I'm sad to say you won't be the last. But you're done with it, okay? You're out. I'm gonna get you set up in rehab, give you some money to get a place together and I'll see if I can get you a job somewhere. I think I know a store that could use an assistant, since it looked like it had been set out by a moron..."

"I can't take money from you, I can't just..."

"I'm not taking 'no' for an answer, so you're gonna shut up and take it, understand?" Carl asked, deliberately paraphrasing the girl's own words from earlier in their conversation.

"Okay," she said quietly with a slight nod.

"Stay here a couple more days, get that stuff out of your system and we'll get you fixed up. Don't worry about the money, I never spend it. Friend of mine ribs me about it something fierce, but I never have anything to buy, so why waste it?"

"Bet you're the kind guy that's married to his job, right? You're a cop when you go to sleep and a cop when you wake up?"

"Yeah. Except I don't sleep that good," Carl half-smiled. "So is there anything else at all that you remember? The guy Taylor was speaking to on the phone, who was it?"

"I don't know, sorry. He never used a name."

"That was probably deliberate," Carl nodded. "Taylor's a big player himself. Anyone he's working for is seriously big money."

"Sorry I can't help you any more," Skye remarked, brushing her hair away from her face.

"I got something to work on, it's fine," Carl assured her. "Look, I have to get going. I'll come and see you again, but I don't want you to worry about anything. Just concentrate on feeling better, okay?"

"Wait," said Skye, kneeling up in the bed as Carl rose from his chair. "I want to say thank you. For everything."

"You already did, and it's fine."

"No, I mean... I want to thank you," Skye repeated, moving her right hand forward so that it was placed over Carl's crotch.

"Skye," Carl said firmly, taking hold of her wrist and moving her hand away. "Don't."

"But you need to know how grateful I am..."

"I know already. I don't know what you're used to, but I helped you because you needed help. That's it. We don't need to—do that. Okay?"

Skye looked at Carl and nodded, but he noticed that tears were filling her eyes. Finally she broke down into a fit of sobs and flung her arms around him. Carl stood motionless for a moment, not knowing what to do with himself, and then reluctantly put his arm around her back somewhat stiffly. He knew what this was, knew that she wasn't upset that he had refused her advances. Rather she was simply overwhelmed with emotion. Invariably she was used to paying for 'kind' treatment in a particular way that Carl had refused. She'd grown used to it, probably even convinced herself it was okay. If it was that or hate herself then the choice was an easy one. But Carl had shown her a different way, and it had been too much after everything else she'd suffered of late.

"It's alright," he said quietly as she cried into his shoulder.

"Thank you," she whispered directly into his ear, before kissing him softly on the cheek.

"You're welcome."

Chapter Twenty-One;
Damn This City

"You're back early," Jimmy remarked as Carl closed the apartment door behind him. "Had expected you to go straight out to work."

"Thought I'd take five first. Shift doesn't start for another couple of hours," Carl replied, tossing his leather coat over the back of his armchair and sitting down with a deep exhalation.

"How was the girl?"

"Her name's Skye. And I actually think she's going to be okay, odd as that sounds. There's something about her, an innocence I don't see very often. It needs to be protected but as long as it survives, she might just get through all of this."

"That's what seventeen year old girls should always seem like, Carl. You just don't see any outside of this crap hole. Here they seem to get tainted fast and then that innocence is lost."

"You're sounding like me," Carl smirked.

"I learn fast," Jimmy shrugged, taking a cigarette and lighting it up.

"Since when did you smart smoking?"

"Just recently. Figured it'd help me lose weight," Jimmy replied, taking a long drag from the cigarette.

"You're an idiot."

"Better than being a fat idiot."

"You're no heavier than I am, you vain old queen," said Carl, wafting the drifting smoke away from his face and coughing rather violently.

"Yeah well it wouldn't hurt you to lose a few, either. And don't go blaming that cough on passive smoking, either!" Jimmy remarked, pointing an accusing finger. "'Cause it doesn't set on that quickly, and the whole thing's a rumour spread by health nuts anyway!"

"Probably that cigar Big Pauly gave me last night," said Carl, covering his mouth with his fist as he coughed again. "Last time I accept a gift from a midget."

"So this girl Skye, you gonna follow up with her?"

"Yeah, I think so. I promised her I'd get her into rehab, clean her up and get her a job and place to stay."

"That's a little extreme," Jimmy remarked with a startled widening of his eyes.

"What do you mean?"

"I know you got this whole 'seeing the victims as humans and not just corpses' thing going on, which is great, and I admire you for it, but taking this kind of interest is a little much."

"Maybe it's because she's actually alive," Carl said with a low tone. "I'm not too late to save this one. If I move fast and hard enough, I can stop her taking a swim in the Styx like all the other girls her age that I've seen before."

"That all sounds plausible and again, admirable, but I think you're not telling me something," Jimmy suggested, resting his chin on his fists.

"Quit analysing me, Jimmy. I haven't paid for it, so I don't want it."

"Who're you making up for? What's making you overcompensate?"

"You're a prick, you know that?" Carl informed his friend with a heavy and weight-filled sigh.

"If you didn't want to talk to me about this then you wouldn't. So go ahead."

"Amber DuBois," said Carl, his voice almost a whisper.

"The dead Escort you pulled from the river?"

"That's her. I saw her the night before last, when I was crossing the Steel Gate Bridge. I slipped and got a little dazed, but I saw her in the water, staring at me."

"You're not about to tell me you see dead people, are you?"

"Don't be an idiot, I'm not saying it was a ghost," Carl snapped. "But it's something. The last time I saw something like that, it was my mind telling me I'd missed something. That the case wasn't as wrapped up as I'd convinced myself."

"You think this is the same? That you've missed something with Amber's murder?"

"I don't know. All honesty, I don't see how I could have. We got the killer, he's where he belongs. It's over, so why did I see her?"

"You can't answer that question, so you're taking your guilt about possibly missing something with Amber and putting it onto this thing with Skye instead."

"I dunno, maybe," Carl rubbed his sinuses and welcomed the brief moment's quiet darkness as he closed his eyes. "I just know that I wanna help her."

"Is she cute?"

"She's pretty, yeah, but if you're suggesting that my motives are—"

"Hey, hey, come on! It's me, I wouldn't dream of laying that on you," Jimmy assured him, his words backed by an honest warmth. "I'm just saying, she's pretty and she's got this innocence to her despite everything you know about her. Just the same as Amber when you pulled her from that river. You see a young, pretty girl and it makes you want to help her twice as much as normal because less than a month ago you saw another young pretty girl laying dead on the ground.

That's called being human, Carl. Nothing to worry about."

"Why did I see her, though? Why did I see Amber? It can't have just been about Skye, I didn't even know her name at that point,"

"Well then maybe you're just messed up in the head."

"Yeah, maybe I am," said Carl, resting his head against the back of the couch and closing his eyes. "Damn this city."

Chapter Twenty-Two
Leather and Lace

Carl opened his eyes slowly, finding them even more unwilling to break their dried-on crust than usual. He'd interrupted his usual sleep pattern to go and visit Skye, and now he'd fallen asleep the first time he'd sat down. Bravo, Carl, real smart. Play the good guy, the nice cop and open the doors to sheer exhaustion. Least the guys who don't give a crap get a good night's sleep. Shaking off the last remnant of whatever forgotten dream he'd been having, Carl brought his head forward to find himself alone in the living room. Jimmy wasn't anywhere in sight, and Carl was a little pissed that he'd left him to fall asleep. A glance at his watch revealed nothing until he rubbed his eyes with his thumb and forefinger, at which point the clock face grew clearer and he could see that it was only an hour since he'd arrived home. He hadn't slept that long, after all. Still, it felt like he needed it. As the last lingering touches of sleep left his mind, Carl was suddenly aware of what it was that had awoken him.

"Hello? Duggan speaking," Carl grunted, answering the ringing phone that rested on the coffee table beside his chair. He had no idea how long it had been ringing, but evidently the person calling had been content to wait.

"Detective Duggan? It's... it's Felicity DuBois," came a nervous, panicked voice at the other end of the line. "I... I don't know if you remember me, but... I kept your number when you called me about Amber's killer... I hope you don't mind me calling you, but..."

"It's fine, Miss DuBois. What is it, what's wrong?" said Carl, his Detective instincts not even required to sense that something wasn't right.

"I... I need your help. Something's happened, I just... please help me. I don't know what to do."

"Alright, just calm down. Where are you, I'll come get you," Carl said firmly, his mind snapping into fully-awake mode at the sound of distress in the young woman's voice.

"Silver Crown apartments, room seven... second floor... please, just get here as soon as you can, okay?"

"I'm coming now, Miss DuBois, just stay calm," Carl insisted, knowing the advise was useless. Why say something like that to someone who was probably close to breaking point for whatever reason? Just a stupid conversational convention, like so many other useless formalities of human interaction.

The Silver Crown apartment building was just over the river, in the area affectionately named 'Limbo'. The reason for that was pretty simple, although like the Styx, no one knew where it had come from. The East side of the city was poor and dirty, the West side was rich and a different kind of dirty. Petty crime and sleazy motels could be found in the West, corrupt casinos and massive fraud in the East. That was the rule, hard and fast for the most part. Limbo, however, was something of an exception. If you looked at the City on a map, took a compass and stuck the needle just in the centre of the Steel Gate bridge, then drew a circle around that point, you'd be drawing a line around Limbo. The area you stepped into on either side of the cold metal walkway. A little bit of the West and East mixed together in a dirty brown pool of paint. In Limbo on the West side you might find a couple of upmarket stores, for instance, but you'd still get robbed in the street outside it. On the East and in Limbo, you might find a cheap motel whose prices suited the other side of the city, but whose clientele were more likely to be rich guys seeking anonymity in a hotel that didn't feature hidden cameras. The Silver Crown was just such a place.

Although the walk wasn't far, Carl hailed a cab to hasten the journey. He didn't favour the idea of Felicity waiting too long for him, especially given that he didn't really know what he was walking into. The cab driver was just what Carl had expected—an ex-con whose prison tattoos were visible all over the back of his hands, wrist and neck. Some of these guys were clean and honest, others would mug their passengers or use their "business" to drive young girls to an old warehouse somewhere, the starting point of their new home in the sex industry. Whilst Carl wasn't a likely target for the latter, he still kept his eyes on the locks above the door handle. If they went down, the driver would find a nasty surprise pressing into the back of his skull in the form of a shiny black Colt.

Carl paid his fare as he departed the vehicle, concluding that the driver was either one of the honest ones or not stupid enough to try something untoward. As the car drove away, tires screeching on the road still wet with snow, Carl moved quickly into the entrance to the Silver Crown. There was a desk with no attendant and an elevator that might as well have had a sign labelled "death trap" stuck to the front of it. Thinking better than to risk it, Carl took the stairs and raced up to the second floor. The speed at which he took the stairs, three at a time, made him glad that the room he was heading for wasn't higher up, as a heart attack might have been on the cards had that been the case. His own welfare wasn't on his mind as he tore up the stairwell, however. All he thought about was getting to Felicity. Saving her from whatever had happened. Making sure she was okay. Not like her sister. Not like Amber.

The door slammed back on its hinges as Carl barged into the room, removing any possibility of a stealthy entrance. He froze for a moment as he stared into the awaiting room, and then swore at himself for not taking more time before entering. What if Felicity had been taken hostage, and this was a set-up? Carl would have just walked right into it. Too busy thinking about Amber. Too busy letting thoughts of dying young girls cloud his judgement. Stupid and careless. That's what emotional distraction will do for you.

The room Carl found himself in was the kind of room where the bedroom was the entire apartment. Bed in the middle, TV on a night-stand and a fridge in the corner. Not the kind of place you spend a lot of time in. Carl finally felt his heart resume its work when he saw Felicity, alive and well in the corner of the room, huddled against the wall with her knees to her chest. She was dressed in a lacy black night-dress over a black leather corset, with black boots that reached her stocking-covered thighs.

"Miss DuBois?" Carl asked gently as he approached her. "Are you OK?"

"No... I didn't...I thought he was okay, I..." Felicity stammered, Carl now noticing that her thick black eye makeup had run down her pale cheeks, her blonde hair sticking to her face with the cold sweat of fear.

"Who? Who are you talking about?"

In response, Felicity pointed at the area of open floor around the other side of the bed. A young man was laying face down on it, naked except for his blue boxer-shorts. Carl cursed himself again for not noticing the body the moment he had entered, but his attention had been diverted solely to Felicity. Taking care not to move the body, Carl gently touched his fingertips against the young man's wrist, confirming what he already knew. There were numerous deep red marks across the young man's back, and his wrists and ankles looked to have suffered some mild rope burn.

"The marks on his back... they're not... I mean, they're..." Felicity stammered, her entire body visibly trembling even as she sat huddled in the corner of the room.

"They were from the Dominatrix thing you had going on with him, I get it," Carl assured her. "The way you're dressed, the fact that he's near enough naked... doesn't take a genius. Or a Detective."

"I didn't kill him. I swear, it wasn't anything we were doing," Felicity insisted, shaking her head over and over.

"You weren't playing at asphyxiation or anything like that? Didn't get carried away with it?"

"No, we didn't do strangulation. He didn't even like it. Just the whip and the ropes to restrain him. Nothing that could..."

"How did he die?" Carl asked softly. "I'm going to need you to tell me what happened, Miss DuBois."

"Am I a suspect? I mean, do you think I..."

"Right now, yes you're a suspect. Technically. But it's only me that knows about this so don't worry about it. You said you needed my help, and I'm here. So I'm going to need you to tell me what happened."

"We were, well he was on his knees, and I was... hitting him. Not too hard, just the way he liked, and... I've been with him before, I know what he can take... and he started to shake, his eyes started blinking rapidly, like he was having a seizure. Then he fell over and just..."

"If he had a seizure then he might have choked, or hit his head, or any number of things. I'm not a doctor but I'm fairly certain that exempts you from any wrongdoing."

"He took a pill, though. I saw him... before we started he took something... if it was a drug, they're gonna blame me. They'll say I gave it to him, that..."

"Where's his clothes?" Asked Carl.

"On the bed," said Felicity, standing up shakily and pointing to the pile of discarded clothing.

Carl nodded and lifted the man's jacket, routing around through the pockets until he found what he had been looking for. With a satisfied nod, he removed something from the inside pocket and held it up for Felicity to see.

"He just took one of his meds for Epilepsy. If he was prone to seizures then it'd make sense he was on these things. You got nothing to worry about, I promise."

"If he took the pill then why did he still have a seizure?"

"All kinds of things can stop a pill from working. Whatever it was, the seizure hit him hard. Probably harder than he's used to if he hasn't had one in awhile. That's what killed him."

"So you don't think this was anything that I did?"

"No," Carl assured her. "Besides, I saw this guy's name on his pill bottle. He's a big-shot lawyer. No way would his family want it getting out what he was into. Hell, if it even got to court then they'd pay you not to talk about what the two of you were doing in here."

"Oh thank God," Felicity breathed an almost tangible sigh of relief back into the room. "I just couldn't deal with that, going to jail. I feel bad for this guy, but he wasn't exactly one of the good ones, you know? He had a wife and kid, can you believe that? Wife and kid and he still comes to me."

"You could have refused his service, Miss DuBois."

"No I couldn't. Dice would have killed me. This guy was a paying customer. I'm not allowed to have moral objections."

"Damn, I hate that guy," Carl grunted beneath his breath. "Okay, here's what's going to happen; we're going to get away from here and let you cool off, then I'm going to call this in and let the blue boys take care of it. You'll give a statement like you just gave me, I'll back it up with what I got from the immediate crime scene, and the whole thing will get covered up by the sleazy lawyer's sleazier lawyers. Okay?"

"I knew that calling you was a good idea," Felicity said quietly, her lips curving into a half-smile. "You just seemed like a good guy, you know? Other cops might have helped me too, but not without wanting me to suck their dick first."

"Yeah, that's not really the way I operate," Carl shrugged. "Guess I'm kind of an idiot."

"Makes me feel bad for slapping you when we first met."

"If you'd dressed like that then maybe I'd have liked it," Carl remarked, forcing a joke to try and lighten the dark air the room had taken on.

"No you wouldn't. There's no way a guy like you would get into this kind of thing. You couldn't give that much of yourself to anything or anyone."

"Got me all figured out, huh?"

"Not quite, but I do know that when I buy you coffee in a few minutes you'll take it black, straight up and simple."

"Some things ought to be simple, Miss DuBois. The things we got control over, at least."

"Seems like I have less and less on that list every day in my life."

"We all do what we can to survive," Carl nodded. "I told you before that I wasn't judging you and I'm not gonna start now. Get dressed, I'll wait outside."

"Wait... can you... stay here. Whilst I change?"

"Um... I know you're used to guys seeing you naked, but I..."

"I just don't want to be alone in here... with him. You know?"

"Sure, I'll stay," Carl agreed, understanding that his experience at being around the dead was not likely to be shared by a woman who'd spent much of her adult life in rich men's bedrooms.

"Thank you," Felicity smiled as she took her clothes from where they hung and started to change back to her normal attire. Carl turned away as she changed, causing her to remark, "You know, a lot of guys would love to watch me undress for them."

"Yeah well, I only got twenty bucks on me," Carl replied, and then felt a shoe hit him on the back of the head. "Okay, I probably deserved that."

Chapter Twenty-Three;
He Ain't Getting
Any Deader

"I hate these places," Carl grunted as Felicity handed him a black coffee in a white mug, the logo of the coffee house emblazoned on the side.

"Too commercial?" Felicity asked as she joined Carl at the table.

"Too busy. I like the quiet."

"I'm guessing you have a lot of that, huh? You don't strike me as the 'married with kids' type."

"Not so much."

"Out of choice?" asked the blonde, stirring her coffee as she looked at Carl across the table.

"Never really thought about it," Carl shrugged. "How're you doing? You calmed down?"

"I'm fine," Felicity smiled, brushing a strand of blonde hair from her face.

"No you're not," Carl shook his head. "Your hands are still shaking, you've been stirring your coffee constantly since you sat down and you're talking about things that don't matter."

"What do you want me to say? That I'm terrified? That I never saw a guy die before, and I just want to burst into tears?"

"If you wanna do that then do it," Carl said, his voice firm but carrying a warmth through its strength.

"Everyone in here would look at me."

"Anyone said anything I'd break 'em in half," Carl smiled.

"What did you do? First time you saw someone die?" asked Felicity, carefully wiping a solitary tear from her eye so that it didn't smear the makeup she'd only recently reapplied.

"Well it was me that killed him, so that was a little different."

"How did you react? Did you cry?"

"I'm not the crying type. I just threw up everything I'd eaten for last eighteen months."

"And now? How do you react now?"

"I don't," Carl said flatly. "The guys I have to shoot deserve it, and I seen enough of the end result of their actions to stop myself feeling guilty. For every guy I put down, there's a trail of girls just like your... just like Amber."

"Thank you."

"For what?"

"For taking care when you mentioned her. I thought you were just some hard-ass cop, stubble and a gun and a leather coat, you know? But you're not. I mean, you are, but there's more. You got a heart under there that's bigger than your fists, but I got a feeling you don't show it all that often."

"You learn to be hard in this place, Miss DuBois."

"I know, I've already done the homework on that one."

"No you haven't. You're still soft, still have some of that innocence in you. You've done crap, sure, but it's not too late for you. Not yet," said Carl, sitting forward as his words suddenly carried more energy than they had before. "You can leave, get the hell out of here whilst you still have that goodness in you."

"What makes you think I have any goodness left in me?" asked Felicity.

"The fact that you cry when a sleazebag dies from a seizure in front of you. He doesn't deserve your tears and you know it, but your makeup's still running."

"Dammit," Felicity whispered, taking out her pocket mirror and checking her eyes.

"Drop it. Stop pretending you're this shallow, hard bitch because you're not. Not yet."

"Why do you even care? Why do you want to save me?" Asked Felicity, tilting her head to one side like a cat studying a mouse.

"Because I couldn't save Amber," Carl said quietly, unable to meet her gaze as he spoke.

"You didn't even know who she was. You'd never met her."

"Maybe I had and didn't know it. Maybe I'd walked past her a hundred times on the street," said Carl. "It shouldn't have mattered that I didn't know her. Girls that young shouldn't have their name on paperwork in my office, Miss DuBois."

"You carry the weight of the world on those shoulders, Detective Duggan," Felicity smiled, taking Carl's large hand and gently kissing the back of it, leaving a red imprint from her deep lipstick.

"So... do you want to cry?"

"Not anymore," she smiled. "Are you going to call your boys to pick him up?"

"No rush, he ain't getting any deader," Carl remarked as he sipped his coffee. "Jesus, that tastes like crap."

"You really don't give a shit that there's a dead guy laying up there, do you?"

"I might if I didn't know who he was," said Carl, taking another sip despite himself. "Two years ago, he and three of his lawyer friends were financing a child prostitution ring that was shipping the kids to Thailand. Oldest one we rescued from the warehouse was twelve. All four of the lawyers walked, friends in high places and all that crap. Couldn't lay anything on them. Took more willpower than I knew I had not to go 'round to their office and put one between their eyes."

"Jesus," Felicity gasped. "How can people do stuff like that?"

"Leave the City, Miss DuBois," Carl said suddenly.

"You sick of talking to me?" she smiled.

"That right there is what I'm talking about. You still express shock that human beings can do things like that. I see it so goddamn often that I expect it. The day I don't hear about a kid being killed or a woman being raped is the day I'm surprised. You need to leave before you've sunk down to where I am."

"Where would I go, Detective?"

"Anywhere you want. World's not as big a place as it used to be. Case in point; I arrested a guy last week that came from Saudi Arabia. Can you believe that? Comes halfway across the world to sell guns for a gang in this shit hole. Idiot."

"What point are you trying to make by telling me that?" Felicity asked, raising an eyebrow playfully.

"That wasn't part of my point, it's just something that pissed me off," Carl replied. "What I mean is that you can go, anytime you want. You stay here long enough and that stops being the case, so you're on a clock."

"And what about you? You're just going to grow old and die here?"

"In my line of work, the second will probably come before the first, Miss DuBois."

"Well, I can promise you that I'll think about it," the blonde smiled, finishing her small coffee with a final tip of her cup. "Are you done with your coffee?"

"Good God, yes," Carl replied with a sigh of relief, his cup still half full. "I better call this in, then I'll walk you home,"

"You don't have to do that."

"Yeah I do, and don't argue with me,"

"You're a weird kind of gentleman," Felicity smiled as Carl held open the door of the coffee shop for her.

"Damn straight."

Chapter Twenty-Four;
Tiny Red Death-Warrant

Felicity wrapped her dark red coat tightly around herself as she and Carl walked down the street, the night air biting against her flesh. The snow had held off for another night, but the sky was growing heavier with gathering weight every hour. When it came, it would come strong and blanket the entire city. All the dirt and blood would be buried beneath a covering of white, masking it in feint innocence. It wouldn't last, of course. Before long the grime would seep through and even the snow would be dirty and red.

Carl walked close beside Felicity and was surprised when she linked her arm with his. There was nothing romantic about the gesture, just the need she evidently had to be close to another human being this evening. Given that any physical human interaction she endured was usually paid for by a stranger, something as simple as linking your arm with that of friend would be welcome. Carl had called the meat-wagon to collect the body and informed the blue boys that the witness statement had already been taken. The further away he could keep Felicity from the whole mess, the better. He'd seen hope in her, a light that was rare in the City. The further into the mire she was dragged, the more that light would be extinguished until nothing remained.

The two of them walked on down the street, Carl welcoming the fact that Limbo was lacking the oppressive neon glow of the West side at its core. His head didn't hurt, he wasn't forced to squint as he glanced ahead. Still, the lights did provide some benefits that the dank, grim nature of Limbo couldn't supplement. Such as the fact that they effectively illuminated every street and passage. Had Carl and Felicity been walking beneath the neon hum of the West Side, they would have immediately seen the black van approaching on the road behind them. The fact that's its own lights were turned off wouldn't have mattered with a thousand others reflecting from its paint-work. In the dark of Limbo, however, approaching silently as it was, the van remained unnoticed until it screeched to a stop alongside Carl and Felicity. At this point the doors slid open and a dozen men clambered out of it. Each one of them was dressed as a pirate in one manner or another, decorated with neon pink, yellow and green makeup as Skye had been when Carl encountered her in the Diamond Heights hotel.

"Stay behind me, Miss DuBois," Carl warned, placing a protecting arm in front of the blonde.

"Hey there, feller, I be wanting a word with ye," said a dread-locked pirate, his face painted over with a glowing green skull. His voice had a heavy Irish accent, but it seemed unnatural and forced, to the point that Carl wondered if it was fake or at least exaggerated. In his right hand he held a large Cutlass.

"What do you idiots want?" Carl asked firmly, keeping himself positioned between the group and Felicity.

"Me and the boys here, we're the Jolly Rogers. Perhaps ye've heard of us?"

"Yeah I have, but that's not what I asked."

"Oh, come on now. No need to be rude, is there? We can all be mates, can't we?" the lead Pirate asked, putting his arm around the smaller man to his left and laughing hysterically. "We're here on a wee bit of work and need yer help with it, ye see. I'm hoping you'll be cooperative."

"You got a name?"

"Ye can call me Willy."

"All right, Willy, I'm gonna ask you politely one more time... what do you want?"

"Yer in no position to be threatening me, matey, but I'll be nice anyway because I like to be helpful. Now, me and the boys here are under instruction from the Captain hisself, he gave us a few marching orders for the night's wee excursion, ye know?" Willy explained, reaching into his tattered grey coat and pulling a brown envelope from within. He opened it and took out two photographs, which he then held up. "Now here I have me some things that I'd like yer help with, if ye'd be so kind. I got me some targets for the evening, some chosen specimens, if ye like. Only thing is, I left me glasses at home and I can't quite tell who I'm looking fer. The picture is all blurry to me."

"That might be something to do with whatever cocktail of crap you got running through you right now," Carl suggested.

"Aye, it probably is at that," Willy shrugged. "Still, if ye'd be so kind as to help me out?"

"You want me to look at the photographs?" Carl asked with a raised eyebrow.

"Ah no, ye see, I think it's yerself and the good lady here that's on these here pictures. Only thing is, I can't be sure, ye know? Now, I could just kill yez anyway, but the Captain was very particular about our work tonight. Only to kill the two on these photos, we are. If that ain't yerselves, then we'd be getting into some trouble. So, what I'd like ye to do is take out yer wallets and show your driving licences to me. Think me eyes can focus enough to read yer names, then I'll be sure, ye see."

"And if it's not us in the photos?" Felicity asked, keeping behind Carl but finding the courage to speak to the obvious nut-case holding the shining cutlass.

"Then we be letting ye go, Miss," said Willy, taking a slight bow as he spoke to his first lady of the evening.

"Why don't I believe that?" Carl asked with a scowl.

"'Cause ye think I'm a liar and not to be trusted," Willy shrugged. "And usually ye'd be right, but not tonight, matey. Like I said, we got ourselves some marching orders and they're to be followed to the letter. So, if ye'd be kind enough to take yer wallets out fer me?"

"Not gonna happen," Carl said firmly.

"Carl, we should just..." Felicity suggested, reaching for her purse.

"Put it away, Felicity. These fuckwits aren't going to let us go no matter what, so don't give 'em the satisfaction of playing along."

"Come on now, don't make me be hurting ye..." Said Willy, placing the point of his Cutlass just beneath Carl's chin.

Carl batted the blade away with the back of his left hand, then smashed his right fist straight into the pirate's face. The blow sent Willy onto the pavement, where he lay flat on his back and clutched at his shattered nose. Scrambling up to his feet in some desperate attempt to regain his dignity, the pirate held his nose with his left hand, blood pouring through the gaps in his fingers and mixing with the green paint on his face. The other eleven pirates raised their weapons, guns rather than swords in this case, and pointed each one of them in Carl's direction. There was a series of clicks as hammers were drawn back, but Willy raised his free hand, his cutlass having been dropped, and signalled them to hold fire.

"Jeezus, that was uncalled for," he groaned, his voice now sounding as though he were suffering from a heavy cold.

"Let the girl go," Carl said. "And I'll show you my driver's license."

"Not much for bargaining, matey. I got me two targets tonight so it has to be the both of ye. Now, we've been playing for long enough, so if ye'll be so kind…"

"Alright," Carl nodded, taking his right hand and reaching inside his coat pocket.

"Now I hope yer not daft enough to be reaching for a gun there, big feller," Willy warned with a forced smile.

"I see at least eleven guns on me right now. I'm not an idiot," Carl informed him, taking his wallet and bringing it out into view of the pirates.

"There's a good lad," Willy smiled.

Carl cursed himself for not seeing a viable way out of the situation, then slowly opened the clasp on his leather wallet. He sifted through the various cards and dollar bills that were found inside, and then finally came to his driving licence. It was dirty and the photo no longer looked like him, but then he hadn't used it in years. No reason to buy a car on the East side. If Carl parked it anywhere near his building then it would inevitably get stolen. If he parked it in a 'secure' garage, it would get stolen. If he parked it far enough away that it wouldn't get stolen, then he might as well walk. Carl often wondered why he carried the licence around, and given the current situation he wished that he didn't. He lifted the laminated card from the wallet, then stopped as he looked once more at Willy.

"Well isn't that something," Carl remarked.

"What's that, now?"

"My driver's licence just became much less interesting, what with the tiny red death-warrant on your forehead," Carl commented, noticing the small glowing red circle that had suddenly appeared between the Pirate's eyes.

"What the fuck are ye—"

The shot rang out through the street and caused Willy's head to snap back suddenly. His skull split open at the front and his corpse hit the ground like a limp rag doll, the life that held the body upright having instantly departed. The other pirates looked around anxiously, gripping their guns and turning them this way and that. Carl saw the red light on the temple of one of the younger pirates, then a second gunshot ended his life as quickly as the first had ended Willy's. A third tore through the throat of the guy next to him, and it was at that point that Carl grabbed Felicity by the arm and dragged her away from the scene.

"What's going on? Did you call for backup?" She asked as Carl took her into the first alleyway they came across.

"Did you see me call for any backup?" Carl asked, catching his breath.

"Well no, but—"

"Then whoever's shooting ain't got nothing to do with me," said Carl, turning to see the metal door locked by a rusty old padlock at his back. "We need to get inside somewhere before those pricks come after us."

"Can you pick locks?" Felicity asked.

"Not exactly," Carl remarked, as three swift kicks broke the rusty padlock from where it hung and left the door ready for access.

"Subtle as always, Duggan," came a voice from behind.

Carl grabbed Felicity and pulled her behind him, drawing his gun in the same fluid motion so that it was pointing to the new entrant to the alleyway. Seeing that the barrel of his gun was pointing at the forehead of a familiar bald man in a floor-length black coat, Carl withdrew the weapon and replaced it in his shoulder holster.

"What're you doing here, Pope?" asked Carl.

"Saving your life, it would seem. And Felicity's."

"You know each other?" asked Carl.

"You might say that. Are you alright?" Pope asked.

"Fine, Charles. Thank you," Felicity smiled, kissing the hit-man on the cheek.

"We'll discuss the insanity of this situation later. Get inside, both of you," Carl instructed, opening the door.

The old metal door opened into a hardware store, locked down for the night. The large front window at the other side of the shop was covered by a large steel grate, the kind that could be lowered of raised with an electrical mechanism. A metal-barred door was secured behind the front door to the shop, barring any entrance from someone attempting to get inside through breaking the glass. Racks and shelving units filled the shop floor, displaying tools, gardening equipment, home barbecue supplies and camping paraphernalia. The shop was dark, but Carl refused to switch on the lights as it would invariably alert the surviving pirates to their location.

"How many did you leave alive out there?" Carl enquired.

"I only killed three, there were nine left by my count. I saw you two come down the alleyway, used the fire escape to join you. I needed to make sure Felicity was alright."

"Thanks," Carl said sarcastically.

"I knew you were fine, it's hardly the first time you've been in a situation like this."

"So getting back to the point, what were you doing on the roof?" Carl enquired.

"I followed the Jolly Rogers from the Casino district. Thirty of them had gathered in the plaza square, around the fountain. They were being given paperwork and instructions by Taylor, their leader."

"I know Taylor," Carl nodded.

"The Rogers split into three groups and drove away in three vans, each taking a different direction," Pope continued. "I was heading home for the night, but this captured my attention. It's not like the Rogers to have any specific goal in mind; Anarchy is their business, which by its very definition is random."

"So how did you know what they were up to? You get painted up and join in the fun?"

"No," Pope smiled, despite himself. "I commandeered one of the vans and asked its surviving occupant to tell me what he knew. He provided me with his photographs and the names attached to them."

"Who was in the pictures?" asked Felicity.

"Detective Duggan and yourself," Pope replied. "I took to the rooftops and managed to catch up to one of the vans, which I then followed here. Luckily it was the right one, had I followed the other you'd have both been dead by now."

"I had it in hand," Carl replied defensively. "How'd you keep up with a van? Even travelling over the rooftops, that's still impressive."

"They crashed the van into three separate vehicles and a streetlight. I think the driver was in some way inebriated."

"Why would these freaks wants us dead? I mean a cop like you, a good guy, they probably hate. But why me?" asked Felicity, rubbing her delicate hands one over the other anxiously.

"Only Taylor knows that," Carl sighed. "I didn't see him outside."

"He didn't leave with any of the groups," Pope commented.

"He's working for someone, but I don't know who yet," said Carl.

"Taylor runs the Jolly Rogers himself. Why would he work for somebody else?"

"God only knows, but I got it on good word that he's been running errands for someone. He called them 'boss' and was promising to clean up some mess."

"Are we the mess?" asked Felicity, her voice raised. "Jesus, what did we do? What the hell did we do?"

Pope quietly shushed Felicity and wrapped his arms around her. Carl admitted to himself that he felt slightly envious of the comfort she took from Pope. The connection he'd made with the blonde earlier had been the closest he'd been to an adult woman for a long time. He'd forgotten what it was like to connect with someone, but his friendship with Skye had sparked something in him. A desire to be close to someone for more than just a night. You don't know you're missing something until you're given a taste of it. It wasn't that he wanted Felicity, so much as the kind of closeness he saw in her and Pope right now. There was a connection between them, anyone could see it. But it would have to wait.

"We need to get out of here," Carl said suddenly. "Without Willy they're not gonna be too organised, but that might not be a good thing. Either they get smart and come in here after us, or they go off and resume the random anarchy they're more familiar with. Lot of civilian deaths, and it'd be on my head. It's me they're after."

"And me," Felicity reminded him.

"This ain't nothing to do with you. It's gotta be me they want, you'll just be by proxy. They saw you with me sometime and that's enough for them. I pissed off enough people, the list could be endless."

"We need to keep their attention focused on us without getting ourselves killed," Pope remarked, his eyes adjusting to the darkness as he walked around the store, taking in the contents of the shelving units and display racks.

"How many bullets you got?" Carl asked.

"Just what's left in this clip," Pope remarked, holding up the laser-sighted modified pistol he was holding.

"That's it?"

"You expect me to carry around an arsenal?" asked Pope. "I carry what I need, nothing more. What do you have?"

"Just the Colt."

"You didn't bring your revolver?"

"I never said I'd sell it to you," Carl reminded him. "By the way, I didn't call you about the poison thing because—"

"It wasn't poison, I know," Pope nodded.

"Christ, is there anyone who doesn't have moles in the police department?" Carl sighed.

"So what are you boys going to do? Charge out there, guns blazing?" asked Felicity, nervously biting her nail.

"We're way too outgunned for that to be anything close to a smart idea," Carl replied. "If we both die, there's no one to guarantee you get out of here safely."

"They're still outside," said Pope, standing beside the steel-grate covered window and peering through the gap. "They don't know we're in here, but they look a little confused. Like they don't know what to do next."

"They're all high as a fucking kite, coherent thought is pretty much beyond them, I'd wager," Carl remarked. "Still, only takes one of them to take a look around where we could have run off to, and they'll storm in through that back door. They do that, we're sitting ducks."

"So we go to them," said Pope.

"Didn't we just cover the stupidity of that plan?"

"I'll distract them, you get Felicity out of here."

"You're not going out there alone, Pope. I know you're more dangerous than any one of those fucks, but you're not invincible. Against that many guns, you're not walking away clean like you usually do."

"I'm not going to get into a gunfight with them. I'm going to improvise," Pope smiled, taking a large gas canister, the kind used for drive-on lawn mowers and home barbecues, and lifting it into view.

"You're insane," Carl stated bluntly.

"What are you going to do?" asked Felicity.

"Give you your distraction," Pope nodded. "Get ready,"

Pope walked over to the side of the large storefront window and placed the gas canister gently on the floor. He then raised a leather-gloved hand and wrapped it around the black metal lever that activated the steel shutter over the window. Carl took Felicity to the back of the store by the rear exit through which they'd entered, and then gave Pope a nod to indicate that he was ready. Pope pulled the lever and the steel shutter creaked and groaned into action, moving upwards and leaving the glass window unblocked. The Jolly Rogers heard the noise from the street outside and turned to face the window. They were only staring into the dark storefront for a moment before the glass was broken towards them by a large metallic cylinder that rolled to a stop just before their feet.

"What the fuck?" one of the pirates asked.

An answer to his question never came before a tiny red dot could be seen hovering over the 'caution; flammable' label on the gas canister.

Chapter Twenty-Five;
Cherry Red and
Smoke Grey

The explosion was still ringing in Carl's ears as he escorted Felicity to her top-floor apartment in the Kootz complex. The Kootz was the best of everything the West side had to offer, all wrapped inside a secure location. Apartments of the highest quality, casinos, night-clubs and restaurants, all in the same overly-illuminated complex surrounding a large decorative fountain. A high wall surrounded the whole thing in a large circle, and the only way in and out was a huge set of steel gates painted gold. If you weren't rich or didn't know somebody rich, you weren't getting inside those gates; it was that simple. Carl felt his skin crawl the moment he entered, backed up by that undeniable feeling that not a single person inside the walls came by their money honestly. It actually made him think a little less of Felicity that she would be here, but he admitted to himself that he barely knew half of the facts in her case.

"So now you're thinking maybe I really am a cold-hearted bitch if I live in this place, right?" Felicity smiled as she brought Carl into her apartment.

"You could make a killing on the casino circuit with those psychic skills, Miss DuBois," Carl smiled, entering the luxurious living space after the blonde. His hands were kept firmly in his pockets, as though the very air of the room would be offensive to touch. He didn't belong here and he could feel it. Every light was mocking him, telling him to go home. To the darkness, to the damp. He felt tense and it was probably written all over his face, no surprise that Felicity had noticed it.

"Dice likes his girls to live somewhere fancy, makes it looks like he treats us good," Felicity explained.

"What's a few bruises when you're lounge furniture is worth more than some people's house, right?" Carl smirked.

"I didn't say I liked it, but you don't argue with Dice. It's just easier that way."

"I'd argue with him. I'd argue with him plenty."

"You'd probably rip him a new hole, and I'd enjoy watching it. But that wouldn't help anything. Lots of girls depend on him for a roof over their heads, and to eat."

"Someone else would fill his shoes, always lots of maggots lining up to take the place of their king," Carl scoffed. "Besides, you wanted me to kill the guy when we first met."

"I thought he'd killed Amber, but when it turned out he didn't, I softened on him. He's a lot of things that are worth hating, but he's not my sister's murderer."

"Give him a cookie," Carl sighed, then closed his eyes for a moment as the references to Amber DuBois had caused the memory of her face in the waters of the Styx to resurface in his mind.

"Do you think Charles is alright?" asked Felicity, sliding a cigarette from a polished silver case and placing it between her deep red lips.

"Pope? Yeah, he'll be fine, he's dealt with worse," Carl replied. "How do you know him, anyway? Can't imagine you met at school, what with him having a few years on you. He hides it well but he's gotta be pushing forty, and you're like what? Twenty-six?"

"Twenty-seven, and how I met him is a long story."

"So give me the abridgement."

"I once hired him to kill my pimp."

"Okay, little more than that," Carl insisted.

"I was young, working in a 'massage parlour' where the owner had the tendency to strangle his girls to death every now and then. I got scared when I learned about it, but he wouldn't let me leave. I got as far as a phone booth once and someone had left Charles's calling card in there. Crazy, right? It says "cleaner", but I somehow got this feeling that it wasn't what it sounded like. Anyway, I called him and spoke with him, met him for coffee. I'd saved up all that I could spare and still eat and I gave it to him to get me out of that place. He wouldn't take the money, said I needed it. He only kept a single dollar, said he had to accept something for it to be genuine, but gave me the rest back."

"And he killed your boss?"

"One between the eyes, then tossed him in the Styx whilst all the girls watched and cheered. I was fascinated with him, couldn't forget about him. So I called him again a few weeks later, not for a job this time. We kept meeting up, and the rest is history."

"You two dating?" Carl enquired.

"Wouldn't call it that. Charles doesn't date people. But I care about him, and I think he cares about me."

"You should take him and leave the City."

"Now you want him to leave too?"

"You got hope, he has faith. Two things that don't belong here. Be good for both of you. Lots of places need a hit-man, he could find work."

"It's a dream, it'd never happen."

"I'm sure it could, if you worked for it. Just like I'm sure there's a few dead Jolly Rogers and few more picking pieces of shrapnel outta their faces even now."

"Why do you think they were after us?"

"They were after me, Miss DuBois."

"He had two photos, Carl. Two," Felicity reminded him, her voice sounding anxious now she was forced to remember the details of what had almost occurred.

"Maybe they were just me from different angles."

"Don't bullshit me, Carl. You're trying to make me feel safe and I appreciate it, but not like this. If someone's after me then I deserve to know it."

"Alright, have it your way, let's say that they really were after you as much as me. Truth is, I can't think why anyone would want you dead, let alone go to the trouble of sending the Jolly Rogers after you. Taylor's not an easy man to hire, he tends to do his own business, so to put that much effort into coming after you... makes no sense to me at all."

"Maybe it's that guy. The one who died whilst I was with him."

"I hadn't reported that ten minutes before they came for us. Based on what Pope said, they were planning to come looking for you and me before that guy even bought it."

"So who have you pissed off lately?"

"How long have you got?" Carl chuckled. "I piss people off every day, sweetheart, ain't no point going down that road."

"So it's gotta be something involving both of us, right? What are we both involved in?"

"Amber," Carl replied without thinking, then cursed himself for mentioning the name.

"What about her? You got her killer, right? You called me and said..."

"I'm not sure," Carl admitted with a reluctant sigh.

"Not sure about what?"

"That I got her killer. I mean, the guy admitted to it, but..."

"But what, Carl?" Felicity demanded, stepping closer to the detective.

"There's a part of my mind that likes to show me things I've missed, okay? Keeps me focussing on things that I'd otherwise let go. Couple days back it showed me Amber, and since then I've been thinking that maybe her case isn't quite as wrapped up as I thought."

"So you saw a ghost of my sister, metaphorically at least, and that's enough for you to think the case isn't closed?"

"My mind wouldn't have shown me that unless—"

"Maybe you just feel guilty that a girl that young had to die because some jackass couldn't stand to lose a few bucks."

"Oh, I know that I do. I hate every minute that I'm reminded another girl had to turn up in that damn river... but I don't think this is that. I think there's more, and as long as I think that..."

"You're not going to let it go, are you? Even on this crazy little hunch based on bullshit, you're going to keep fighting for her memory?"

"Yeah. I guess I am," Carl shrugged.

Felicity put out her cigarette and took hold of Carl's face with both hands, bringing him close and kissing him passionately. Carl froze on the spot; he hadn't expected this and didn't know how to react to it. His hands remained rooted to his sides despite a voice screaming in his head to grab hold of her and return the kiss. The voice sounded a lot like Jimmy, which pissed Carl off all the more. Even here and now he was nagging him.

"I'm sorry, I shouldn't have..." Felicity said quietly, keeping her slender arms around Carl's neck and staring at him from barely an inch away. "I just... I don't know what me or Amber ever did to get someone like you trying to help us."

"I'm just a cop, Miss DuBois."

"You need to start calling me Felicity. Seriously, it's getting annoying now," she smiled. "And you're not just a cop. In this City, the cops are the guys who help you for a blowjob, or a few bucks in their back pocket. The guys who help you because it's the right thing to do... who follow hunches and put themselves in danger because they want to help a dead stranger to rest in peace... they don't exist. Except for you, the guy whose tired eyes I'm looking into."

"I'm always tired," Carl shrugged.

"You should relax."

"Don't know how. Think I forgot a long time ago."

"What are you thinking, right now?" Felicity whispered as she stared into Carl's eyes, her nose almost touching against his.

"I'm thinking that I wanna have sex with you on that couch."

"Very forward of you, Detective."

"Yeah, well... I'm also thinking that it'd be wrong for about three reasons."

"Which are?"

"One—you're in a bad place right now. Two—I know it's not going anywhere. We're not gonna get married or anything because neither of us is looking for that, so it'd just seem like a cheap fuck, which I don't want to be responsible for. And three—you're gonna be thinking about Pope the whole time, which I could do without."

"Okay..." Felicity nodded with a raised eyebrow, then cocked her head and replied; "One—I'm in a much better place than I would be if I hadn't met you. Two—

sometimes sex can just be a moment of happiness between two friends who want to share in each other's company in a special way. It doesn't always have to be a marriage proposal. And Three—this has nothing to do with Charles. If I wanted to be with him, I would. But right now I'm with you."

"You make a good case."

"So? You have a verdict, Detective?"

Carl answered by way of grabbing the back of Felicity's head and forcing her lips onto his once more. He could taste her immediately, the combination of cherry lipstick and grey smoke forcing its way into his mouth. It was some time since he'd felt a woman in this way, pressed against his chest and wanting him as much as he'd wanted her. Sex or physical pleasure in general wasn't something that Carl spent a lot of time on. But now, holding this soft, firm woman in his strong hands, something was reawakened in him. A desire to be inside her, to feel her wrapped tightly around him as they embraced.

His leather jacket dropped to the floor with a heavy thud, and he noticed the arousal in Felicity's eyes as she removed his shoulder holster, filled with a gun as it currently was. Was the crazy chick actually turned on by the fact that he was packing? Her connection to Pope suddenly made a lot more sense if that was the case. Carl placed his hands on the back of Felicity's blouse, looking for a zip or button that wasn't there, and then cursed and ripped it off her instead. The blonde gasped in shock and pleasure as he tore her clothes away, causing Carl to look at her and remark, "That wasn't expensive, was it?"

"Oh, shut up, Duggan," she insisted grabbing his head and kissing him so passionately that he thought he was in danger of choking on her tongue.

Carl removed his own shirt with equal disregard to the damage he might cause to the garment. When he tossed it aside, Felicity ran her hands over his muscled chest, taking particular attention to the scars on his flesh.

"What was this?" she asked as her fingers laced over a patch of scar tissue just below his left pectoral muscle.

"Buckshot. Just grazed me but hurt like hell."

"And this?" she touched the long, deep scar next to his navel.

"Punk stabbed me when I tried to arrest him. Don't worry, I broke his jaw."

"And this one?" she brushed her fingers against a scar on his abdomen.

"Where I had my appendix out."

"That's not too sexy."

"And the others are?"

"What can I say? I'm a crazy chick."

"Damn fucking straight," Carl agreed, flicking open the button on Felicity's jeans and letting them drop down to her ankles, revealing her long, slender legs. "Always knew you'd have some killer gams."

"Why thank you, Mr Detective," Felicity smiled as she jumped up and wrapped her legs around Carl's waist.

Holding onto her with a single hand, the strength of his arm easily bearing her weight, Carl walked over to a wall and slammed her back into it, causing her to gasp out as he ripped off her underwear and lowered his black suit trousers. With a grunt he forced himself inside of her, relieved to see the look of shock and pleasure on her face as she felt him there.

"Jesus Christ, you're so fucking..."

"Don't say it. I appreciate it, but I can't get out of my head the fact that you probably say it to every..."

"Don't make me slap you," Felicity said sternly as she gasped for breath with each of Carl's thrusts.

"Hey, I might like that," Carl shrugged.

Felicity reached behind her and pushed herself off the wall with her hands, so that she and Carl were still fucking as they walked across the floor. Finding the floor in the centre of the room covered with a soft fur rug, Carl threw her down on it and immediately got down on top of her. He held her wrists above her head as he moved into her once more, causing her to moan so audibly that his eardrums rattled.

"Cuff me... right now... fucking cuff me..." she gasped as Carl thrust in and out of her.

Carl didn't need asking again, snapping the cuffs off his belt and wrapping them around the blonde's wrists and locking them above her head. The feeling of being unable to stop him even if she wanted to evidently worked for her, as her moans and gasps suddenly doubled in volume and Carl felt her tighten around him even as she wrapped her legs around his back.

"Of fuck, you are good..." she gasped.

"Gotta say... always thought you'd like to be the one doing the cuffing," Carl smirked as he continued to give her everything he had.

"I always am... that's what they pay me for... so fucking nice to have it the other way..." gasping again, her breathing short and fast. "Oh God, you're gonna make me..."

Carl winced as Felicity's scream cut through his ears, so loud and piercing that he thought the windows or at least the light fittings were going to crack. As she stopped, she looked up at him and her eyes widened.

"You're not done yet... are you?" she asked with a look of alarm.

"Um... no..."

"Oh God, you're gonna fucking kill me," she smiled, laughing despite her physical exhaustion.

"You want me to stop?"

"You dare and I'll kill you with your own gun," she warned.

Carl continued for several minutes more until finally he reached his own climax, Felicity having done so twice more before they were done. He removed her handcuffs and then kissed her softly. Their breathing was heavy and Carl actually felt light-headed as he stood up. He took a few steps to reach for his shirt and fell to the side, catching a chair to keep himself upright.

"I'll take that as a compliment," Felicity smiled as she stood up and began dressing herself.

"It's been awhile," Carl admitted.

"Didn't feel like it."

"I'll take that as a compliment," he smiled softly.

"So are you going to ask me to marry you?"

"Huh?" Carl asked, freezing in the act of buttoning his shirt.

"Joke," the blonde smiled as she realised her blouse was actually damaged to the point of being unusable. "Hope that wasn't too awkward for you."

"No, it was... well, I think I needed it. Unprofessional as all holy Hell, but... thank you."

"We all need to feel close to someone now and again. Like I said, sometimes sex can just be about friendship."

"Yeah, it's nice to..." Carl stopped himself as he leaned against Felicity's marble kitchen table, his eyes feeling glassy.

"Carl, are you alright?" Felicity asked as she walked over to him, her top half still naked save for her bra.

"I just... something's wrong. I don't remember the last time I did this with anyone, but... I know that it hasn't been that long... and thinking about it makes me feel dizzy."

"That doesn't really make sense."

"I know," Carl sighed, looking down at the marble table and trying to get his eyes to focus. "My head doesn't feel right."

"Let me get you some aspirin," Felicity suggested.

"It's alright, I got something," Carl replied, rooting through the pockets of his leather jacket until he found his wallet. He opened the button for the section where loose change was kept and took a white pill from where it rested there. With a single motion he tossed it into his mouth and swallowed it, then took a drink from the glass of water Felicity handed him.

"What are those for?"

"Some kind of vitamin deficiency. Been taking them since I was a kid," Carl shrugged. "I'm okay now, don't worry about it. Think you just blew my mind."

"I'm a little worried about you."

"Don't be, I'm fine," Carl assured her. "Look, I don't really know what I'm supposed to—"

"You don't wanna stick around because you have stuff to do, but you don't just want to fuck and run because that makes you feel like a jerk?"

"You're good," Carl smiled.

"For what it's worth; I don't think you're a jerk because you have to go, and I know that a guy like you probably has a ton of stuff to before you hit the sack tonight."

"And you're sure you're okay to be alone? I mean, those guys are still after us... for whatever reason that might be... I could arrange for a couple of cops to watch the place."

"The Jolly Rogers won't get in the Complex, don't worry. I can tell the guards downstairs to keep Taylor out, makeup or otherwise. It's just going out to work that might worry me a little."

"Tell Dice you have some personal business to take care of and won't be seeing clients for awhile," Carl suggested. "Least 'til we get sorted."

"He really won't like that."

"Then I'll tell him. Or better yet, have Pope tell him," Carl smirked.

"Oh, that does sound fun," Felicity laughed.

"You got my number, right? In case you need anything?" Carl asked, pulling his leather jacket on.

"I do, and I won't hesitate to call you," Felicity smiled, straightening Carl's shirt for him as she rested her hands against his chest.

"Thank you for a wonderful evening, Miss DuBois," Carl said warmly, brushing a strand of blonde hair from her face.

"Goodnight, Mr. Detective," she smiled as he took his leave of her apartment.

Chapter Twenty-Six;
Discharged

Whatever weight it was that kept Carl's eyes tightly closed refused to relinquish its pressure at the sound of his alarm clock. To actually get his eyelids open was more of an effort than he could have imagined. When finally the lids parted, the clock read "6 p.m.". Earlier than he usually woke, but still enough that he should have enjoyed a good sleep. He wasn't aware of being restless in the night, so why was he exhausted this way? The state he found himself in was like some waking coma, his mind unwilling to drag him from the dream world and into this one. Carl came close to turning off the alarm and going back to sleep, when he remembered the reason he was waking early. With a groan and a curse muffled by his pillow, Carl rolled out of bed and shuffled into his bathroom. When he emerged into the living room a few moments later, Jimmy was sat watching the TV, the volume turned quiet.

"Hey, hope I didn't wake you," said Jimmy.

"Nah, the alarm did. Wanted to get up early enough to make a visit to Skye at the hospital. See how she's doing,"

"You look like shit,"

"Thanks," Carl nodded, pouring himself a black coffee, pleased to find that the pot was still warm.

"I only got back a couple hours ago. Been taking in some of the local eateries. To say this place is such a crap hole, there are some good restaurants."

"Eating's about the only honest thing to enjoy here, so we do it well," Carl smiled. "Make any friends?"

"Oh yeah, I brought him back here. Look how handsome he is," Jimmy said sarcastically, pointing at the empty couch at his side.

"Well keep trying. The cheap floozy of your dreams has gotta be out there somewhere," Carl joked.

"For someone who looks like the walking dead, you seem awfully happy this morning," Jimmy remarked. "You have some fun last night?"

"I may have," Carl shrugged as he leaned against the kitchen counter.

"Dish! Don't you dare hold out on me!"

"It was Felicity. I took her home, we got talking and, well you know how it goes."

"She's the hot blonde, right?"

"That's the one."

"Nicely done, Mr. Duggan. Even I'd consider mowing that lawn!"

"Lovely use of metaphor there, Jimmy. Tasteful," Carl nodded.

"You going to see her again?"

"Not in that way, I don't think. It was a one time thing, a special night. Nothing more."

"Those are often the best. You're not expected to make breakfast."

"Romance is alive and thriving in the gay community, I see," Carl smirked, before taking one final sip of his coffee and grabbing his coat.

"Tell her I said hi," Jimmy called after him.

The walk to the Seven Saints hospital seemed to take less time than it had before, and Carl wondered whether it was the new sense of hope he was feeling regarding the whole situation. An eagerness in his muscles to get there quickly, to see how the young friend he'd made was doing. Quite a few weeks it had been, Carl thought to himself. He'd made a friend who'd probably remember him the rest of her life and slept with a woman the likes of which he could only have dreamed of. It wasn't all roses, though. There was still the matter of why Taylor and his gang boys had marked him and Felicity for dead, why Amber was still haunting him, and who had murdered Queen Bea, the drag artist. Carl didn't mind, though. He liked being busy. Kept his mind active, kept him focussed. Downtime was bad, it would lead to too much time alone with his thoughts, which always went to dark places given the chance. Not tonight, though. Tonight Carl actually felt a warmth in him, a feeling of excitement at seeing Skye's happy smile as she saw him arrive. He stopped at a store vendor and purchased some flowers as he walked by. Carl couldn't remember the last time he'd even contemplated doing something like that. Maybe for his mom on some birthday decades ago.

The colourful bouquet contrasted greatly with the grey and dismal interior of the hospital as Carl walked through the door. The desk attendant was a young male this time, skinny and with glasses that kept sliding down his nose. He was sorting through some paperwork when Carl walked in and didn't seem to notice the Detective until Carl tapped on the raised desk.

"Hm? Oh, hello," the receptionist smiled.

"I'm here to see someone. I called in a couple days ago, her name's Skye."

"Do you have a surname for her?"

"Um, no..." Carl said meekly, rolling his eyes and cursing himself for never having asked the girl.

"That's okay, I'll be able to find her if you give me a few more details?"

"Well she was being treated for drugs, heroin to be exact. Purple hair, about seventeen years old. She was in room number twelve."

"Ah, that helps a lot," he smiled, pushing his glasses back up the bridge of his nose once more as he started sifting through some files. "Room twelve... ah here we are. Oh, it would seem she was discharged earlier today."

"Discharged by who? She was supposed to be signing up for a rehab programme."

"There's some notes, it says she was taken home by a friend. He paid for her meds and said he'd arrange for her to be taken to the rehab clinic over the bridge. It's much better than the one we have here, I wouldn't worry about her. I can get you the address if you..."

"What friend?" Carl asked as a thick black bile began to fill his guts.

"Hm?"

"Who was it that took her home?" Carl said again, trying to keep his voice calm despite the black ooze seeping up into his throat. He could hear his heart beating behind his eyes like a massive drum pounding away the feelings of happiness and hope that he had felt mere moments ago.

"He signed the sheet here, let me just... ah, it was a very generous gentleman who actually made a donation as well. His name was Taylor."

"No... dear God, no..." Carl said quietly as he heard the Devil laughing over his shoulder.

The flowers dropped to the floor at Carl's side as he turned and ran out of the hospital, his shoulder banging against the door that he hadn't fully opened before passing through it. The pain didn't even register; all he was aware of was the pounding of his feet against the cold, hard street. The shockwave of each footfall travelled up his legs and resonated with the beating of his heart. Carl knew where he was running, even though it seemed like his feet would take him there before his mind had remembered the directions; The Electric Dragon, an underground music club that was once the height of live music in the City. Live bands had long since crossed the City off their tour list, so it became home to illegal raves and whoever else could break in and hold their own "event's" there. Over the last few years it had become the party-central base of operations for the Jolly Rogers. If Taylor had said he was taking Skye 'home', then the Dragon was where it would be. Carl took his phone from his pocket, dialling a number as he ran across the Steel Gate Bridge.

"Pick up pick up pick up..." he muttered as his breath struggled to reach his lungs fast enough to give him the oxygen needed for this sudden excursion.

"Hello, Detective. Calling to ask if I'm still alive?" Came the voice of Charles Pope.

"Pope, listen to me and don't ask questions, alright?" Carl yelled as he ran.

"What is it?"

"Get to the Electric Dragon... *now*. I'll pay you whatever you want, just get there fast, and wait for me," Carl instructed. "And Pope?"

"Yes?"

"Bring guns."

Chapter Twenty-Seven;
Who Went First?

The sign outside the Electric Dragon was illuminated with a series of bright blue bulbs, despite the fact that the club was long since closed for legitimate business. Still, if you had enough money you could rent the place no questions asked, legitimate or otherwise. Taylor had enough money, more than enough in fact. The club itself was little more than a basement with a stage set up and a bar in the far corner. It used to be plastered with posters of bands that had played there and reviews from local newspapers, but now it was painted with hideous neon tones in the style of the Jolly Rogers themselves.

Pirate flags hung from the walls and some fake palm trees had even been stuck in the corners alongside empty barrels labelled 'Whisky'. There were two doors to enter the place, one at the front and one at the back, both of which led to a small set of stairs down to the club floor. It was at the front entrance that Carl now stood, his fists clenched so tightly that he could almost hear the skin stretching across his knuckles.

From behind the metal door, Carl could hear the pounding, angry bass of whatever it was the Rogers called music. They played it loud through the speakers to cover up the sounds of their activities down there. It was just easier for them if nobody knew; less people to pay off. But Carl knew, he'd fished enough young girls out of the Styx to know exactly what the group of hedonistic pricks got up to in the Electric Dragon. He hoped that tonight might be different, but he'd already been screwed over once for allowing himself to believe in something as fragile as hope. Best case scenario was that they are all shooting up listening to their Hard-House bullshit, Skye back on the needle like any other junkie. The worst case scenario was something that Carl couldn't bear to think of.

A deep breath entered Carl's lungs, the ice cold biting against his insides as he sucked it in, and then his foot slammed into the metal door. The crash it made against the adjacent wall was so loud that it caught the attention of the dozen-or-so Jolly Rogers crowded round on the floor below, even over their pounding music. Carl leaned over the rail to stare at the faces looking up at him, and his eyes instantly recognised the face of 'Captain' Zack Taylor. His makeup was a neon green skull, no different than any of the rest of his crew, but Taylor was audacious enough to wear a black tri-corner hat, effectively marking him out in the crowd. With a satisfied nod that he was in the right place, Carl descended the stairs and kept his hand ready to draw his gun.

The firearm against his left side was comforting to him, much more so than it had been the previous night when faced with this many neon pirates. The difference now, of course, was that they weren't armed. Taylor had his rules about this place, one of which was 'no guns allowed'. The reasoning behind this was simple; getting a bunch of crazy freaks high on drugs in a small room with pounding music often led to raised tempers, and fights were inevitable. Having his crew smack the crap out of each other was fine, having them shoot each other in the skull was another matter. It had happened once and Taylor was forced to start a recruitment drive to replenish his numbers. Since then, the nights spent in the Electric Dragon were strictly gun-free. Idiots.

"I'm sorry, Boyo, this club is for Pirates only. If you're looking to be a member, there's a joining fee,"

Taylor smiled, taking a slight bow as Carl stood before the small crowd.

"Not interested."

"Wait, wait... you're Detective Duggan, aren't you? Well isn't that interesting, I've been trying to make your acquaintance for—"

"Move aside. All of you," Carl instructed, catching a glimpse of something soft and white on the floor behind the numerous baggy trousers and boots that blocked his vision in the already-dark club.

"We're just having some fun, no reason to be—"

"Move aside... now." Carl said again, this time drawing his gun and pointing it directly at Taylor's forehead.

"Alright, calm down big guy." Taylor conceded, taking a step to his left and letting his fellow pirates part like the Red Sea.

Carl's speculations about the night's activities for the Rogers were answered in cold and brutal fashion as he saw what had caught his eye behind the gathered throng—it was the worst-case scenario. Skye was laid on the floor, naked and badly bruised, blood staining her inner thighs in the aftermath of repeated rapes. Her eyes were wide open but lifeless, her jaw swollen from where her screaming and crying had been forcibly brought to an end by whoever had been the first to grow sick of it. Her purple hair was half-covering her face, stuck there with the mixture of sweat, blood and semen that clung to her skin. Carl walked over to her and crouched down at her side, touching his fingers against her neck despite knowing that it was a pointless effort. With a long sigh, he gently closed the girl's eyelids, then took his phone from his pocket and dialled a number. He let it ring twice, and then without saying a word he hung up the phone. The rear door to the club instantly opened, much to the surprise of the gathered pirates.

"Holy shit, that's..." one of the Rogers trailed off as he saw the silhouette of the tall, long-coated bald man stood in the doorway.

"I know who that is, you idiot," Taylor snapped, trying to hide the obvious panic in his own voice.

Pope looked down at Carl and the girl he was crouched beside. Carl met the hit-man's eyes and solemnly shook his head, to which Pope made the sign of the cross on his chest and mouthed a silent prayer.

"Okay, we obviously have a problem here, Detective," said Taylor, raising his hands in submission, "But I'm quite willing to solve it for you. If this girl owed you some money, I can repay it for you. If you were expecting the pleasure of her company, I have plenty of girls that—"

"Who went first?" Carl asked, his eyes fixed on the broken young girl at his feet.

"I'm sorry?" Taylor asked, leaning forward slightly.

"Who got their rocks off first? Who broke her in?"

One of the Rogers raised his hand and said; "Well, I guess that'd be me, but—"

The speaker didn't finish his sentence before Carl's bullet tore through his throat and out the back of his neck. Blood spurted forward like a fountain as the pirate dropped to his knees, then slumped lifeless to the ground like a marionette cut from its strings. The other Pirates took a step back and glanced at the rear exit, only to find that Pope was now stood on the club floor at their back, each hand holding a Beretta.

"We can discuss this... anything you want, I can get you..." Taylor insisted.

"Pope," said Carl, looking over at his partner. "I need Taylor alive. That's all."

Pope nodded and the carnage began. Bullets from the only three guns in the club tore into the Jolly Rogers, ending the lives of those they hit with deadly accuracy. Three of the pirates tried to escape by taking the staircase down which Carl had come, but the Detective wasn't going to let them leave. No one was going to leave here. Not tonight. If Skye couldn't walk out of here, then the rest of them could join her in the blackness. They could end the night laying in a pool of their own blood on the cold, dirty floor, just like her. Carl's bullet tore through the kneecap of the first would-be escapee, sending him crashing back down the steel staircase and bringing his two companions with him. As they landed in an awkward heap at the base of the stairwell, Carl simply leaned over them and placed a bullet in the head of each one of them.

The detective turned in time to see Pope holding a gun against Taylor's head, who was now bleeding from his right thigh and struggling to stand upright. A quick glance around the floor revealed that every other attending member of the Rogers was dead, Pope's guns having done what they always did with disturbing efficiency. Carl nodded at Pope and then walked over to Skye, wrapping her in his leather coat and lifting her limp, frail form off the ground.

"I need to know why he was sent after me and Felicity," said Carl, looking directly at Pope. "I need to know who he was working for and what they want. How you find out is up to you, I won't tell you how to do your job."

"I'll call you with the information," Pope nodded, keeping the barrel of one of his guns pressed firmly against Taylor's head.

Carl turned and started to walk back up the staircase with Skye in his arms, forcing himself not to cry but finding that a single tear still made its way down his cheek to drip onto her soft white face.

"Detective Duggan," Pope called after him. "She will be at peace now. God will welcome her into his home."

"He'd damn well better," Carl replied with a low growl as he left the club with the dead girl in his arms.

Chapter Twenty-Eight;
Two Dots Make A Line

"Glass will take care of everything, Duggan, don't worry about it," Detective Trent insisted as he spoke to Carl on his cellphone. "He can make her look just like she was alive, you've seen his work. She'll look beautiful for her funeral, and we'll get the state to pay for it and—"

"No. State funded means 'cruddy'. I'll pay for it," Carl insisted.

"Funerals ai't exactly cheap, Duggan. They can run up to—"

"I'll pay, Trent."

"Okay, if it means that much to you. Glass says he'll sort all the arrangements, you just send him a cheque, alright? He's going out of his way to help you here, I couldn't help but notice. I asked him why and he just said that he owes you a favour."

"Yeah, I guess he does."

"What'd you do? Catch him high as a kite again?"

"Something like that," Carl replied.

"You going to tell me how she died?"

"Glass can tell you that."

"Glass already told me she was gang-raped and beaten, but I get the feeling that you can tell me who was responsible."

"You're right, I could."

"But you're not going to, are you?" Trent sighed.

"No."

"Any particular reason why?"

"Because they're already dead, so it's not like you can arrest any of 'em. And even if they weren't, you still wouldn't arrest any of 'em."

"Why wouldn't I?" Trent asked, somewhat defensively.

"Because they're not the kind of guys we arrest, Trent. It's all in the pages of the unofficial rule book."

"What did you do, Carl?" Trent asked as he swallowed the lump in his throat.

"Nothing you're gonna hear about because the only person who witnessed it and walked away isn't likely to be contacting the police."

"Who was it you messed with? Tell me a name, Carl."

"Taylor and his boys."

"Oh Christ. Oh Jesus fucking Christ," Trent whispered. "What are you... why... Jesus, Carl, there's a reason we don't mess with guys like him!"

"I've heard all of 'em a thousand times from guys higher up the chain than you, Trent. And you know what? None of them are worth shit when weighed against the fact that there's a dead seventeen year-old lying in Glass's morgue right now."

"I know, Carl, it's all messed up, but—"

"But nothing, Trent," Carl stopped him. "Taylor crossed a line, one that the rule-book of bullshit corruption wasn't going to protect him from. The law couldn't touch him, so the law didn't. It's that simple."

"Is he dead?"

"Probably is by now. Depends how long he holds out."

"I'm not going to ask what that means."

"Better that you don't," Carl agreed.

"Can we forget about this now? 'Cause if you're up for it I have something for you. I wanted to tell you when you brought the girl to the morgue last night, but... well you had enough on your plate and I didn't want to... over-burden you, I guess."

"I appreciate that," Carl said quietly. "What do you have? More information about our drag artist?"

"Yes and no."

"What kind of answer is that?"

"The kind where we got another victim killed with the same M.O. The kind that makes us think we now have a serial killer on our hands."

"Two dots make a line, not a pattern, Trent."

"The vic was an 'out there' gay guy, lived alone, friends with his neighbours, and now he's dead. Didn't have enemies, wasn't a performer or a man-whore or anything like the first guy. Nothing in common except the fact that he was queer. That sounds serial, Duggan."

"Maybe, but I don't want to jump to that conclusion without at least looking into it," Carl conceded. "Look, I take it the crime scene's already been worked over?"

"Yeah. I know this is your case, but they found him last night and like I said I didn't want to force you to—"

"It's fine, Trent," Carl assured him. "Get the details sent over to me, would you? The reports and whatever Glass makes of the body. I'll take it from there."

"I'll get right on it. Take it easy, buddy."

Carl replaced the handset of his house-phone and turned to see an anxious Jimmy staring at him.

"Who was that?" he asked.

"Trent, just work stuff."

"You said something about gay guys and I overheard something else about a serial killer," Jimmy said nervously.

"You shouldn't be listening in on my work conversations, Jimmy."

"I wasn't, but when I overheard that, I just—"

"Alright, come on, let's talk about this," Carl surrendered, taking a seat on the couch whilst Jimmy took the armchair opposite. "I'm going to tell you about a case I've been working on, but I don't want you to worry, okay? I'm only telling you so that you get the real deal and don't panic when you hear whatever bullshit the press might come out with."

"So, is there a serial killer?"

"I don't know," Carl admitted. "Trent thinks so, but I'm not convinced just yet. Making that kind of conclusion based on just two deaths... well, at this point, it's as likely to be unrelated as it is to be the same guy."

"But both the victims were gay guys, right?"

"Yes, but that might not be what links them," Carl pointed out. "Might be the fact that they're both tall, or slim, or had blue eyes. You'd be surprised what shit can attract a killer."

"But what if it is some crazy homophobe? Should I be scared to go outside?" Jimmy rubbed his hands one over the other in an effort to fight off the imaginary chill that had evidently descended over him.

"No, look..." Carl sighed. "This is what I was trying to avoid, and now I'm kinda making it worse. Whoever this guy is, he picked up his first victim at a queer club and even had sex with him. Some crazy redneck homophobe wouldn't go that far, it'd be a simple 'beat him to death in the street' kind of job."

"Comforting," Jimmy remarked.

"The guy took his victim home, fucked him, then killed him. He was invited to the victim's home, who had no idea what was going to happen until it was too late. I don't know the details from the new crime scene yet, but if they're similar to the first, and it is the same guy, then we're not dealing with the kind of killer who grabs people off the street or breaks into your home. He meets you, talks to you, gets you to trust him, then does his thing when your guard is down."

"So as long as I don't invite anyone home, or go home with them, I should be okay?"

"Yes," Carl assured him.

"Thanks for explaining that. I know you're not supposed to tell me, but—"

"It's fine. You're here alone a lot of the time, I don't want you worrying about it. But if you're really concerned, I keep a spare gun in the second drawer next to my bed. It's an old revolver, the first I had given to me on the force. Kind of legendary, actually, as this guy named Pope wants to buy it from me."

"Why would someone want to buy an old gun?"

"Long story," Carl smiled. "But the gun's there if it makes you feel any better. You do know how to fire one, right?"

"Pull the trigger and point it at the bad person?" Jimmy asked sarcastically.

"Bingo."

Chapter Twenty-Nine;
Serial

Carl found a cup of cold coffee and his pill bottle waiting for him on his bedside table as his alarm clock greeted him once more. He hadn't remembered putting either of them there, so he could only assume that Jimmy had preempted his usual difficulty in waking up. The thought was nice enough, but Carl would still rather be getting a good night's sleep. Once more he didn't remember stirring in the night, but his body told him otherwise. Forget it, take the pills, down the coffee. Let the caffeine hit your system, force your eyes to focus and splash some cold water on your face. One more night in the city.

Yet again Carl was forced to enjoy even less sleep than usual, having been sent over the documents relating to the most recent murder. He wanted to take the time to look over the details of the crime scene before heading out to speak with the friends and neighbours. If he managed to get both done tonight, then it would all be in time for Glass to contact him with the findings of the autopsy. All of which sounded great on paper, but it meant further exhaustion for Carl. He'd been running on coffee and adrenaline for days now and wasn't sure how much longer he could manage it. Carl thought that maybe he should go and see a doctor, get some sleeping pills prescribed. With that thought Carl checked the side of his own pill bottle to make sure they were compatible, then gave it up as a bad job when his eyes refused to focus on printed words so soon after their first opening.

After taking a shower and getting dressed, Carl ventured into the living room and opened the envelope that had been delivered to him earlier in the day. He was grateful for the fact that he'd caught the courier as he arrived back home from his shift, otherwise the poor guy would have met a torrent of verbal abuse for daring to wake Carl from his sleep. The envelope was heavy, containing a plastic file inside of which were photographs and crime scene notes from the CSI's who had been on the case. Carl looked down the list of names of the officers present and was pleased to note the name of CSI Reeve. One testimony he could trust, at least.

The first thing the detective took from the file was a colour photograph of the victim, and the relevant notes attached. The guy was lying face down on his bed with a bullet wound to the back of his head. Just like the first guy. No sign of struggle, no evidence of forced entry. Not even any bruising on the guy's wrists. He wasn't held down against his will, he had no idea that this freak was about to pull a gun on him. Just like the first guy.

"Dammit," Carl muttered to himself.

As he read on, Carl was finding his instincts leaning further and further towards Trent's 'Serial Killer' theory. He didn't want it to be that, of course. The City had enough dead bodies turning up as it was, without a maniac taking more at his leisure. Still, Carl wasn't stupid enough to think that blindly hoping against something would actually make any difference. Whatever God it was that answered prayers of hope had long since died as far as the City was concerned. The only monument left to him was a desolate shell attended only by a devout man who killed for money.

The next page of notes was titled 'witness statements', which caused Carl to swear out loud and bang his fist against the coffee table. Another officer had already spoken to the witnesses, had got their first-hand recollection of what they might have seen. Carl wasn't one to brag about his skills, but it was safe to assume that whoever spoke to them did a half-assed job compared to Carl's methods. They wouldn't have cared, for one thing. One more dead guy to stuff in the morgue, one more load of paperwork to do. Other cops didn't see the victims as people, not like he did. Trent still tried, but now and again Carl would see the way his attention would drop. He'd think about how late he'd be getting home tonight, how he might miss the big steak that was waiting for him, and how the latest dead guy was one more queer off the streets. If Trent didn't retire soon he'd become one more zombie with a badge, Carl just knew it.

The witness statements would be far from what Carl had hoped for, but they still had their use. Carl also knew that talking to the witnesses a second time was pointless, as the best information always came when the events were fresh in their minds. Others, 'experts' mostly, would say that time to think on the events and get them clear in the mind was a better approach. Carl knew better than any of those educated pricks. An adult life spent patrolling the streets would teach you that the longer people thought about what they'd seen, the more diluted it would become. Other's people's comments on the same subject, the fluidity of memory, and even additions of stuff they'd seen on the news would all screw up what they'd actually been party to. Best to get in there early, before any of that crap set in. With that in mind, the documents in Carl's hand were the best he was going to get as far as the latest victim was concerned.

Carl didn't recognise the names of the officers who'd taken the statements, which could either be a good thing or a bad thing. If the officers were rookies, new to the City, then there's a chance that the corruption hadn't set in yet and they actually did a good job of taking an interest in the case. On the other hand, they might be officers who weren't good enough to work in a different precinct so transferred somewhere that no one gave a crap. Somewhere like the City was a welcoming ground for such officers, and Carl had seen more than his fair share of them.

The notes on the pages in front of him were written in longhand, which was a source of relief as trying to understand another man's code was a nightmare. The first person spoken to, was an old lady who lived in the apartment opposite the victim's. She saw him coming home in the evening with a gentleman, but it wasn't someone she recognised. The lady knew that the victim was gay, so wasn't surprised to see him with another man in an obviously familiar fashion. She even said hello to them and gained a response. What she did note as being odd was the fact that the man accompanying the victim was wearing a dark red opera mask.

"Goddamn it," Carl grunted again, banging his fist down on the table for a second time.

It was the same guy. The story hadn't hit the papers yet, no way this could be a copycat. Unless it was a gang thing, like Taylor and his pirates. Maybe the opera masks were a new thing, their calling card. Carl read on, clinging on to that fragile hope, the one last desperate belief that this might not be a serial killer. The old lady's description of the man tore through it like a knife through tissue paper; the man was quite tall, broad, and wearing a denim jacket. Carl sighed heavily and resigned himself to the fact that the same killer had now clocked up two victims. Same description, same M.O. Could still be a gang but it was seeming unlikely. There had been no evidence that the victims had been robbed, either, so what would be the gang motivation? Taylor's crew were the only ones who killed for the hell of it, the reason for that being the simple reality that every one of them had more money than God to begin with. Carl allowed himself a small smile at the fact that the Jolly Rogers would probably dwindle into nothing given what had just happened to the majority of their number. Good riddance.

The second witness was the janitor who saw the red-masked guy leaving later in the evening. He commented in his statement that he saw lots of people coming and going and it wasn't even unusual for them to come home dressed up in some weird way. What caught his attention this way was the fact that the guy was leaving the same night, and that he was still wearing the mask. The janitor didn't say anything to the guy, of course, why would he? But he did consider it so strange that he neglected to mop up the guy's footprints, in the event that the crime lab could use them. Carl smiled as he read this, endearing to this guy without even having met him. Reeve had taken images of the footprints, but there was no tread left on the tyre. Whoever was wearing the boots had been wearing them so long that matching the pattern to anything was impossible. You could get the size of the shoe, but that was next to useless.

The final witness statement was from a street vendor selling glow sticks on a small cart. Glow sticks, Carl thought. How the ell could a guy make a living selling glow sticks? Must be selling crack on the side, at least. Anyhow, Glow Stick Man... who refused to give his name... couldn't be because his name was already in the system, could it? Claimed that he saw this burly guy walking down the street towards him. Saw the opera mask, thought the guy must be heading to the club, and was invariably the perfect mug to buy his crap. So the vendor did what vendors always did, he followed the guy down the street waving his crap in the masked man's face. Until he got a punch to the stomach that doubled him over. Guy had a bruise like a sledgehammer had hit him, or so he claimed. Addicts tend to bruise easily, but they're also prone to exaggerate.

The remaining paperwork consisted of photographs of the crime scene from different angles and general information about the victim. Twenty-eight years old, worked for a coffee shop, came out of a long-term relationship some months ago, or so the old lady had assumed when the boyfriend had stopped coming round. Were if not for the mask and the description, the boyfriend would have been a suspect. Carl wouldn't rule it out, he never did until something was resolved, but it was doubtful given everything else. The victim had been coming home from work when he met his murderer. He'd texted a friend to say he'd be going out to the clubs later and had never shown. That was when one of them came looking for him and found him dead. Carl felt for whoever had found him that way. Try as they might to forget it, that would be their last memory of a friend. Whenever his name was mentioned, even at his funeral, the image of him laying dead and naked with a hole in the back of his head would force its way into the mind.

"Alright," Carl sighed to himself as he concluded his perusal of the paperwork. "We got a serial killer."

Chapter Thirty;
Big Money

The second cup of coffee went down as well as the first, Carl's energy stores eagerly taking what the caffeine had to offer. Deciding that he might still need to pick up a third beverage from Stu the coffee vendor, Carl checked the contents of his wallet and satisfied himself that he had enough loose change on him. He tossed his jacket on and reached for his keys when he felt his cell phone vibrating against his pocket.

"Duggan," he answered.

"Good evening, Detective," came Pope's eternally-calm voice.

"You got something for me, Pope?"

"Everything you asked for, as much as was possible."

"What do you mean, exactly?" Carl enquired, resting against the kitchen counter as he eagerly hung on the hit-man's every word.

"Taylor wasn't aware of too many details, but what he did know he was very willing to tell me."

"I'll bet he was," Carl chuckled. "How many of his own teeth did you make him swallow?"

"Only two. He's not quite as resilient as you might think."

"Shame, I was hoping he'd suffer," Carl admitted.

"I assure you that he did," Pope replied. "So are you interested in the answers to your questions, or did you just want to satisfy yourself that he'd met as horrible an ending as that young girl?"

"You're telling me Taylor's dead?"

"I'm not a man to leave things unfinished, Duggan," Pope reminded him.

"So what did you get out of him first?"

"He and his crew had been sent after Felicity and yourself by their current employer. I'm aware that it was unusual for them to work for anyone, which is why I made a point of enquiring about it. Apparently one of Taylor's largest clients in his more legitimate enterprise... such as it is... requested his services with regard to killing both of you."

"He was an investment banker, right? So one of the guys on his books has a beef with me and Felicity. Why did Taylor say yes to that? It's really not like him."

"Apparently this particular investor was not a man that Taylor was likely to say 'no' to. A Mr. Carlito Petroni, it would seem."

"Petroni? The US Senator-slash-big Mafia player? You serious?" asked Carl.

"My reaction was the same, but Taylor was in no position to be lying at the moment he screamed that name to me."

"Petroni hasn't done any business outside of Washington D.C in years, what's he doing back in the City?"

"Evidently he found a lucrative operation here and thought it worthy of his attention. Whatever it was, you and Felicity were somehow in the way of it, as was Fei Ling White. She wasn't a random killing either, but part of the same 'clean-up' operation."

"So are you saying that Taylor didn't know what Petroni was actually doing?"

"Apparently not. If he knew, he'd have told me. Men rarely lie with an eye-socket full of battery acid."

"I'll remember to get that on an inspirational poster," Carl commented, involuntarily wincing his own left eye. "He tell you anything else?"

"He told me the name of someone else involved with the operation. He wasn't sure how the man was involved, but he'd been informed that part of the scheme was wrapped around him. The name was Kenny Smedley, it didn't mean anything to me."

"Kenny Smedley? He runs the pharmacy in Limbo. Only decent one in the whole damn city, since the others attached to the hospitals are constantly stolen from either internally or externally."

"Does he have a record?" Pope enquired.

"Hell no, he's just a pharmacist. Hands out prescriptions, pills and over-the-counter meds. This is making less sense the more I hear," Carl sighed with a weary rubbing of his sinuses. "Anything else from Taylor? Anything at all?"

"Just that he'd leave the City and was sorry about the girl and any number of things that he thought would get him out of that nightclub alive. Nothing useful, to me or to him."

"I appreciate your help in all this, Pope."

"I'd be lying if I said that it was just for your benefit, but for what it's worth you're welcome."

"You need to leave, Pope. I said it to Felicity and now I'm saying it to you. Get out of the City."

"Why would I do that?"

"Firstly, the two of you got some connection and no-one has that kinda thing here. You need to take it and run with it whilst is lasts. Secondly, this shit with Taylor and Petroni is gonna have a price. I'm willing to pay it, but you shouldn't have to."

"I appreciate your concern, Duggan, but I can take care of myself."

"I'm intimately aware of that fact, but we're talking Big Money here. Taylor had friends, Petroni has more of 'em. If they get to me then I'll cross that bridge when I come to it, but I don't want Felicity dying any more than you do. Take her and get out of here. Lots of places need a hit-man, Pope."

"I'll take it under advisement, Detective," Pope conceded. "Look after yourself, especially now. However bad it's been out there, I have a feeling it will get worse soon."

"Sweet Dreams to you too, Pope."

Chapter Thirty-One;
Over the Counter

Carl's mind was a mess as he walked the distance to Smedley's pharmacy. It would have been quicker to take a cab, but he needed the walk and the time it would bring him. If his head wasn't at least partly clear when he arrived at his destination then nothing would be gained from going there in the first place. How could Smedley be mixed up with Petroni and his large-scale operations? There was 'out of character' and then there was this. The Smedley's pharmacy had been there as long as Carl could remember; first run by the current Smedley's grandfather, then his father, and now Kenny himself. All three of them had been honest guys making an honest buck. They wouldn't even overprice their products, which could easily be done given what dumbass sick people will pay for meds they think they need. Something was very wrong at the pharmacy, and no question.

Limbo greeted Carl with its usual mixed aura of light and dark, a thin veil of fake joy wrapped around a black core of desolation. The whole damn section of the city could be summarised with the image of smiles painted on toothless grins and neon light-bulbs filled with dead flies. Smedley's Pharmacy had its own illumination outside, but it was a simple logo of a red cross and the name of the owner in the middle. Carl came here a lot, every month in fact, and had done as long as he could remember. He refused to pick up his pill prescription from the hospital pharmacies as he could never guarantee that it would actually be there waiting for him. With Kenny there was no such worry. Carl would turn up on the seventh of each month to find a neatly rolled-up brown bag waiting for him. As he approached now, Carl noticed something that caught his eye immediately;

there was no board over the large window nearest the till. That window was always boarded up, because every time Kenny replaced it some crack-head dipshit broke into the place. Now it was a clean sheet of glass, unbroken and naked to the world. Carl supposed that it could be new, but why would Kenny change his mind about never paying to have the damn thing replaced again?

"Hey Kenny," Carl nodded as he entered the pharmacy, squinting as he always did under the bright strip-lights on the roof.

"Little early for your refill, Carl," the small, overweight pharmacist smiled at him between handfuls of the potato chips he held. "Not overdosing, I hope?"

"Nah. If I was gonna do that then I'd take better stuff than the crap you give out," Carl joked. "So how have you been, Kenny?"

"No change since last month," Kenny shrugged.

"You sure about that?"

"Yeah, why wouldn't I be?"

"I hear otherwise, that's all," Carl replied with a slightly narrowed gaze as he studied Kenny and noticed the beads of sweat forming on his forehead.

"So my doctor says I gotta lose a few pounds for my heart, or whatever. Who cares? I know medicine, I know about shit like that, it ain't up to him to tell me about my own health, you know? Arrogant prick," Kenny scoffed as he wolfed down another handful of potato chips.

"Not what I'm talking about, Kenny."

"No? Then what's bugging you?"

"What's with the window? Thought you were done replacing it?" Carl asked, nodding towards the new pane of glass on the left-hand wall.

"Insurance is a wonderful thing, Carl. I ain't got to pay for shit anymore."

"You don't believe in insurance, you never did. Used to say it was like paying for stuff that might never happen."

"A man can change, Carl."

"Yeah, that's what I'm worried about," Carl sighed. "Who paid for the window, Kenny?"

"I paid for it, who else would have?"

"Then let me ask you another question; who was it that gave you a guarantee your store wouldn't be broken into again?" Carl asked as he walked over to the counter where Kenny was sat.

"I, uh... I don't know what you're..."

"Cut the crap, Kenny," Carl demanded, slamming his open hands down on the counter with such sudden volume that Kenny dropped his bag of potato chips on the floor.

"Carl, you don't understand, man... they just... I..."

"What happened, Kenny? What have you gotten yourself into?"

"It's... it was my mom. She needed medical stuff, Carl. Stuff I couldn't afford... they got her on this gas tank thing just so she can breathe. That stuff ain't free, Carl! I got to pay to help her breathe, can you believe that?"

"That's why you have insurance, Kenny," Carl said with a soft sigh. "Go on."

"I couldn't afford it, my business doesn't make enough to... but I couldn't just... so I started to sell some pills, for more than I usually would. Only, um... not to people who, um... need them."

"You were selling them to crack-heads?"

"Please don't arrest me, Carl. If I went to jail then my mom would... I mean, she wouldn't have anyone to..."

"Keep talking, Kenny, 'cause I got the feeling you ain't told me everything yet," said Carl. "Then we'll decide what I'm obligated to do about it."

"Well, I was selling some pills to the addicts and stuff, the ones who used to rob me, ironically... and I started making enough to help my mom get her stuff, but then, well... it got out of hand. I couldn't fill my actual prescriptions so I, um... started to substitute pills..."

"For what?" Asked Carl.

"Sugar Pills. Basic painkillers like ibuprofen. Anything that wouldn't be harmful, you know?"

"Holy shit," Carl gasped, as things started to piece themselves together in his mind. "Was Judge White getting his calcium meds from you?"

"Um, yeah, he was. His wife would pick them up. Man, she was hot, I used to look forward to Wednesday when she would..."

"She's dead, Kenny," Carl snapped.

"What? She... she is?"

"Taylor's pirate crew killed her. Just like they tried to kill me."

"Kill you? Oh shit. Oh shit, Carl, they didn't say that they'd... oh shit..."

"And the Judge died because he took a lot of pills everyday that ended up firing up his heart a little too much. Could Ibuprofen do something like that if you take too much and are kind of heavyset to start with?"

"Yes, it could. But I didn't think that he was taking so many that it might..."

"How many prescriptions have you been substituting, Kenny? What else is going on here?"

"I just picked a few names at random, you know? If I chose all the diabetics or all the guys with bad hearts then it would be obvious that something was wrong if they got sick or..."

"If they died."

"Carl, I swear to God I didn't want to... but... my mom, if you could see her..."

"Did you change any birth control pills? Meds to stop epileptic seizures?" Carl asked, recalling Amber DuBois getting pregnant despite her pills, and her sister's client who died in front of her.

"Yeah, a couple of each I think..." Kenny nodded nervously, sweat dripping from his podgy nose onto the counter.

"Jesus, Kenny... do you have any idea what you've... there was a girl, nineteen years old, who got killed by her pimp because she got pregnant. You're responsible for that, do you understand?"

"Carl, I'm sorry... I'm sorry, all right? I didn't want it to go this far. I started to get worried, started to think about the people who might be... might get sick and stuff, so I... I wanted to stop doing it. But..."

"Someone else got in on it, didn't they?" Carl asked with a deep exhalation through his nose.

"Yeah," Kenny nodded, wiping the sweat from his head.

"How did Petroni hear about it?"

"I was giving meds to one of his nephews for a rash he'd gotten. It didn't go away so he came back and threatened me, said I'd given him bad pills. I realised that he was one of the ones who—"

"Fucking Christ, Kenny! You switched the pills for a family member of a Mafia boss? Are you insane or just retarded?"

"I didn't know who he was, I don't know about stuff like that..." Kenny said quietly. "But I had to tell him what had happened, he threatened me, he... he had a gun... he said he'd forget all about it if I let his uncle in on the deal. I didn't want to, I was done with the whole thing, but..."

"Carlito Petroni isn't a man you say 'no' to, is he?" Carl nodded. "So now he's paying for your mom's medication, your new window, and keeping the shit-heads away from your door. And you're stuck in the great big hole that you started to dig yourself."

"I know, I know... I want to stop all this, but..."

"And now they want me dead because your new benefactor evidently heard about the cases I was investigating... wouldn't surprise me to learn he had moles in my own station... and he thinks I might be getting close to the truth. Fei Ling White and Felicity DuBois are just side lines, people who were close to the victims and it's smart to get rid of them 'just in case'."

"I'm sorry, I didn't want any of this. I just needed some money, I swear to God."

"You should have called me, Kenny."

"I didn't think... I just... I've never been in any situation like this, I don't know what I'm supposed to do, Carl!"

"I want to help you, Kenny, I do," Carl sighed. "But I keep picturing the face of the girl who washed up on the shore of the Styx because of you... and it's all I can do not to pull my gun on you."

"Please don't hurt me, Carl. I... I'll testify, I'll do whatever it takes, but... I can't go to jail or anything. My mom doesn't have anyone else. You gotta understand that."

"I do," Carl nodded, shaking his head and rubbing his eyes. As he opened them again he put his hands on the counter and suddenly noticed something just under the lip of the customer-facing side where he was stood. "Kenny... you had any other customers in here tonight?"

"A guy came in about ten minutes before you," Kenny nodded. "He wasn't one of Petroni's boys, I don't think."

"What did he look like?" asked Carl, putting his hand around the small object he had noticed and removing it with a sharp pull.

"Quite tall, bald head. Weird tats on his hands," Kenny said nervously. "Is he one of Petroni's boys? Are they checking on me?"

"He's not one of Petroni's boys," Carl said with a deep swallow, looking at the small black microphone surveillance device that had been placed under the counter. "Did he say anything to you?"

"Just bought some headache pills, I think. Over the counter stuff..." Kenny stammered as he wrung his hands one over the other.

"There might be more of these things, if you didn't notice this one..."

Carl moved around the store quickly checking for any further devices that might have been planted there for the purpose of listening in on what Kenny had to say. Pope had known the pharmacist was involved with the death of Amber DuBois from his earlier conversation with Carl, but the detective had never imagined that he'd go to this much trouble to find out how. Why did he even care what this pharmacist had to say? It was Carl who'd been targeted, not Pope.

"Alright, I can't see any others. He must've known that I'd most likely talk to you right there at the counter, and..." Carl stopped as he saw that Kenny had left the counter, taken his coat, and was quickly making his way to the exit. "Kenny, don't go outside!"

The warning didn't come quickly enough to save the fat pharmacist from the gunshot that split the cold night air in half. It screamed down from the roof of his own store, tearing through the back of his skull as he ran away from whatever invisible opponent he was imagining. Terrified out of his mind and not even close to logical thought, Kenny hadn't even known what he was trying to escape from or where he was going. He'd just wanted to run. Evidently he wasn't fast enough.

"Shit. SHIT!" Carl yelled.

He glanced left and right and noticed the door at the back of the counter, then quickly made his way towards it. The door opened onto a stairwell that led up to a small apartment. As Carl ran through, he noticed that it had signs of being lived in, and it occurred to him that perhaps Kenny had actually lived above his own store. Not anymore. Kenny had slept in this dump for the last time. Carl found the emergency exit that led to a final staircase and finally the roof, which he came to just in time to see a black-clad figure vaulting the small gap between the roof of the pharmacy and the adjacent building. With a deep breath Carl ran after him and leapt the small gap, landing badly on his ankle and stumbling forwards to keep his balance.

"Pope!" Carl yelled, hoping to distract his prey as he knew he had no hope of physically catching up to him.

"What do you want, Detective? What's to be gained by following me?" The hit-man asked as he turned to face his pursuer.

Carl didn't answer as he closed the gap between himself and Pope, but merely leapt at him in a football tackle and grabbed him around the waist. They both hit the roof hard, but Pope took the brunt of the fall on his back, leaving Carl free to instantly hit him across the jaw with a hard right hook.

"You didn't need to kill him, you prick!" Carl yelled.

Pope narrowed his eyes and moved himself beneath Carl's weight, positioning his arms in a way that he could flip the larger man from his person and get back up to his feet. Carl came at him again, swinging with a right hook that Pope successfully blocked, and then a straight left jab to the chest. The hit-man wasn't so lucky with that one, staggering back and holding his chest where the blow had forced the air from him.

"He was part of it," Pope said weakly, one hand on his chest as he hunched over slightly.

"I told you to take Felicity out of here, then you'd both be safe!" Carl yelled as he kept his fists clenched and his arms raised, just as he would have done when squaring off against an opponent in the old boxing ring.

"This wasn't about the hit that was put on you and her," Pope explained as he stood upright, grimacing slightly at the pain in his chest. He's forgotten how hard Carl could hit and now he was suffering through a tough reminder. "Felicity loved her sister more than you could know, Detective. Do you have any idea how many times she tried to stop her getting involved in the same industry that she herself was forced to work in? She's famous in her trade because she does things… allows things to be done to her... that others don't. Do you know why? Because she saw it as the only way to make enough money to get her sister out of here!"

"And now she's dead before Felicity got the chance, I know," Carl nodded. "And that's gotta sting like hell, but what exactly does that have to do with you?"

"I love her!" Pope yelled, losing his cool for the first time in Carl's recollection. "The first time I met her... she was so young and fragile... I just wanted to wrap my arms around her and take her somewhere safe... but I didn't. My life should have been kept well away from hers. Then her sister came out to the city as well, and she finally had a reason to leave. By that time she didn't know me the way I wanted. I'd kept away, I thought she'd forgotten about me."

"She hasn't," Carl stated firmly. "You're pissed off at yourself because you didn't get both of them out of here when you had the chance. Now it's too late. I get that, I really do. You have no idea how much of a goddamn failure I feel as a cop every fucking time a girl her age finds her way to a slab in the morgue at the back of my office... but you didn't need to kill Kenny. That was out of line, even by your standards."

"He was part of it," Pope repeated. "His little money-making scheme led to her getting pregnant, which led to her running from Dice and being killed by her new pimp. It all starts with that fat coward down there."

"It doesn't end with him, though, does it? What about Dice? And Petroni? You actually going to go after a US Senator as well?"

"I'll do what I have to." Pope nodded.

"Get out of here," Carl sighed. "Just go."

"I was expecting you to actually arrest me this time."

"If I make a move on you then one of us is going to end up dead, the other something close to it. That leaves Felicity alone, and right now that's not a good idea. Petroni still wants her dead, so—"

"She needs us both."

"We're not okay, Pope, you understand? Taking Kenny down that way was over the line. The guy just wanted to help his mom, for Christ's sake. Don't you understand that?"

"I understand, but that doesn't grant him absolution. He ran his own business, he could have taken a bank loan, committed insurance fraud, or even some form of embezzlement. There were numerous options available to him that wouldn't have cost any lives."

"He was desperate and he was an idiot. That doesn't always lead to the smartest decisions."

"For what it's worth, I'll light a candle at the church for his safe passage. I may not be able to grant him forgiveness, but the Lord will."

"Hallelujah," Carl sighed, turning to look out across the city. Despite the fact he hadn't heard a sound, he knew without question that Pope would long since have gone by the time he turned back around.

Chapter Thirty-Two;
Rest in Peace

Carl had waited for the meat wagon to come and collect Kenny's body, and the CSI's to examine the scene. He explained what Kenny had told him, and that he was shot by an unidentified assailant on the roof. Glass would back that up from the trajectory of the bullet wound, but he'd be unable to trace the bullet itself. The guy had probably pulled dozens of unmarked bullets from Pope's targets over the years. Perhaps he knew who they came from, perhaps he didn't. No one in the police department would go after Pope either way, as that would require growing a pair of balls. The crazy thing was, if they actually bothered to send a SWAT team after the guy, they'd take him down no question. He was dangerous as hell, sure, but he wasn't a superhero or a vampire or some other comic book bullshit. Pope was a well-trained, ahletic guy who could kill six people with five bullets, but if you hit him between the eyes with one of your own, he'd go down as easily as anyone else. It'd never happen, though. Any mention of "His Holiness" around most of the City's crooked cops would be enough to make the boys in blue wet their regimental pants. If ten of them went after him, Pope himself would be brought down, but maybe six cops would come back. No one had the guts to risk being one of the other four, so he was left to carry on doing what he did best.

Whilst his fellow officers took care of the crime scene, Carl left the pharmacy and went for a stroll out of Limbo and back onto the familiar territory of the East side. He'd spent too much time in the recesses of its brighter sister lately—it was comforting to feel the grime and cold of home. The sky above had finally released its hold on the heavy grey clouds that filled it, and a snowfall had started almost immediately after Carl had climbed down from the roof. It was almost symbolic, he thought, like a weight had been lifted now that the root of Amber's death had been cut out. The sky could finally exhale. It wasn't completely done, of course. Senator Petroni himself was still alive and living it up in Washington, his work done through his cronies in the City like everywhere else. Dice was a part of it too. If his treatment of his girls hadn't made Amber so afraid of him, she never would have run to Big Dog's arms when she got pregnant. Still, Carl hoped it would be enough. That she could rest now.

Without realising it, Carl had strolled along the banks of the Styx, finding himself now stood at the very spot where he and Trent had first seen the body of the nineteen-year old girl who had been the start of the recent troubles. The detective's mind had led him here without informing him, like it wanted him to see the place where it began as it all came to an end. The sound of heeled shoes coming to a stop at his side led Carl to the conclusion that he wasn't the only one with such thoughts for the night.

"Evening, Miss DuBois," Carl nodded, turning his collar up against the snow.

"Hello, Carl," the stunning blonde smiled at him, her red lips giving off enough heat to melt any snowflakes that would dare to fall towards them. Her neck was covered by a black scarf, her hair hung down loose, and she wore a long scarlet coat that almost reached the floor.

"Pope call you and tell you what went down?"

"Yeah. He said you'd had a little altercation."

"I didn't rough him up too much," Carl shrugged.

"Is it wrong that I'd get very excited watching the two of you throw down?"

"Very much so."

"Oh. Guess I'm a little weird, then."

"I wouldn't say that. The thought of you and another chick having a cat fight isn't without its charm."

"I can arrange something like that if you like, but you gotta pay for my time and the other girl's." Felicity remarked with a coy smile.

"I'll pass. My paycheque doesn't stretch that far."

"Charles knew I'd come to find you. He said to tell you he was sorry you lost a friend tonight."

"That's rich, coming from the guy who shot him."

"Well... Charles is a complicated guy, Carl."

"No kidding," Carl chuckled. "Kenny had it coming, I guess. Desperate or not, he'd gone over the line the moment people started dying. Amber probably wasn't even the first, just the first we got to. So how'd you know I'd be here?"

"I just knew you'd want to pay your respects, and this was where you first saw her, so..." Felicity smiled, wrapping herself around Carl's arm and holding close to him. "Where else would you go?"

"I hope she can rest now," Carl said quietly, the words leaving his mouth in a cold grey whisper.

"I remember when we were kids, it was anything I could do to get her away from me, you know?" Felicity commented with a soft smile and a shake of her head. "But now... God, I'd do anything to have her back."

"The Gods of Hindsight like nothing more than to point and laugh," Carl agreed. "So what now for you, huh? You going to leave the City?"

"Would you miss me if I did?" she smiled.

"Yeah, but probably not the way you think. I mean let's get it out in the open, you're smoking hot, and if I live another four decades I wouldn't get close to a woman half as fine as you," Carl explained. "But what I'd miss about you is what's beyond that. The passion you have for those you care about, the innate goodness that even this cesspool hasn't managed to stamp out of you... you got a soul, and that's rare. Even rarer to be wrapped up inside a broad that looks like you."

"That's probably the nicest thing anyone's ever said to me," Felicity said softly as she looked up at Carl through tired eyes. "I get complimented all the time by the guy's I'm, you know, with, but... you sounded like you meant that."

"I answered your question, you didn't answer mine. Are you leaving?"

"I don't have an answer to give you."

"You don't know?"

"It's not that simple. I know how Dice would react if he lost me."

"Just leave in the night, what's he gonna do?"

"Kill some of the other girls in anger, probably. Or at least beat the hout of them."

"I fucking hate this place," Carl sighed, spitting into the river with an almost symbolic gesture of his contempt for the waters that formed it.

"I don't even know how we ended up here, Amber and me. I mean, I heard there was easy money to be made, so I thought 'what the hell'. I had no idea I'd get stuck here, and that Amber... God, I just feel like I failed her."

"I could come out with a load of therapeutic crap about how it ain't your fault, how nothing could have changed what happened yadda yadda, but you know all that already. Me saying it isn't gonna change the way you feel, so I won't waste my breath. What I will say is that you should remember the good stuff about her, not just how she died."

"She was smart to choose you to be the one to find her. Anyone else… she might never have found her answers," Felicity smiled.

"Speaking of which, if you're still pondering whether or not you should leave the City, I'd advise that you remind your boyfriend that the both of you are still in danger. Taylor's boys might be dead and gone, for the most part, but Petroni's got a lot more soldiers where they came from."

"If you've exposed the case and the pharmacist guy is dead, then the whole operation's bust, right? Nothing for him to gain by killing us now."

"They got this whole thing about honour and vengeance. Basically he'll want us dead even more so now. Me included of course."

"Then why don't you leave?"

"I got nowhere to go and no one to go there with."

"You could come with us."

"Threesome with you and Pope? No thanks. Don't relish the idea of having another punch up with him over who gets which end."

"If I weren't scared my hands would fall off from the cold, I'd slap you something fierce," Felicity teased with a playful scowl. "Seriously, though, if you wanted to get away—"

"You gotta realise that Pope's gone outside of his normal actions on this one, Miss DuBois. A little for me, but mostly for you. He's done that because he cares about you in ways that are probably unfathomable to him. If you're the same about him, you should do each other a favour and leave. There ain't no room in there for me, and that's the way it should be. Besides, I still got me a serial killer to catch."

"A serial killer?" asked Felicity.

"Yeah, that's what it looks like. Don't worry though, his thing is gay guys."

"That's one guy I don't have to be watching my back for then."

"You shouldn't be walking around on your own at night, though..." Carl said, and then stopped him and remarked, "Pope's here, isn't he?"

"He's close by," she smiled.

"Tell him it's annoying as hell when he does his Batman thing."

"He probably knows, but I'll tell him from you anyway."

"Goodnight, Miss DuBois," said Carl, taking her leather-gloved hand and kissing the back of it gently.

"Goodnight, Detective Duggan."

Carl watched as Felicity walked away into the ever increasing snowfall, and then looked once more into the dark waters of the Styx. Satisfied that he could no longer see Amber's frozen face staring at him longingly, he nodded to himself and walked the rest of the way home.

Chapter Thirty-Three;
Dirty Game

"What the fuck is this?" Carl yelled as he held up the newspaper. The other police officers in the station stopped in their tracks and stared at him. "Who was it? Which of you idiots is responsible for this?"

"Duggan, cool it," Trent insisted as he approached, still holding a mug of coffee.

"You seen this, Trent? The rags got a story about a red-masked serial killer stalking the city. How'd they found that out, huh? We ain't done a press release."

"Could have been any number of ways, Duggan. They—"

"What about you, Dooley, huh?" Carl demanded as he angrily pointed the paper in the direction of a young officer. "Still trying to fund that coke habit of yours? Selling stories to the rags really helps keep your nose stocked up for winter, doesn't it?"

"It wasn't me, I didn't even know about that thing," Dooley said defensively.

"Bull...shit," Carl retorted.

"That guy who sold glow sticks, he could have told the papers what he knew," Trent suggested as he took Carl to a quiet corner of the office.

"All he knew is that one guy had been killed, Trent. You don't get 'Serial Killer' from that, and that's exactly what the headline reads."

"Okay, listen… it was me. I told them."

"You serious? Trent, you moron! Do you know what..."

"I know what I'm doing, Carl, alright? Listen to me..." Trent said calmly. "We get something like this, the fewer people on the streets the better. If people think there's a nutjob serial killer on the loose, then less of them will go out getting hammered; they'll be more careful, not talk to strangers, stay in groups, play it safe. Makes it harder for this guy to get his next prey, which means he gets desperate, which means he gets careless..."

"Which makes it easier for us to catch him when he slips up," Carl nodded. "Maybe you're not just an asshole looking for easy cash."

"I got paid for the story as well, but I agree with the 'not being an asshole' bit. You're not the only cop out here who knows how to play the game, Duggan."

"Kind of a dirty game, Trent."

"True, but if it works, it works. And you've played far worse yourself."

"You're right, I'm sorry. I just... I hate half the pricks in that office and that we have to work with 'em. I see something like this and I think it's gotta be one of them making a fast buck."

"They're not all bad, you know," Trent insisted. "Some of the newer recruits are quite promising."

"Yeah, this week. Until someone from the other side of the river flashes a shiny penny at them."

"Anyway, you come down here this afternoon just to yell at the boys? Shouldn't you be asleep?"

"I want to be asleep, I promise you that," Carl sighed. "But Commissioner Grant called me, said he wanted to speak with me.

"Good luck with that," said Trent, backing up his words with a firm pat on Carl's shoulder.

Carl reminded himself where Grant's office was and entered immediately after seeing that the Commissioner was alone inside. Grant was a huge black guy that wore braces instead of a belt, the reason being that a belt probably wouldn't get around him. The braces weren't much better of course, as they just gave him the appearance of bread baking around two pieces of twine. His appearance aside, Grant wasn't really a bad guy. He looked like the kind of boss who'd tell you that you had forty-eight hours to get the job done or he'd take your badge, but the truth was he was much softer. Too soft, in fact, which was why so much crap happened under his shift. He was clean himself, but he did far too little to keep his officers that way. Carl had always thought the guy would have been better served as a school principal than a commissioner of police, but it wasn't his place to suggest it.

"Good afternoon, Detective Duggan. Thanks for waking up to come down here," Grant smiled as he offered Carl a seat across the other side of his desk.

"It's fine, I don't sleep that good lately anyway," Carl replied as he sat down.

"Sorry to hear that. You eating okay?"

"Yeah, it's nothing," Carl forced a smile, having been given a full-force reminder of the fact that this guy was too damned friendly to be of any use in this City.

"So you're probably wondering why you're here, right?"

"It did occur to me."

"Well... it's about this guy," said Grant, taking a photograph from the file in front of him and sliding it across the desk towards Carl. As the Detective looked at it, he saw a photograph of Charles Pope leaving St. Michael's Church.

"Huh. Didn't think he'd show up on camera," Carl remarked.

"So you know who it is, right?"

"Sure I do."

"Then you're probably aware that he's been rather active lately, am I right? More so than usual, given his past work."

"Maybe lots of people got beefs with folks they don't like these days."

"I know you don't believe that's what this is, Carl," Grant said with a soft sigh, using Carl's forename as a way of softening the fact that he had to call him up on the fact.

"Okay, let's cut the crap, shall we? This is about the fact that he killed Taylor, who probably owns half your damn police force, and now you're getting heat from whoever's pockets that jackass was lining."

"I couldn't give a rat's ass about Taylor or his crew, and if some of my men have to go back to one paycheque per month, I won't lose sleep over it," said Grant, his honesty gaining him a little respect in Carl's eyes. "I'm worried about you."

"I'm touched, but really, I'm fine."

"Carl... you were involved with Pope once before, weren't you? A few years back."

"Yeah but he never called so I broke it off," Carl said sarcastically.

"Help me out here, Carl. I don't want to have to be a bear about this."

"Okay," Carl conceded. "Yes, I was involved with Pope before now. You were there at the time, you gotta remember how that went down, so why don't you tell me? This is obviously leading to something."

"We heard that Pope had been hired to kill my Chief of Police, and you were tasked with stopping him. You got close, closer than anyone had ever gotten to Pope before, and then you let him by. The Chief still bought it and you didn't lift a finger to stop it. I found out later it was because of what our guy was involved in, child prostitution and worse. You let him die, Carl."

"To use your own words, I didn't lose any sleep over it," Carl said flatly.

"I'm not saying that you should have, but the fact is you let a hit-man take out one of our own because you had moral issues with what he was doing," Grant explained. "And now Pope has been wading into gangsters like there's no tomorrow, following the disappearance of a girl who you yourself took to the hospital."

"How do you know about that?" Carl asked, his attention suddenly captured.

"The hospital called us to say that there'd been something of a scene following a homeless girl being discharged. After what 'a large man in a leather coat' had to say on his visit, they were worried that there may have been something suspicious regarding the girl leaving their care. The receptionist who called told us who had discharged the girl, and the rest kind of fit together after that."

"You're better than I thought you were," Carl admitted.

"I wasn't always a fat ass who sits behind a big desk, Carl," Grant smiled. "I used to be a fat ass walking the beat."

"So where are we going with this, Grant? You know that I had something to do with Pope getting to Taylor, and that's so far out of the rule book that you probably don't even have a disciplinary code for it."

"I'm not writing any of this down, you may have noticed," Grant remarked. "This isn't a disciplinary hearing or anything, Carl. I just need to get this clear in my head so I know I can trust you."

"Are you asking me why I let Pope kill Taylor?"

"Who was the girl?"

"Just a girl I got out of Taylor's gang. She needed my help and she got it. In return Taylor dragged her back to his world and had her gang-raped and killed for the insult."

"That son of a bitch," Grant sighed. "And what's this with the pharmacist? Guy on a roof taking someone down with a single bullet? That's got Pope written all over it."

"That was something else, personal stuff for Pope. It also has to do with the fact that I have a hit out on me right now."

"You do?"

"Apparently. Taylor was supposed to be working on it but obviously that's not going to happen. I'm just waiting for the next hammer to fall right now, but what are you gonna do?"

"Who was paying him to kill you?"

"Carlito Petroni, he was in on the whole thing with the Pharmacist. I was getting too close for his liking, apparently, and it pissed him off. How dare I do my damn job, right?"

"Senator Petroni? I've heard the rumours that he's Mafia-connected, but..."

"They're not rumours, Grant," said Carl, shaking his head.

"We can get you some cops on your door, keep you covered and..."

"I'd feel safer alone. I don't trust more than half the guys you got out there. Most of 'em are probably in Petroni's pocket anyway."

"You don't seem particularly concerned right now."

"Why worry about it? If I get all paranoid and nuts then I'm less likely to see it coming. Better to stay sharp and focused, concentrate on the job. Like this serial killer with the mask, for instance."

"From the row outside, I'm guessing you heard about Trent's plan with the media?"

"Yeah, it makes sense come to think of it. Serial killers always get sloppy eventually, speeding up the process seems smart."

"Guys?" Trent interrupted as he opened the door to the office. "We just got a call. Dead gay guy number three."

"Talk of the Devil," Carl sighed, getting up from his chair.

"Carl," Grant said before he left. "Be careful, alright?"

"Hey, you know me."

"Yeah I do. That's the problem."

Chapter Thirty-Four;
End of the Line

"So talk me through it," Carl requested as he sat in the passenger chair of Trent's battered grey Sedan.

"We got a call saying some big guy in a red mask had dumped a heavy-looking sack at the old train station. Description seemed to match our guy, so one of the guys on patrol checked it out. Masked guy had gone, of course, but he found the sack and what was inside it. Dead body, of course. That's when he called us," Trent explained.

"So we're going to be the first ones on scene this time?"

"CSI's are already there, but no one's taken any statements yet. We get to hear what the crazy bums and addicts have to say first hand."

"Ain't our life wonderful, huh Trent?"

"Very," the grey-haired detective nodded as he pulled to a halt at the cracked red streetlight. "I gotta tell you, I'm not sure about this one."

"Why? 'Cause the guys who called it in were homeless? They used what little cash they had to call the cops, I hardly think they're gonna be screwing us around."

"That's now that I meant. Like you said, can't have been easy for 'em to decide to call us, so if they did then I'm pretty sure they saw what they said they saw—a big guy in a red mask dropping off a sack filled with a corpse. What seems weird to me is that it totally goes against this guy's M.O," Trent explained as the light turned to a dull green, the bulb barely working, but giving him passage to continue down the road nonetheless.

"Victim wasn't left at the scene, and the body was dumped," Carl nodded. "In view of witnesses. Seems a little careless."

"I guess that is what we wanted, although now I'm curious as to what caused him to be so careless. The newspaper article didn't get out 'til this morning, the body was dumped last night," Trent mused. "You think he panicked or something?"

"I can't say that this seems anything like the actions of a guy losing his cool. There ain't no residential area within a couple of blocks of the station, Trent. Guy had to have walked a long way to dump the body. Or maybe he drove, put the body in the car and pulled up here. But if he was getting in the car then why not take it further, somewhere where he wouldn't get seen?"

"You know, I remember reading once that all serial killers want to get caught. That they like the attention, which is why they deliberately get sloppier towards the end. Even if it's subconscious."

"This one's more than sloppy, it's downright stupid," Carl remarked as the car pulled up at the train station.

The train station wasn't easily accessible from any direction, given that it had long since closed down and been blocked off. It was this that led to it becoming a haven for derelicts and drug addicts. Their own little home, cold and dark, but sheltered. To get to the main doors—which had been boarded up long ago but forcibly pried open shortly afterwards—was only possible by crossing through the bus station. The two were located next to each when constructed for ease of transport around the city. Take a bus to the station then jump on a train to wherever. That was back in the days when people actually had somewhere to go. Long time ago, longer every day. As he and Trent crossed the cracked tarmac, snow drifts pooled up against the benches and trash cans, Carl remembered the last time he was here—the first time he'd met Skye, saved her from one sleazy predator only to lose her to another a few nights later. Taylor was dead now, and he didn't die happy. Big Dog might be dead or he might not, but he'd have been raped repeatedly at least, which was some comfort. Neither brought Skye back, though. Nothing would bring her back now, all that was left of her was just ten minutes' worth of happy memories for Carl. The ten minutes he'd spent with her in the hospital and actually let himself feel some hope for her. Soft idiot. Should have known better.

Trent came to the train station door first and let it swing open with a gentle push. Like the others lined up next to it, the door had been glass at one time, but it was now covered with rotten wooden boards which had been nailed haphazardly one over the other. The door opened and the two detectives entered, not really expecting any need for their guns but keeping their hands tensed and ready to draw just in case. The inside of the station was large, with a high roof and two levels. On the upper level had once been coffee bars and magazine stores, on the lower level the ticket offices and the doors which led to the only three platforms in the station. It wasn't exactly a huge station even in its prime, but it had served a purpose, at some point in time. Now it was just a dank old husk of forgotten memories.

The station interior wasn't as dark as the two men had expected, illuminated as it was by several flaming trash cans around which groups of men and women were huddled. There were beds made from old sheets and folded boxes, and steel shopping carts full of whatever had been scavenged in the day. Carl could feel the fragile glass of old syringes breaking beneath his boots, and this too haunted him with memories of Skye and the life she had once led. In the centre of the room, Carl and Trent could see a police officer stood guard over the corpse that was surrounded by police tape. CSI's were already working on the body, the scene illuminated by their strong beam torches and lamps.

"You guys the detectives?" Came a gruff voice in the far corner of the room.

"You the guy who called the cops?" Trent asked as he approached the bearded man who had spoken. Unlike the other denizens of the station who were huddled over fires in groups, this man was stood alone by his warming trash can. Trent wondered if he was unpopular with the group already, or whether they just didn't want to speak with the police.

"Your boys came to look at the body a few minutes ago, wasn't sure if they'd actually send anyone to speak to us," the homeless man replied. "Name's Jed."

"Why didn't you think we'd be coming to speak with you?" asked Carl.

"You know how it is. They get a call from one of us, they'll come and pick up the body then leave. They ain't interested in what we got to say, particularly if the body is one of our own."

"Is the body one of your own?" asked Carl, seeing no need to try and argue with the point.

"Nah, the guy in the mask brought it in with him and dumped it on the floor there."

"What did he look like?"

"Big guy, broad shoulders, blonde hair and wearing a red mask."

"Blonde hair? You sure?" Asked Carl, raising an eyebrow.

"Yup. Tied back in a ponytail and everything."

"The descriptions we have of this guy put him with short, dark hair, right?" asked Trent.

"Yeah," Carl nodded. "This is starting to make more sense."

"It is? How is that, exactly?"

"It's not him. Whoever did this is someone else, the mask might just be a coincidence."

"Pretty weird coincidence, don't you think? Not like they both wear the same shoes or something."

"So do I get a reward, or what?" asked Jed.

"Don't go anywhere, I might have more questions," Carl remarked as he handed the homeless man a couple of twenty dollar bills.

"What'd you pay him for? He was only doing his civic duty," Trent commented as he and Carl walked back outside of the station.

"You think he cares about that? He did a good thing so I gave him a little credit for it. If his friends see him buying some good smack or some actual food in the next few days, it might encourage them to be a little more forthcoming when we next ask them stuff like this," Carl shrugged.

"Did you see how many people were in there? Kinda sad to think that this place might be the last home some of them ever see."

"Most of 'em, probably. They come here when they've run out of options. End of the line," Carl sighed. "So why are you here, Trent? We all know this ain't your thing."

"What? Investigating crime scenes? 'Cause that kind of is my thing."

"You had reasons for giving me this case instead of taking it yourself, and those reasons haven't gone away.

The victims are still queer, far as we know. You just want a piece of it now it's the City's first serial killer?"

"Hey, that's outta line," said Trent, his tone a little hurt. "I just wanted to help you out a little cause I've been worried."

"About me? Why?"

"You look like hell, Carl," Trent sighed. "You got bigger bags under your eyes than the guys in that train station! You're running on fumes and since you never talk about yourself nobody knows why! Telling you to see a doctor would be useless 'cause you don't listen, so I just wanted to keep an eye on you."

"I appreciate that, but I'm fine. I've just been having some sleep issues."

"You're not getting to sleep? My wife has these relaxation candles and tapes that you could borrow."

"I'd sooner die, but tell her thanks," Carl managed half a smile. "No, it's not that I ain't getting to sleep. The sleep I'm getting isn't doing any good. I wake up as tired as when I laid down."

"Do you sleepwalk?"

"How the hell would I know that?"

"Cousin of mine used to do it. Use up all her energy walking around watering plants and stuff, so she'd wake up tired."

"I got a friend staying with me, I think he'd have noticed if I was doing things like that."

"You're up during the day right now, which means this can count as your shift. Take the night off, sleep in until tomorrow night, see if that does you any good. That's like a full day's rest, should help you out a little."

"Yeah okay," Carl agreed, knowing from experience that when Trent was playing the 'concerned buddy' it was easier to shut him up if you just did as he suggested.

"Aren't you supposed to be working on some arsonist thing, anyway?"

"Just some punk torching cars," Trent shrugged.

"Then go look into that, I'll wrap up here," Carl insisted. "I don't need babysitting, I'm fine."

"You call me if you need anything, alright?"

Trent patted Carl firmly on the arm and then left the station in the direction of his car. Carl decided to leave the two CSI's and their accompanying officer to attend to the body whilst he walked around the exterior of the building. Old, rusted train tracks could still be seen beneath the overgrown grass and weeds, and Carl had to watch his step to avoid tripping over the damn things. There had to be tire tracks around here, no way had a guy walked this distance with a body slung over his shoulder. The daylight hurt Carl's eyes, unused to working in it as he was. Still, it made it easier to look for evidence as he walked around the surrounding area. Whatever tire tracks might have been there had been covered by the fresh snowfall, but still Carl kept on walking.

Before he realised how far he'd walked, Carl found himself in an open area of flat dirt that had the last, dying remnants of a construction site. There was a rusted old port-a-john, a battered old ball and chain that had somehow broken and detached from a crane, and a stack of cracked cinder blocks. As he looked at the scene, Carl remembered hearing that a company had, about three years ago, decided to try and reinvigorate the area by rebuilding the train station. Bigger, better and brighter than ever. The money dried up fast, like they always do when newcomers are forced to pay protection rackets, and the project was abandoned. Now all that was left was the ghost of what might have been. Hope and opportunity stifled before it took its first breath.

"You look a little lost," a voice sneered.

Carl turned to see two men dressed in black suits, one wearing a red shirt under his jacket and the other a dark green. The taller man in the red shirt was broad and had long blonde hair tied back in a ponytail. The smaller man in the green shirt had thinning black hair and wore leather gloves. In his left hand the smaller man played with a switchblade, whilst the taller man was unarmed.

"I'm working here," Carl remarked, noticing the fact that the large man fit the description given by Jed.

"So are we," the smaller man smiled.

"So... 'cause I think I have this figured out but stop me if I'm wrong..." Carl remarked, keeping his gaze fixed on the men as he walked, like a tiger circling its opponent. "You boys work for Petroni... one of your inside men on the force told you about the other case I was working... so you decided to set me up by staging another murder to get me out here, correct?"

"Hey, he's smart," the small man remarked.

"Shame that you're not," Carl chuckled. "Dumping the body in front of witnesses? Not even close to how our man operates."

"Doesn't matter, it got you here didn't it? Now, all we wanna do is have a nice chat, ain't that right Shirley?"

"Yeah, that's right," the tall blonde man nodded.

"Shirley? His name's Shirley?" Carl laughed.

"Won't seem so funny when he's pounding your face into the dirt."

Shirley stepped forwards and clenched his fists, a leering smile on his face at the prospect of what fun he was about to have. Carl tensed himself and moved out of the way as the large man lunged at him, turning in time to strike Shirley in the back with a straight jab. Shirley swung out with his fist and Carl narrowly avoided being struck by it but was unable to avoid the second blow that sent him to the floor as it struck his face. It was unusual for Carl to fight someone who was bigger and stronger than he was, and he hadn't actually planned for it. As the tall blonde came towards the prone detective, Carl kicked out at his knee and snapped it to the side. Shirley roared in pain and staggered to one side, struggling to keep his balance on his broken joint. This gave Carl the opportunity to stand up and draw his gun, at which point he fired a shot into the blonde's other kneecap. The smaller, dark-haired man now approached with his blade, but Carl spun around and pointed his gun directly at him.

"Think about it," Carl warned, his reddened and already swollen face betraying the fact that he was in no mood.

"All right, look... we didn't mean to get into this, we just get carried away, you know? Particularly Shirley, he... well he enjoys his work," the small man stammered, his arrogance gone given that his burley friend was crying in pain on the floor, the advantage well and truly taken from him. "We were just here to warn you that Petroni ain't happy."

"I know that already."

"Well, just watch your back, that's all, 'cause next time it might be worse than just us."

"I should hope so, else I'd start to think a lot less of Petroni," Carl remarked. "So who was the dead guy in the sack?"

"Just a stooly who'd been blabbing lately, no-one important."

"Two birds with one stone. Very economical of you."

"You gonna let us go now?"

"Hmmm," Carl pondered deliberately loudly. "Your friend ain't walking out of here, is he? You're gonna have to carry him."

"I got a cell phone."

"Course you do, big-shot like you. What am I thinking?" Carl sighed, forcibly taking the phone from the smaller man's pocket and then smashing it against the floor. Keeping his gun trained on the small man, he then walked over to the fallen Shirley, who was now unconscious from pain and blood loss, and removed his own phone, breaking this one with equal disregard. "There we are. Now won't this be a fun afternoon for you?"

Carl smiled mockingly and patted the smaller man on the cheek, before walking away from the scene.

"Oh wait, I almost forgot," Carl stopped himself, turned and fired another bullet straight into the dark-haired man's right shoulder, causing him to cry out in pain as the arm instantly became useless to him. "Now it'll be really fun."

"You're not just gonna leave us here, you're a good cop!" the man cried as Carl resumed his act of walking away.

"Thanks to guys like your boss, that means less in this town than it does anywhere else."

"You're just gonna let us bleed to death out here in the cold?"

"Yup."

"You serious?" The man screamed erratically as he clutched his shoulder, the blood spraying out between his fingers which had no hope in hell of applying an effective tourniquet.

"Yup."

"You're a crazy motherfucking son of a bitch!"

"Yup."

Carl walked on until he returned to the train station, at which point he took out his own cell phone and dialled 911.

"I need an ambulance down at the old train station, there's been a bit of an incident. What? No, nothing serious. Take your time."

Chapter Thirty-Five;
One Man's Trash

The third-to-last stair on the way to Carl's apartment let out its same, regular creak as the detective's foot pressed down on it. Best security system in the world, better than any alarm that could be deactivated by cutting off the power. As Carl ascended the final step, he put his hand on the doorknob and then froze. Something was wrong, he could feel it. That innate sense a cop gets after years on the force. The sense that tells you to watch yourself, that something isn't quite right. Some guys ignored it, some passed it off as paranoia, particularly when they'd already been threatened in the way that Carl had. Carl himself didn't avoid the feeling, but neither would it stop him from doing what he wanted to do. Instead, he drew his gun and gripped it tightly as he turned the knob and entered his apartment. There was no sign of a break-in, but Carl could immediately hear one of Jimmy's CDs being played at low volume. He looked over to the corner of the room where the stereo was located, the one Jimmy had bought upon realising that Carl didn't actually own one, and saw a tall, black-coated bald man holding an album and studying it.

"I must admit, I never would have took you for a Madonna fan," Pope commented.

"Never would have taken you for the breaking and entering type either," Carl remarked, keeping his gun in hand. His past acquaintances with Pope were complicated to say the least. Whilst his gut told him that there was no need for the weapon, he couldn't ignore the fact that a hit-man was stood in his own living room. Carl doubted that Pope would accept a contract on his life, but he couldn't be sure. A job was a job, after all.

"I apologise for that, but I didn't want to wait around outside for you. It's becoming rather dangerous out there, and I had no wish to make my presence known."

"You been attacked by Petroni's boys too?" asked Carl, flipping the switch on the kettle at his side.

"Yes, there was a single man sent to attack me outside the church, of all places."

"Am I going to be finding him in the Styx in the next couple of days?"

"His head, perhaps," Pope shrugged as he continued to study the album. "Is this the album that carries 'Like A Prayer'?"

"Are you going to burn it if I say yes?" Carl enquired as he made himself a cup of tea, deciding that coffee would be a poor choice given his desire to get a good night's sleep. He considered offering Pope a drink but decided against it as this would only give him reason to stay for longer.

Pope chuckled and replaced the record, then asked, "You were attacked yourself, I assume?"

"Yeah, couple of jerks in Italian suits."

"Are they still alive?"

"What am I, a doctor? I called 'em an ambulance after we had our conversation, didn't wait around to see the verdict."

"You're an interesting man, Detective," Pope remarked. "You condemned me for judging the value of human life differently depending upon an individual's actions, and yet you gladly do the same. If they are innocent victims then they get your help, if they are beyond innocence, they get your fists or your bullets."

"I have a badge that expects me to do just that. You just have a gun and a musty old book."

"That book is my badge, as is this," Pope replied, pointing to the tattoo on the back of his head.

"How about we get to the question of why you're in my home?"

"I am considering your advice regarding Felicity and myself, and have some unfinished business to take care of," Pope explained. "One of which is the matter of you being the only man to have bested me/"

"So you here for round two? Or three, if you count the roof of the pharmacy."

"After our encounter on that roof, I was worried you had broken one of my ribs... again. So if you were to 'count' it, then I'd say it went to you. But no, I am not here for anything of the like. I've told you before that I have no grievance with you, Detective, and that hasn't changed. What I am here for is to make a purchase." As Pope spoke, he took a brown leather wallet from his inside pocket.

"If you want the Madonna album just take it, I'd be quite glad to get that crap out of my apartment."

"I want your old gun. The one you scarred me with," Pope explained, pointing to the narrow scar across his cheek.

"You want that old thing? I thought you were joking about that."

"One man's trash is another man's treasure, as they say. It is important to me, as a reminder to stay humble. A reminder that we are all of us mortal, no matter our skills."

"Glad I could be of service in providing that after school special, but I can't sell you the gun right now. I'm sure you've heard about the serial killer situation we have?"

"I do read the papers, yes."

"Well a friend of mine is worried that he might be on the list of possible victims, so I said he could use the gun if he needed to, as a kind of reassurance. I don't actually expect him to need it, but... well it makes him feel better."

"We all need to feel safe," Pope nodded. "I understand, of course. If you change your mind then please contact me. I'm considering mounting that weapon."

"Have I told you before that you're nuts? As in, cartoon character crazy? You probably have an underground layer where you keep other people's guns and crap like that, don't you?"

"Not currently, but it might be something I invest in should I purchase a new home," Pope smiled, causing Carl to wonder if he was playing off the joke himself or whether he hadn't actually understood it.

"Well I'm going to have me a nice long sleep and hope the sandman doesn't screw me over tonight," Carl remarked with a weary sigh. "Unless there's anything else, I'd appreciate you not being here when I close my eyes."

"I find prayer often leads to an untroubled night. You may wish to consider that," Pope said warmly as he walked past Carl towards the door.

"Thanks for the suggestion, but I prefer not to waste my time."

"I prayed for your purple-haired friend the night she died. Would you consider that a waste?"

Carl stared Pope directly in the eye for a moment, and then looked down at the floor and quietly replied, "No. No, I wouldn't."

"Goodnight, Detective. Sleep well."

"Night, Pope."

Carl closed the door behind the Pope, listening for the sound of the third stair creaking on his way down, only to find that no such sound was made under the hitman's footfalls.

"Creepy sonnova bitch," Carl sighed as he walked back into his apartment. All was quiet for a moment until the bedroom door opened and Jimmy came through.

"Is he gone?" he asked sheepishly.

"What were you doing in there?"

"Um, hiding? What did it look like?"

"Would you like to tell me why you were hiding?" asked Carl, sipping his tea.

"I heard someone working the lock... don't ask me how he opened it... and so I went for your gun, the one in the second drawer? Anyway, I looked through the crack in the door and saw who it was. I recognised him from your descriptions of him—the tattoos, the coat, who else could it have been? Anyway, gun or not, no way I was getting messed up with him, so stayed hidden under your bed. Not too brave, huh?"

"Sensible," Carl assured him. "You must have been silent like a goddamn ninja for him not to have known you were there."

"I was scared to even breathe. Now I can't stop shaking."

"Well, in the unlikely event that he ever comes back, you don't need to be afraid of him, okay? Just tell him who you are and he'll be fine."

"He's one of the good guys, then? A friend of yours?"

"Not exactly... I mean, he's not technically a bad guy, but... it's complicated. Just trust me when I say that he's okay."

"Oh and when he started looking through my albums! How dare he insult Queen Madge?"

"He didn't insult her, technically. He just asked if a song was on the album."

"He's Catholic, he probably hates her. What does he know, anyway? Stupid hit-man with his baldness and his coat."

"I almost wish you had come out of that room, been funny as hell to see how he dealt with you," Carl laughed.

"Can we talk about something else now?"

"Well I gotta hit the hay soon, but okay, what's on your mind?"

"I saw the papers this morning."

"Brilliant," Carl sighed. "Look, papers have a way of blowing everything—"

"Oh, I know all that, that's why normal people read news on the net," said Jimmy, pushing the comment away with a flip of his hand. "It just got me thinking. Have you ever actually gone after a serial killer before?"

"Yes and no," Carl replied.

"What kind of answer is that?"

"Well, we thought it was a serial killer but it was a gang of three people doing the same type of murders, so..."

"What were they doing?"

"Drilling through the side of people's skulls."

"Oh my God! Why were they doing that?"

"I didn't ask, I just shot two of 'em and arrested the third."

"How'd you find them?"

"Once the CSI guys figured out that it was three guys... forensics showed it somehow, some clever shit to do with the angles of the injuries suggesting different heights and bodily strength and stuff... anyway, we found out that the idiots had been dumb enough to pay for the drills on a single credit card. We traced the card, found the owner, and found the two friends who'd been living with him."

"There must have been a reason why they were doing it," Jimmy protested.

"Poor little rich kids looking for something more exciting than Playstation," Carl shrugged. "The surviving one is probably back on the streets now, given the money his dad can throw at the legal system."

"Why don't we just kill all the bad guys. Wouldn't it be easier?"

"No," said Carl, backing up the word with a firm shake of his head.

"Why not?"

"Because where do you draw the line with stuff like that, and who gets to draw it? Do we kill the starving kid selling dope to buy his next meal? What about the homeless addict who buys it? What about guys like Pope, who are murderers themselves but get rid of people who are even worse? It's impossible to judge, and once you open that box there ain't no putting everything back in."

"You've shot a lot of guys dead though, right?"

"Not a lot," Carl replied. "Maybe twenty, I think. I know you read these magazine interviews with guys who say they see the faces of everyone they've had to shoot every single night... but it's bullshit. If I took the decision to kill them, then I knew there and then that they weren't worth being haunted over."

"Would you shoot this serial killer if you had the chance?"

"Depends on the context of the situation in which I was given the opportunity."

"What do you mean?"

"Well, if I had him bang to rights and he wasn't going anywhere, I might shoot him in the leg or something to make sure he didn't try and run for it. But killing him would be a little out of line. If he was coming at me with a weapon of his own, or I knew there was no way to physically stop him and keep him alive, then yeah I'd kill him."

"So if you came home and he was here—"

"Oh for God's sake, I knew it'd come back to this," Carl sighed, rubbing his tired eyes.

"You can't blame me for worrying about this, Carl!" Jimmy protested.

"If I came home and he was here, I'd empty my clip into his head and then load up another and empty that one as well. Happy?"

"Thank you Carl," Jimmy smiled. "You always make me feel safe. I wish I could do the same for you."

"You don't need to do that."

"I've always wanted to. All I ever wanted was to be like a brother to you."

"Well you already are, buddy. More like a sister sometimes, but still..."

"If there was ever a situation where it could be me protecting you for once, you know I'd do whatever I had to, don't you? And that whatever it was, I'd only be looking out for you?"

"Yeah, I know," Carl assured him. "But don't be going after Pope or the serial killer with my gun or anything stupid, alright?"

"I wouldn't even know how to reload it."

"Remind me to teach you," Carl smiled as he moved towards the bedroom. "Time to hit the sack."

"Sweet dreams," Jimmy called after him. "Am I okay to quietly play my Madonna albums whilst I read?"

"Depends if you want your ass kicked or not."

"Okay, I'll just read in silence."

"You do that," Carl nodded as he closed the bedroom door behind him.

Chapter Thirty-Six;
The Real Number Three

Carl awoke to see the neon pink of the "Jesus Saves" sign buzzing in his window, the night sky set against it as a soft snowfall drifted lazily down to the street below. He reached for the alarm clock and read the time as 8.pm, the date next to it revealing that he had indeed slept for almost a full twenty-four hours. To his surprise, he did seem to have lost the weariness that had been creeping up on him more and more with every day. Carl wasn't sure if he had actually slept solidly through twenty-four hours, but he certainly felt rested; so much so that his eyes remained willingly open as he got out of his bed. A stretch and a yawn preceded his trip to the bathroom, where he was glad to see that the bags under his eyes had lessened considerably. They weren't gone completely, of course; a single day's rest wouldn't achieve that given the depth of exhaustion he'd been feeling, but any improvement was something.

A shower, a shave and an actual breakfast of toast and cereal, and Carl felt more ready to venture out into the night than he had done in weeks. The detective found some confirmation that his sleep might have been somewhat restless to start with, in the form of the bruise on the back of his right knuckles. It looked as though he'd banged it against the bedside table, but he hadn't remembered doing it when awake. The skin was a little tender but nothing more, so Carl ignored it and began to dress for work. He actually chose a fresh shirt to wear for the day, a dark purple in colour that went nicely with his black leather jacket and black tie. He didn't actually remember buying the shirt, but it was in his size, so it was quite possible that Jimmy had purchased it as an unannounced gift. It was also ironed, which made it even more unlikely that Carl himself had placed it in the closet. He had just finished forcing his tie to remain straight despite the poorly crafted knot when his house phone started ringing.

"One day I'm gonna be up more than five minutes before you start mouthing off at me," Carl grunted as he reached for the phone. "Duggan."

"Hey, Carl. How you feeling?" Trent asked. "You sleep okay?"

"Yeah, actually I did. Please don't tell me you're just calling to ask about that, you soft sack of shit."

"No, afraid not. We have a real number three. Another dead gay guy."

"Where and when?"

"He was killed last night, looks like. In his own place, like the others. Landlord heard a ruckus, called the cops."

"Did he go and help out?"

"He said the guy his tenant came home with was huge, so no. Anyway, we got CSI's on it already and the witness statements were taken under my supervision."

"I thought you weren't in on this one?"

"I'm not, but I know you'd want someone you could trust so I worked a little extra shift."

"Great. Make me feel guilty for taking the night off."

"Never mind that, the fact is I think our newspaper idea worked, to some degree at least. He's broken his pattern."

"What's he done different?"

"No gun," Trent replied. "Glass is looking into the specifics, but from the state of the bed, I'd say the guy's head was bashed repeatedly against the headboard. And not in the way he might have been hoping."

"The back of his head?"

"Yeah."

"So the vic was facing his killer this time. Any evidence of a struggle?"

"Yeah, the guy had bruises on his forearms, like he'd been held down, and his jaw was broken, like he'd been hit hard to shut him up."

"He'd somehow figured out what was going to happen and fought back. So the guys grab his head and bashes it into the headboard until he's done," Carl thought aloud, allowing the scene to play out in his mind. "Why no gun?"

"No clue, no evidence it was fired at all on the scene. No empty cases or the like," Trent replied.

"Maybe he didn't take it. Or maybe he did take it and the thing jammed on him or whatever."

"This does seem kind of desperate," Trent agreed. "Like a last ditched attempt to salvage the kill."

"Who were the witnesses?"

"Just the landlord himself, no one saw the murderer leave. Must have taken the fire-escape."

"And was our guy wearing a mask?"

"No, he was wearing makeup, white theatrical stuff, kinda like that movie where the guy comes back from the dead, you know?"

"He changed his look, the son of a bitch," Carl hissed. "The papers were all over the red mask shit, so that's what everyone is looking out for. Guy turns up to a gay bar with a painted face... no-one bats an eyelid."

"I think I messed up," Trent admitted. "Should have left the mask part out when I spoke to the papers."

"Spilled milk, and all that crap. Better to focus on what we can do now."

"That's another reason I called you. Glass finally made a breakthrough with the bullets we found in the other two guys."

"What do we got?"

"Carl..." Trent said quietly, then took a breath. "You still got that old service revolver? The one you asked to keep when everyone else gave 'em back in?"

"Yeah, it's in my drawer."

"You sure? You might wanna check."

"I'm not liking this, Trent," Carl said grimly was he took the cordless phone with him into his bedroom and opened the second drawer in his beside cabinet. "Oh shit."

"Bullets matched your gun, Carl," Trent said with a sigh. "Serial number's still on file from the days it was standard issue. Can't be sure it was your exact gun, but only cops would have that model, and to my knowledge no one else still owns one."

"Son of a bitch," Carl said under his breath.

"Any theories? You haven't pawned that thing or something lately, right?"

"No, but Charles Pope said he wanted it. Something about keeping it as a souvenir, but..."

"You don't think Pope is behind this? That really wouldn't make any sense, would it?"

"Not in the slightest," Carl admitted, deciding against telling his fellow detective the depth of his recent experiences with the hit-man. "But right now he's the only lead I have here."

"You know where to find him?"

"Yeah, I think so."

"Carl... I hate to be the one to tell you this, but you're kind of a suspect as of now."

"You are fucking kidding me."

"I wish I was. But... well, you're a big guy, the murderer's a big guy... it's your gun that's been used—"

"For Christ's sake, Trent, you don't actually think—"

"Of course not, Carl. Come on!" Trent assured him.

"Still, I gotta keep an eye on your movements until we get this sorted. Technically I should bring you in for questioning, but I ain't doing that 'cause it's retarded."

"I'm going to go speak with Pope," Carl informed him. "I'll let you know how it goes."

"Thanks, Carl. Don't go nuts about this, okay? Don't get reckless and angry, it makes the situation even more dangerous."

"I'll be fine," Carl insisted.

"It's not you I'm worried about. It's Pope."

Chapter Thirty-Seven;
Clutching at Straws

The stained-glass windows of St Michael's Church were illuminated from within, shining their message of hope and faith onto the streets outside. The message fell on deaf ears and blind eyes as it had done for years. The largest window bore the image of an angel holding a candle before it, the light from inside the church causing it to glow with an unnatural warmth that seemed eerie and out of place given the filth of the surrounding area. Carl didn't believe in angels, he never had. Even if there were any out there in the ether, they'd long since turned their gaze away from the City. If the angels themselves had given up hope of making the place any better, then who else should be dumb enough to try?

The door to the church was unlocked, free for anyone to come inside and rob the place if they chose. Strangely enough, no one ever had done. The devout would say that even the vilest of criminals would think twice about breaking into God's house. The more sensible would suggest that it was something to do with this being the Church of His Holiness. Pope was here at least once a day, which the City at large knew. If you were a crook looking for an easy break-in, a church frequented by the most dangerous man in the entire City would be a poor choice. Not even worth the risk, anyone would agree.

Carl swung the door of the church open and entered, leaving the snow and the cold behind him, save for that which still clung to his boots and rested on his shoulders. The church was lit by hundreds of candles, as it had been the last time the detective had seen it. It occurred to him that in the past few weeks he'd been in church more than he had in decades. Not for a wedding or funeral like normal people who avoided church, but to speak with a man who kills people for money. The same man who now stood at the far end of the church lighting candles on the altar.

"Why'd you steal from me, Pope?" Carl demanded as he walked down the red-carpeted aisle, drawing his gun and training it at the hit-man's head in one fluid motion.

"Please put your weapon away, this is a house of God," Pope requested as he blew out the match he held and tossed it aside.

"Normally I might respect that, but tonight I care to the sum of zero," Carl replied. "Answer the question, why did you steal from me?"

"I don't steal, we've discussed this before. The last time you were here, I believe."

"Maybe you don't class it as stealing because in some weird way you think it belongs to you, I don't care. The fact is you took my old gun!"

"I assure you that I didn't."

"You wanted it, and now it's gone. What's more is it's being used to kill people. Never occurred to me before that our serial killer might just be a professional trying to make his work look like that of someone else."

"You seem confused and agitated," said Pope.

"What do you expect? My gun has been stolen without me even knowing it, and now it's being used to kill people!"

"You're telling me this serial killer of yours is using your own gun?"

"That's exactly what I'm telling you."

"And you actually think that I'm the serial killer?"

"Are you telling me you're not?"

"I can tell you that the only lives I have taken recently are those you are party to," Pope said sincerely. "And that I did not steal your gun. Why would I have come to your house two nights ago to buy it if I had already stolen it on some previous occasion?"

"To cover your tracks maybe, I don't know," Carl suggested. "The fact is there's not many people that could break into my house without me knowing it. Actually that's a short list, the only fucking name on it is yours!"

"Then perhaps your home wasn't broken into," Pope offered. "You may have misplaced the gun or sold it."

"I think I'd remember something like that."

"You'd be surprised what we forget. When was the last time you even used it?"

"I don't know," Carl admitted. "It wasn't long after I gave you that scar, I remember that much."

"If it has been out of your sight for such a long time, it could have been stolen at any point. You're only now aware of the fact, and would you please holster your gun?"

"Alright," Carl conceded, placing the gun back inside his jacket.

"So are you willing to accept that I had nothing to do with this?"

"I'm not willing to accept anything just yet. I'm a suspect in my own damn investigation!" Carl remarked with an angry laugh.

"They made you a suspect? That's ridiculous."

"Glad you think so. Although I hardly think your character testimony would hold up in court."

"I'm assuming this has less to do with the likelihood of your actually being the murderer, and more to do with the corrupt elements of your police force wanting to see you swing from the rafters? Metaphorically, at least."

"Or literally, given half the chance," Carl sighed. "Lot of the 'high-ups' don't like the fact that I do my job the way I'm paid to do it."

"They'd never make any charges stick, just because it was your gun that was used."

"If they own the judge, jury and witnesses they can make any case they like," Carl explained. "Thankfully I have friends on the force who've got my back right now. Not many of 'em, but better than nothing."

"So your plan is to keep on with the case and find the real killer before they start to round up the necessary 'evidence' to pin this entirely on you?" Pope enquired.

"That's about the size of it."

"And you honestly thought I was likely to have broken into your home and stolen from you?"

"You broke into my home earlier this week, remember? Who's to say you didn't take it before I arrived?"

"If the purpose of that break-in was to steal from you, I certainly wouldn't have waited for you to arrive home. I'm also fairly confident that you know this, and don't honestly believe me responsible for your missing weapon."

"I'm pissed off and I'm a little crazy right now, Pope. I'm clutching at straws."

"I can help you."

"I've already taken more help from you than I should have."

"I'm not going to kill anyone else for you, I meant help of a subtler kind. Let me take you somewhere. It's not far to walk."

Chapter Thirty-Eight;
House of
Ghosts

Madam Chong's House of Ghosts was about a five-minute walk from the Church in good weather. When the ground was covered with ever-deepening snow and the wind pushed against you like the hands of a thousand invisible demons, it was more like fifteen minutes. Still, Carl had walked further than this in worse weather, so he didn't complain. The weather was bracing, it kept him focussed. With Pope walking at his side he needed that focus. No matter what they'd been through, he still didn't feel like he could entirely trust the guy, and probably never would. Refusing to give your full trust to a hit-man was a sensible place to be, in any case.

The House of Ghosts was a tall, black building with dark windows and black wooden doors. From the exterior it was impossible to tell what went on inside, and Carl was forced to admit that he had no knowledge of the place.

"If you've never been told about it, then you wouldn't know," Pope explained.

"So what is it? Chinese hookers, Chinese food or Chinese drugs?"

"Whilst you're here, you can get all three," Pope smiled. "But none of that is for us tonight."

"I'm not a fan of the cryptic, Pope, so drop it and explain what this place is and why we're here."

"Do you recall stories of the old Opium dens in the late nineteenth and early twentieth centuries?" Pope enquired. "Well this is something similar."

"Chinese drugs?" Carl repeated.

"Yes, but with a purpose. Madam Chong specialises in a herbal tea that she refers to as 'Blue Dust Lily'. It is inhaled as much as it's consumed, and it provides a singularity of purpose."

"Makes you high?" Carl shrugged.

"Interestingly enough, no it doesn't. Hallucinogenic drugs normally provide the effect of taking the mind to realms it is unaccustomed to, places outside of normal human experience. The Blue Dust Lily has the opposite effect, forcing the mind to take a journey deep within itself, to the recesses that are not often accessed."

"Why would I want to do that?"

"It's very good for memory loss," Pope explained. "It's commonly accepted these days that the mind holds onto every experience it is ever given. Things that we believe we have 'forgotten' are merely stored in a deeper area of our mind that the conscious part of it cannot access. The tea of the Blue Dust Lily allows us to see what is stored there, so that we might utilise it."

"You're freaking me out a little with all the psychology know how, Pope."

"I read a lot."

"So how do you know about this place?"

"I used it myself, some time ago," Pope replied. "I had forgotten something that it was necessary to recall."

"What did you need to remember?"

"I had misplaced a sock."

"You're kidding," Carl asked with a frown.

"Not at all. When you do what I do, details are everything. I had become careless and misplaced a single item of clothing. In and of itself it may not seem like much, but one act of carelessness leads to another. One day I am misplacing a sock, the next I neglect to correctly count the number of rounds I have discharged. It was therefore necessary to recall where I had placed the sock so that the pattern could be corrected before it began."

"And you found it after drinking this blue tea?"

"Of course," Pope nodded. "And it will help you recall what happened to your gun. If nothing is shown to you, then it truly was stolen."

"You know, I remember the first thing I ever heard about you," Carl chuckled with a slight shake of his head. "Before we even met, it was something they used to tell newcomers to the force. They'd say, 'two things you need to know about living in the City—don't drink the tap water on East Side, and don't make an enemy of Charles Pope.' Sound advice, I think."

"You're not my enemy, Detective."

"If I come out of this place alive then I'll accept that statement," Carl nodded. "All right, I guess I've come this far. Just let the record show that I think this is insane."

"Duly noted," Pope nodded as he knocked upon the black wooden door and awaited a response.

A small slot in the centre of the door was slid open, and two dark eyes stared out at Carl and Pope. The eyes looked at one man and then the other, and then the slot was closed. Seconds later the door was unlocked and opened, revealing an ageing Asian woman dressed in a long purple Kimono.

"Good evening, Mr Pope," she smiled with a slight bow. "And your friend."

"This is Detective Duggan, he is in need of your speciality."

"Ah, he has forgotten something that must be recalled. Very important for a police officer."

"Can we get this over with?" Carl suggested.

The Chinese woman led the way into the dark building, as Pope whispered to Carl that she was in fact Madam Chong herself. Carl was somewhat surprised, expecting that the owner herself would never be seen amongst her customers. Madam Chong led them through the winding hallways, passing doors that opened onto scenes of drug-induced sex and delirium. Carl found his nostrils beset by a thick smoke that was a concoction of the various herbs, legal and otherwise, that were being burned in each of the rooms. He coughed a little but ignored the scent, focusing instead on keeping sight of the small Asian woman who seemed to flutter down the hallway with a speed that hid her age. Pope walked behind them both, the hallway being too narrow to fit two people side-by-side. After passing more doors than Carl had thought possible, so many in fact that he wondered if they had gone around in a circle, Madam Chong opened a red door into a small room. The two men followed her inside to find a quaint little room, illuminated by candlelight that shone from paper lanterns adorning the walls. On the floor was a circle of red mats, in the centre of which was a grey urn with a single incense stick placed inside.

"Please, sit," Madam Chong insisted as she ventured to a table placed in the corner of the room. On the table rested several pots and jars of varying shapes and sizes.

"I have no need of your services today, Madam, but if it does not insult you, I shall be content to observe," said Pope.

"As you will," she nodded, taking three of the jars and bringing them over to where Carl had seated himself on one of the mats.

Madam Chong poured the contents of each jar into the urn and reached beneath it with a lighted match. It was only then that Carl realised the urn was full of water and placed over a small iron furnace, inside of which were chippings of dark wood. As she dropped the match into the grate, dark red flames licked upwards and embraced the base of the urn. Carl hadn't expected the fire to start so quickly, but the smell of the flames revealed that the wood chippings were probably laced with an accelerant of some kind. Before long, steam began to rise from the urn, at which point Madam Chong used the incense stick to stir it gently, before lighting the top of it. The flame flickered around the incense stick and then travelled downwards into the liquid below. At the point of contact the liquid ignited momentarily in a blue flame that was gone as soon as it had burst into life. Madam Chong then took some metal tongs and used them to place a cup inside the urn and fill it with the herbal mixture. This she then placed on the floor in front of Carl.

"Let it cool," she instructed.

"And what, just drink it?" Carl enquired.

"No. You must first breathe in the vapours; let them fill your head. Only then can the waters fill your stomach."

"This is stupid."

"Your Eastern medicines dull the mind. Our Western ones sharpen it. Which would you say is better, Detective?"

"How long am I going to be in the can after drinking that?" Carl asked as he caught sight of Pope, stood in the corner of the room. In his hand he held something that he had removed from a white envelope. Upon catching sight of Carl watching him, Pope replaced the envelope in his coat pocket.

"It is cooled. Take the cup and close your eyes when you have drank from it," Madam Chong instructed, regaining Carl's wandering attention.

Carl swallowed his pride and lifted the cup, touching his fingertips against it first to ensure it wasn't likely to burn his hands. He was glad to find that the cup was made of a thick porcelain that succeeded in insulating the exterior from the heat found within. As he stared into the cup, he found that the liquid was indeed a blue colour. Carl wasn't sure what he had been expecting, but he had wondered if the name had actually been literal. With a deep breath, he allowed himself to inhale the steam that was slowly rising from the liquid below, letting it bathe the inside of his throat and nostrils with a tingling, warm sensation. After taking three more such breaths, he drank deep of the cup and forced himself not to wretch at the awful, perfumed taste of the tea.

"So why do they call this the House of Ghosts?" Carl enquired as he closed his eyes.

"Memories are the ghosts of things that once were. They are still here, but only in our minds, if we choose to see them," Madam Chong explained.

"Right, well I don't think this crap is working, because I ain't seeing much of..."

Carl opened his eyes and immediately stopped his protestations. He had expected to see the figures of Madam Chong and Charles Pope observing him in the bizarre tea-room, but instead he was faced with something else entirely. Neither of his companions were visible to him, although he had the sense that they were still present. What he now saw was the hallway of a house that was familiar to him but somehow distant and detached from any emotional state. There was a plant-pot to his right, and a staircase to his left. Through the gaps in the wooden spindles of the bannister he could see photographs hung from the wall leading upstairs, but the pictures themselves were obscured. Everything seemed to loom over Carl as though he were much shorter, and the image itself was entirely drained of colour. It was like viewing his old black and white TV screen through a fishbowl. Carl then heard a sound coming from directly above him, but it was distorted and warped like it was being heard through water. He looked up and could see a man staring down at him, shouting angrily, his words unclear but spoken with such ferocity that each one carried a weight of spittle to accompany it.

"What do you see?" Madam Chong enquired. Carl could hear her voice but could not see her in the vision that now surrounded him.

"I'm in a house... my parent's house, I think. The one I grew up in."

"You are not sure?"

"I don't know. It's different... not the way I remember it..." Carl explained as he tried to focus on the words of the faceless man above him. "It's something from when I was a kid, I think... there's a guy shouting at me... I can't see his face or hear what he's saying."

"If you do not hear it now, you did not hear it then," Madam Chong explained. "You refused to hear the words that came from his mouth. Perhaps they were too painful."

"Then why can't I see his face?"

"Perhaps you refused to believe that it was who you knew it to be, so you placed a blank slate over his image."

"The belt buckle he's wearing..." Carl remarked, squinting at the phantom image of the bull-shaped belt buckle he was observing. "I think it's my dad."

"Why is your father shouting at you?"

"I don't know, I was a kid. Could have been any number of things," Carl shrugged.

"Then why would you remember it so strongly that your mind still holds onto such a picture? It must mean more to you, on a subconscious level if nothing else."

"He's not just angry, he… it's like he's full of hate..." Carl said softly. "He's pointing to the back door... wait, I can make out a few words now... something about being irresponsible, not looking after things... and queer. He's saying that word a lot. Jesus, I think he's talking about Jimmy."

"Who is Jimmy?" asked Madam Chong.

"Friend of mine, he's gay. Knew him as a kid, and even then it was obvious that he was... I don't remember this. I don't remember my own dad hating Jimmy so much that he'd yell like this for me hanging around with him."

"Perhaps you forced yourself to forget, to fabricate a different memory of the man you wanted your father to be."

"You a councillor now?" Carl asked sharply.

"Actually she is," Carl heard Pope's voice remark. "It helps with allowing people to correctly interpret what they see here."

"Ain't that dandy," Carl sighed. "Wait... I'm moving... walking down the hall to the back door, my Dad's gone now... my face hurts. I think he hit me.. .but he never hit me, I don't think..."

"The Blue Dust can only show what is, nothing more," Madam Chong reminded him.

"Yeah yeah, my dad was a prick and I repressed it, big deal. My dad's been dead years, I don't see the relevance of this," Carl stated as he saw himself opening the back door onto the small garden.

"I cannot choose what the tea shows you any more than you can. It is merely what your mind needs you to see."

"Well right now I see the garden... it's kind of overgrown, hasn't been tended in awhile. It should be green, and that fence was brown... but everything is black and white."

"You have disassociated yourself from the memory, to the degree that you cannot truly live in it."

"Jimmy is here," Carl remarked suddenly. "He's stood by the fence, and he's holding something."

"What is it?" Madam Chong enquired.

"It's a chain and a bike lock... and the bike isn't fixed to the fence like it should be... holy crap, I remember this..." Carl's voice increased slightly in volume. "I let Jimmy ride my bike, take it out for awhile. He brought it back but forgot to lock it up, so the thing got stolen. He was always forgetful and clumsy with stuff like that, and... my dad got pissed 'cause of how much the bike cost... wait... Jimmy forgot to lock the bike up..."

"Duggan?" Pope stepped forward as Carl's head started to sway slightly, as though he were close to losing consciousness.

"Pope, that you?" Carl asked as he bit his bottom lip and forced himself to remain awake.

"I'm here."

"The gun... it got stolen... no one could break into my home without me knowing it, except for you, probably... so maybe they didn't break in," Carl explained, his vision of the black and white garden blurring and crackling like a picture on a television that was suffering from interference. "Jimmy's been staying with me... he must have left the door unlocked... someone just walked right in and took it... I never use the gun anymore so never noticed."

"Who knew it was there?"

"Other cops." Carl said through gritted teeth.

"Are you sure that is all the vision has to show you?" Madam Chong enquired.

"It's breaking up, I think... I can still see the garden... the empty bike lock... but Jimmy's gone... it's only me stood by the fence... I can hear my dad yelling..." Everything went white before Carl's eyes, and then he once more found himself staring at the withered face of Madam Chong. "It's gone."

"Was that helpful to you?" She smiled.

"Amazingly, yes," Carl nodded. "But I feel like crap."

"You should eat something," the elderly Asian woman smiled again. "Come now. If there is nothing else, I have other customers."

"Pope, lead me out, will you? If I have to find my way out of here alone, I'm gonna wind up in a closet."

Pope did as requested and he and Carl left the House of Ghosts, finding themselves once more in the darkened alley outside. The snowfall was quite heavy now, but Carl was okay with that. The cold air against his skin and the chill filling his lungs removed the last remnants of the haze that the Blue Dust had brought about, sharpening his vision and his thoughts.

"So are you willing to accept that it wasn't me who stole your gun?" Pope enquired.

"Yeah, I guess so. Which is a shame, because it would be so much easier if it was you."

"Instead you are faced with the reality that one of your fellow officers is setting you up."

"Joyous revelation, huh?"

"Which officers knew the gun was there?"

"Well let's see... I had to fill in some paperwork to keep hold of the thing when everyone else turned it in... included on that form was a box where I had to make a note of my 'secure location' for storing the gun. That being the locked drawer next to my bed. So the only cops who would know it was there are the ones who had access to those records."

"That should be a small number, then? Surely your station has sufficient controls in place to limit unnecessary access to such information?" Pope inquired.

"You'd think so, wouldn't you?" Carl sighed heavily.

"Then you need to ask which officers hold a personal grudge against you?"

"Probably all of 'em, except for Trent and the Commissioner. They don't like me because I actually do my job and I do it for one paycheque only," Carl explained. "Make it easier for a lot of 'em if I was gone, one way or another."

"You're not that good at making friends, are you?"

"I'd never claim to be a people person," Carl conceded. "But still, this is a big set up, Pope. To go the length of killing three random gay guys this way? No way is this all about me, it can't be. Whoever killed those guys wanted them dead anyway, framing me for it is just a sidebar."

"So that would mean your serial killer is a police officer," Pope nodded.

"Yup, and one who hates gay guys. Or is one himself, I'm not clear on that yet," Carl spoke his thoughts aloud so Pope could keep up. "You see, the crime scenes show that he actually slept with the guys first, which is a big step to take if it's a standard homophobe murder."

"Perhaps he is homosexual himself and yet hates it anyway? A double-edged sword?"

"You should be a police psychologist," Carl remarked as he snapped his fingers in agreement with Pope's suggestion. "I gotta put me a list together of possible suspects. I seen the guy on tape, he was pretty burly, so it can't be any of the younger guys; they're all skin and bone. Hard to believe half of 'em actually passed the physical. That should narrow down the list a little."

"Would you like me to assist you?"

"You've done enough, and besides, you're leaving."

"What makes you say that?"

"I saw you looking at something that you took from your pocket. They looked like tickets, and I don't see you as much of a movie goer."

"They're coach tickets," Pope nodded, taking the items in question from his inside pocket and holding them up for Carl to see. "Two, for tonight."

"Should I guess who the other is for?" Carl asked.

"I think you know."

"Nice to see that someone listens to me."

"She deserves better than this, Duggan. You were right."

"Gotta ask, Pope. Why do the tickets state 'Washington D.C' as their destination? Why not take her to Florida? What's there to do in D.C?"

"I never said that would be the only place we would go," Pope smiled as he returned the tickets to his pocket. "The tickets can be rearranged if you need my help."

"Thanks, but no. You need to get out of here, before things with Petroni start to heat up. He still wants me dead, probably you too. At least one of us should survive, and I got a better chance of doing that and solving this cop-murder debacle if I ain't worrying about you and Felicity."

"If you change your mind, you have my number," Pope nodded, shaking Carl's hand. "Take care, Detective."

"Look after her," Carl returned.

Chapter Thirty-Nine;
True Friend

Carl walked on through the increasing snowfall, his leather jacket refusing to keep out the worst of the cold. The wet snow slid off it to the ground, keeping him dry as was intended, but the cold air itself just bit straight through the cowhide like it wasn't even there. The night wanted everyone in the City to feel its presence, and Carl wasn't putting up much of a fight. He had departed from Pope and was heading home, determined to start work on his list of possible suspects whilst his thoughts on the matter were still fresh. He could feel the snow deepening on the ground, his boots had to press down through several inches of the soft white crust before reaching the harder pavement beneath. As he walked on, he heard the sound of a car driving slowly not too far away from him. Carl glanced over his shoulder and saw a battered grey vehicle making its way down the street with the headlights dipped. The manner of the driving was that of someone taking it steady in dangerous conditions, but Carl knew better. It couldn't have been more obvious if the cops had placed a damn flashing cherry on the roof. If you want to tail a suspect, make sure it's not someone who knows every undercover car on the books for a particular station. Goddamn morons.

As he passed a dark alleyway, Carl suddenly felt someone grab his arm and pull him off the street. It was so sudden and unexpected that he had no time to resist it, just as he had no time to block the hard blow to his face that sent him reeling back into a collection of garbage bags discarded at the side of the alley. Carl shook his head in an effort to clear it and saw three average-sized men stood over him, each wearing expensive-looking black suits and shades.

"Nice night for a walk," one of them smiled as he flicked a switchblade from his pocket.

"It's December and you're wearing sunglasses at night... what're you, an idiot?" Carl commented as he stood up, tensing himself for what he knew to be inevitable.

"Oh, he's got a mouth. I'm gonna cut it out of his face," one of the men remarked, lunging at Carl with his knife.

Carl grabbed the man's wrist and twisted it until it cracked, causing him to drop the knife and scream simultaneously. He then turned his opponent around and kicked him in the small of his back, feeling something dislodge beneath his foot as the man went down to the floor. Facing three opponents at once is difficult for anyone, even a fighter as adept as Carl. You can't be everywhere at once and you can't dodge every blow that comes. Or every knife blade. The detective felt the cold steel thrust itself between his ribs on the right side of his body, causing him to grimace as his nerves suddenly blurted into life. Carl managed to raise a fist and drive it into the face of the attacker, causing him to let go of the knife and leave it in Carl's side as he backed away.

"You ever feel like you brought a knife to a gunfight?" Carl groaned as he drew his weapon and fired a single shot into the chest of the man who had stabbed him.

He went down hard, and fast, the bullet tearing straight through him and out the back of his chest. Despite the success of the action, Carl instantly regretted using his gun given that the shockwave it sent down his arm could be felt in the gaping wound at his side. If he wanted to remain conscious then firing the gun again would be a poor idea, but the third and final suit wasn't looking to give him an option. He drew his own gun and aimed it directly at Carl's head. The detective kept his weapon aimed at his final opponent whilst taking the knife from his side and pressing his left hand against the wound in a desperate attempt to hold off the blood-loss. To his gratitude, the cold night-air was also doing its part by slowing his blood flow.

"Petroni's not a guy who lets things go, is he?" Carl chuckled as he struggled to keep his hand from shaking as he held the gun.

"You insulted him."

"I'll lose many a sleepless night over it," Carl nodded.

"He's not a man you should make an enemy of. He wanted you to know that."

"Oh, so he has a message, does he? Was wondering why you guys didn't just kill me the moment you dragged me down here. I'm gonna black out any second, so come on, let's hear it."

"He says you—"

Carl didn't let the suit get close to finishing his sentence before he put a bullet between his eyes. The talkers always did carve out their own gravestones.

"Moron," Carl groaned as he staggered past the body, kicking it in the ribs as he went.

With a severe grunt of pain, Carl reached inside his jacket and took out his cell phone, hit one of the speed-dials and waited for the call to be answered.

"Trent, come pick me up. I'm in the alley next to that store where they sell the donuts with the cherry glaze. Don't ask for directions, you know where it is, you fat prick."

Carl forced himself over to the wall, where he then slumped down to the floor, keeping all of his strength focussed on holding his hand against the wound at his side. He glanced to the left and saw the three bodies of the men who had tried to kill him. One of them was still alive, but he wasn't going anywhere, Carl thought to himself. At least one segment of his spine had been broken or dislodged, so he wasn't likely to be getting up and trying anything. With that knowledge in hand, Carl felt that it was safe to close his eyes, just for a moment. When he opened them again, he was in a white room being attended to by a young female nurse he didn't recognise. She was pretty despite the lack of makeup, and her dark hair was tied back in a ponytail.

"Am I dreaming this?" Carl groaned.

"You don't have very exciting dreams, do you?" she smiled as she continued to stitch up Carl's side.

"I dunno. Hot chick in a nurse outfit? I've had worse."

"I'll take that as a compliment and not file a harassment complaint on account of your delirium," the nurse smiled.

"I appreciate that," Carl smiled as he looked around. "Hey, am I in Seven Saints?"

"You certainly are," she nodded.

"I knew you'd play hell if I took you to the hospital across the river," came Trent's voice. Carl turned to see the elder detective stood with his arms folded in the doorway. "How you doing?"

"I've been worse."

"I know, I've seen it," Trent nodded. "Is he going to be alright?"

"Of course," the nurse smiled as she cut the thread on the last of Carl's stitches. "The blade didn't cut anything important, so as long as he rests he should be fine."

"Fat chance of that," Trent sighed. "What the hell happened?"

"Petroni still wants to ask me to dinner. He ain't happy when I keep saying no," Carl grunted as he tried to sit up. The nurse narrowed her eyes at him and pushed him back down in the bed.

"You stay there until I saw otherwise, do you understand? I just put those stitches in you and if you rip them straight out I am going to be very annoyed!"

"Jesus, you're hot," Carl smiled at her.

"Sorry to disappoint you but you're not my type. I'm actually dating one of the other nurses. She's blonde and six-two," the nurse smiled as she wrote something on the clipboard at the end of Carl's bed.

"I'm not sure if I want you to be kidding or not," Carl said with a confused expression.

"Go easy on those stitches and you should be fine," the nurse commented before leaving Carl and Trent alone in the room.

"So Trent, can I ask you a favour?" Carl inquired.

"Of course."

"Next time you got someone tailing me, tell 'em to maybe come and help me when I'm getting stabbed, alright? I think 'blowing your cover' comes further down on the list than letting another officer get killed."

"I didn't ask anyone to tail you," Trent said defensively. "But there's lots of folks who want to see you go down in flames, so I guess they're looking for any opportunity to catch you out."

"A cop stole my gun, Trent. I'm sure of it."

"OKAY, well that does make some kind of sense. Who else would know it was there?" Trent said humbly. "So what do you want to do about it? I wanna help, but I can't just start questioning the entire force, based on nothing more than accusation, no less."

"Just get me home, to start with. I need to speak with a friend of mine. I'm pretty sure he left my door unlocked and didn't tell me about it. If that's what really happened, then I know I'm right about this. I gotta confirm that before I do anything else."

"You've finally learned that it's a bad idea to go charging in without taking your time to get everything in order. I'm so proud," Trent said mockingly.

"If I could move my right arm, I'd hit you. Luckiest day of your life," Carl said with narrowed eyes. "Now help me up, will ya?"

"Your shirt and jacket are on that chair," Trent informed him as he helped Carl get out of bed. "I didn't let her cut you out of 'em, 'cause that looked like a new shirt and I know you only buy those once a decade."

"Thanks for not letting them put me in one of those little white dressing gown things," Carl remarked, fastening his shirt, slowly so as to not disturb the tender flesh of his side.

"That was for my benefit. Those things tend to gape open, and I didn't wanna be seeing your ass," Trent remarked.

"You're a true friend."

Chapter Forty;
Brotherly Love

“So let me get this straight... it’s you that’s tailing me now?” asked Carl as he sat back in the passenger seat of Trent’s car.

“I’m not ‘tailing’ you, Carl. Someone has to watch you, though. Keep an eye on you, that’s the rules. I volunteered ‘cause, well… it should be me, I guess.”

“Is that ‘cause you wanted to rib the crap out of me for it, or ‘cause you were the only cop who was likely to give an accurate report of my actions?” Carl inquired as he adjusted himself so that his side wasn’t causing him as much pain.

“Bit of both,” Trent shrugged. “You gotta admit, you being a suspect in your own investigation is a little funny.”

“Funny as in ‘ridiculous’, definitely.”

“For the record, no one with any sense actually believes this crap, Carl,” Trent assured him. “Even the guys that don’t like you know this is a set up. They just don’t care.”

“That doesn’t bother me so much, let ‘em think what they want. I’m more concerned with the fact that our serial killer is a cop.”

“Lot of the guys wearing a badge in this City are involved with all kinds of crap, you know that as well as anyone,” Trent reminded him.

“Yeah, but this is different. Taking bribes or being addicted to drugs, that’s to be expected here. But how could our evaluations miss the fact that someone is a complete psycho?”

“I don’t know, but my gut tells me it has to be someone that’s been on the force for awhile, to get around us like that.”

“Yeah, mine too,” Carl agreed as the car pulled up outside his apartment building. “I know you gotta wait outside whilst I'm done talking to Jimmy, so don't insult me by making up some other reason for hanging around, okay?"

"Wouldn't dream of it," Trent assured him. "So now that you've had your little 'biting back' moment, why not admit that you actually need my help getting up the stairs?"

"Fine. But one joke and you're dead. Stitches or otherwise, I can still kick your ass."

Carl opened his car door as Trent walked round to accompany him. He needed a little help standing up, but once on his feet he was fine until they reached the staircase. The act of lifting his legs up one after the other seemed to pull at his stitches and make him short of breath, so Trent had to help him slightly by bracing him up. The nurse had said the knife blade had avoided doing any serious damage, but Carl could still feel how deep it had gone. It felt like a hole had been torn in his innards, making it impossible to do something as simple as putting one foot in front of the other without causing pain. Still, he ignored it and carried on. He had work to do before letting himself rest tonight, and it was crap that wouldn't wait. The sleep in the hospital hadn't exactly been voluntary, but at least it had brought him some time to build up a little energy. Every step was currently taking far more out of him than it should, so Carl was increasingly grateful for what rest he'd had.

"Okay, here we are," Carl said with a grateful sigh at the sight of his apartment door. "Wait here, I don't want Jimmy to think he's under arrest or being interviewed or anything."

"No problem. Am I okay to smoke in here?" asked Trent as he removed a cigarette from the packet.

"Probably not, but knock yourself out anyway," Carl shrugged as he unlocked his door and entered the apartment.

The door closed behind him and Carl instantly found himself resting against the kitchen sideboard. Damn stairs. Damn knife wound. He closed his eyes for a moment to shut out the throbbing pain, and then glanced around the living room.

"Hey Jimmy, you here?" He called out to the empty room.

There was no answer so Carl walked into the bedroom, where he found Jimmy stood by the window biting his fingernails. On the bed was an open rucksack.

"Who's car is that?" Jimmy asked he looked out of the window.

"Trent, he dropped me off."

"You okay? You look a little tired."

"I got stabbed, but it's fine."

"You got stabbed?"

"Yeah, and I also said that it's fine," Carl assured him. "I got patched up, no serious injuries, nothing to worry about. What's with the bag, you going somewhere?"

"What? Oh, no, I'm just getting rid of some stuff," Jimmy smiled as he walked into Carl's bathroom and started to apply some eyeliner.

"You heading out tonight?" Carl inquired.

"Thinking about it, but I dunno." Jimmy called back.

"Listen, I need to ask you about something," said Carl, feeling somewhat awkward. "When you go out, either at night or whilst I'm asleep... have you ever left the door unlocked?"

"Why would I do that?"

"Not intentionally, jackass. I mean, you always were kind of forgetful. I'm not mad, it's just kind of important."

"Important how?"

"My old gun, the one I told you about? Someone's been using it... that serial killer."

"Um... you sure?"

"Yeah, they matched the bullets. I'd have known if someone broke in here, which means the door was open for 'em. Only people that know about my gun are other cops, so..."

"You think a cop did this?"

"Yeah, but I can't pursue that line of investigation until I'm sure about this."

"They have you as a suspect right now, don't they?" asked Jimmy, biting his thumbnail as he returned from the bathroom, his eyes now painted with black eyeliner.

"Yeah, but I can sort the whole thing out. Come on, Jimmy, did you leave the door unlocked?"

"They shouldn't think it's you. They shouldn't! After everything you've done for them, how hard you've worked... it's not right. It's not!"

"It's fine, just calm down."

"I'm just trying to protect you, Carl. That's all I've ever done..." Jimmy said quietly as he shook his head and stared at the floor. "You need to understand that, okay? I love you, like a brother."

"What are you talking about? I only want to know if you left the door unlocked. I'm not even pissed at you!"

"There's a lot you don't understand, Carl. There always has been," Jimmy protested, involuntarily glancing at his rucksack and causing Carl's own attention to be diverted to it.

"What's in the bag, Jimmy?" Carl questioned, swallowing the heavy black lump in his throat.

"I just want to keep you safe, Carl. I never wanted to ruin anything for you..." said Jimmy, reaching for the bag.

Carl grabbed the bag before Jimmy could and pulled it open. Inside were some clothes that he removed, including a denim jacket that he stared at for a moment before dropping it to the floor. Underneath the jacket were two items that caused Carl's blood to run cold; his old service revolver, and a dark red opera mask.

"Holy Christ, Jimmy, what did you do?" said Carl, his voice so low and quiet it was almost a whisper.

"I can't deal with this... I can't... you won't understand..." Jimmy sobbed, pushing past Carl and running out of the bedroom.

"Stop right there, Jimmy," Carl demanded as he pursued Jimmy into the living room.

Jimmy turned to see that Carl was now aiming his gun directly at him, his hand shaking from a combination of the physical effort of aiming the weapon with the pain in his side, and the act of being forced to hold it towards the last person he would ever have expected. The old wooden framed mirror was at Carl's side, so that out of the corner of his eye he could see his image aiming the gun at his friend. He hated it, despised it, but still couldn't bring himself to lower the weapon.

"You don't understand," Jimmy repeated. "You never have. I have needs, but... I wanted to keep you safe. To protect you. You're like my brother, Carl! You always have been, I needed to protect you!"

"From what? Gay guys I don't even know? How does killing them keep me safe?" Carl yelled. "Jesus Christ, Jimmy, what the hell happened to you?"

"I couldn't help it! I have needs, you know that! I didn't want them to know who I was, to ruin your reputation and everything you've worked so long to build up!"

"You think I care if they know that I live with a queer? You think that's worth killing people?" Carl screamed.

"You don't understand!" Jimmy cried again, black eyeliner streaming down his face as he took a step closer to Carl.

"Stay where you are, Jimmy! I'll fire, I swear to God!"

***

Out in the hallway, Detective Trent couldn't wait any longer. He'd heard the voices from within the apartment getting louder and louder—Carl's and the other voice, not quite identifiable to him. Finally when the yelling turned to full on angry shouting, he knew that waiting any longer could risk something bad happening, one way or the other. Carl had a temper, that much was obvious to anyone that knew him. If the guy he was speaking to could push his buttons to this degree, then there was no telling what might happen. Stamping his smouldering cigarette out on the floor, Trent drew his gun and then marched towards the door. With a silent count to three, he kicked the door open and aimed his weapon inside. Whatever he had expected to see upon entering, it wasn't this.

Carl was stood on the far side of the room, his gun pointed at a large, wooden-framed mirror. He was shouting and aiming his gun at the reflection, his face red with more anger than Trent had ever seen in it. When he heard his fellow detective enter the apartment, Carl turned towards him, still holding his gun. It was then that Trent noticed Carl's face was stained with twin streams of black eyeliner.

"Jesus Christ..." He muttered under his breath.

"I won't let you take him! I won't!" Carl screamed in a voice that was a little more high-pitched than his usual, gruff tone. It was so bizarre that Trent could have sworn it sounded like a different person.

Carl dropped his own weapon and grappled with Trent to force him to do the same. Trent kept a firm grip on the handle of his weapon, forcing himself not to let go despite the best efforts of his friend and fellow officer. The two men struggled with all the effort they could muster. Carl was the stronger of the two, but in his weakened state Trent was able to hold his ground. For a second, Carl let go of Trent's wrist and punched him in the face. Reacting on instinct Trent immediately altered the angle of his gun and pulled the trigger.

Chapter Forty-One;
The Other Side
of
the Mirror

"So... let's talk about what happened," Commissioner Grant said with a heavy sigh, breathing into his hands as he looked at Trent across the desk.

"You can read my report."

"I need to hear it from you, Detective."

"I heard Carl yelling at someone, went in to see what was going on and found him staring at a mirror and screaming. He ran at me, we struggled, and my gun went off. The bullet went up through his chin and into his brain, killing him instantly. It wasn't intentional, I wasn't even aware that I'd fired it. And I feel like shit. Anything else you need from me?"

"Your report will be given to internal affairs, as well as my statement that Carl was under tremendous pressure. There were threats on his life, and he cracked. There will be no mention of his being this serial killer or anything else. With enough money in the right hands, we can make it stick and save his reputation, at least."

"So you're going to protect him using the very methods he hated?"

"I'm afraid so."

"Well that makes me feel wonderful, Sir," Trent said with a tone of angry sarcasm. "Now why do you need to speak to me about this? You can read my report."

"Carl Duggan was your friend and there are some things you don't understand."

"Some things? Try EVERYTHING!" Trent yelled, leaning forward and slamming his hands on the desk.

"Alright, I understand how you must feel. I will explain everything to you, but it cannot leave this office, do you understand?" Grant said, keeping a calm tone in the hope that it would encourage Trent to do the same.

"I don't care what anyone else wants to know, I just need to understand how my friend could be... this."

"Carl joined our force straight out of the academy... that was back in the days we had our own academy, not just transfers from other cities. His scores in everything were off the chart, best damn cop we'd ever seen. More important than that, though, was his resilience. His determination. There was this logical deduction puzzle all the cadets had to figure out, and Carl could not get his head round it. So he stayed in that classroom all damn night until he got it. Stayed awake for twenty-four hours solid until he found that answer."

"Sounds like Carl," Trent nodded.

"We don't get cops like that in this City, Trent. Do you understand me? If we had half a dozen of 'em, we could turn the entire place around. But we don't. Until Carl."

"He was the best, I know. Reminding me of that doesn't make me feel any better, Sir."

"We couldn't take him on. Not once we'd gotten his medical report through," Grant said with another heavy sigh. "There were some irregularities that would have kept him off the force. But he was too good to reject, so we buried them. I buried them."

"What kind of irregularities?"

"He ever talk to you about his childhood?"

"Not really."

"There's good reason for that," Grant explained. "You see, Carl was what you might call an effeminate child. The kind of kid who likes dolls and jump rope instead of sports and army men, you understand? Modern attitude on the subject is that people can be gay from a young age, it's not something they decide in later life. I don't know if that's true or not, I'm not a sociologist, but if it is true, then Carl was gay, right from the start. His dad wasn't the liberal type. Apparently he was... well, kind of like you. But worse."

"Thanks for that," Trent said quietly.

"You know what I'm getting at Trent, just go with it. He hated his own son, looked at him and saw the exact opposite of everything he'd wanted from his kid. So he tried to do what guys like that always do; beat the problem away. Admittedly I've only read the reports on this, but it sounds like Carl got the worst treatment you can imagine from his dad. The kind that damages you for life. Verbal as well as physical. His dad used to tell him he hated him, that he wasn't his son, that he was nothing to him."

"No kid needs to hear that."

"No, they don't. But one day, Carl changed. He suddenly started acting all tough and manly, playing the roughest sports he could find, kicking the crap out of other kids who used to pick on him. He became a little bruiser, everything his dad had wanted... half the time, anyway."

"And the other half?"

"He was still effeminate and soft, the way he used to be," Grant replied. "Carl's mind forced itself to become the only thing he could become to stop his dad treating him like dirt. Only it didn't work, not entirely. He effectively became two different people. The therapists call it DID, Disassociative Disorder. Carl actually started to believe that he was two people—he could talk to the other half of himself like it was a separate kid. He even named it, Jimmy Galante, he called him. They were like best friends, brothers, an imaginary friend that was actually part of himself."

"Christ, he was messed up," Trent remarked.

"Very much so," Grant nodded. "Which is why his parents... or his mom, at least—his dad having called it quits by this point—took him to therapy. He got his own psychiatrist, who managed to figure out everything I just told you. Even she said that it was unusual, though. Split personalities, they often hate each other, or at least they don't get along. Carl and Jimmy were different, though. They actually cared, each about the other."

"So wait a minute... was Carl aware of this? Did he know about all this crap?"

"Carl? No. Jimmy? Yes," Grant replied. "You see... and I only know this from the psychiatrist's notes... apparently it's quite common for one of the personalities to know the whole truth, and the other to be ignorant of the fact. That was what went on with Carl. Jimmy knew the whole score, knew that he and Carl were one and the same, everything. Carl, on the other hand, actually believed that Jimmy was a separate person; he never learned otherwise. I mean maybe the psychiatrist told him about it, but he obviously didn't believe her, or didn't take any notice of it."

"I've known Carl for years, I don't know how all of this could have slipped by," Trent admitted.

"Well there's more yet," Grant continued. "All the techniques the psychiatrist used to try and 'integrate' the personalities didn't work, so she had to turn to drugs. Strong drugs, the strongest you can get. Anti-psych pills that actually repress one of the personalities, leaving just one complete person. Carl started taking them around the time he was twelve years old, which was the legal minimum, given the strength of the drugs."

"So he went a few years thinking Jimmy was actually a separate person?"

"He had to, the therapy wouldn't work and the doctor couldn't legally prescribe the meds. That's why the identity got so strong; it was allowed to grow and develop. Jimmy was his own person, in every way imaginable. He liked different music, different food. There's even evidence to suggest that he had different allergies."

"Is that even possible?"

"This psychiatrist says so in her report," Grant nodded, at which point Trent realised that the Commissioner was actually looking at the report amongst the other files on his desk. "Mind over matter, and all that. Anyway, the pills worked the way they were supposed to. One of the personalities was repressed, and it was Jimmy. Now, apparently it's never clear which identity is going to remain, and sometimes they fight each other for dominance. There was no such case here, it was actually like Jimmy allowed Carl to remain, because he loved him. So Carl became all there was, despite the fact that Jimmy was actually the original, real version of him."

"And how did Carl deal with this?"

"He had no idea what had gone on, but he obviously noticed that Jimmy wasn't around anymore. His mom told him that Jimmy had moved away, and everyone went on with their lives. Carl grew up mean and hard, joined the academy, and because we buried all this stuff he became a cop, then a detective."

"Okay, I'm with you so far," Trent nodded, taking a deep breath as though the sheer influx of information was exhausting him. "I understand why none of this was ever mentioned. It was buried, put to bed, didn't matter anymore. So how did we get from there to the point where Carl... or Jimmy... is a masked killer?"

"Carl had been taking his meds for close to thirty years, Trent. He thought they were for some form of vitamin deficiency, that's what his mom had told him. So he happily takes them every day without ever thinking twice. Well, guess where he'd been getting his meds?"

"Holy crap..." Trent gasped as realisation dropped on him like a great big sack of bricks.

"Kenny's Pharmacy, the one where real meds had been substituted for sugar pills for months now. Evidently Carl was one of the customers who had been getting something other than his actual prescription. And that's been the case for long enough to allow Jimmy to make a return appearance. Only now, he's an adult, of course. So he 'turns up', and Carl thinks his old friend is back. Only Jimmy has thirty years of repressed sexual urges to deal with... so he hits the town, hooks up with some guys... only he has a problem. Like I said, Jimmy knows that he and Carl are one and the same, so if he's seen making out with a bunch of guys..."

"He's going to completely ruin Carl's reputation for being a tough bastard..." Trent nodded as he wiped the sweat from his brow. "Jimmy's only memories regarding his sexuality are of Carl getting the crap kicked out of him for it. Jimmy wants to protect him... so he wears a mask."

"And decides to cover his tracks even further by killing the guys he sleeps with. Using Carl's old gun; the one he knows about because he has access to Carl's memories and everything. The reverse isn't true, of course, so Carl has no idea what's been going on."

"Carl wasn't getting any sleep. When he thought he was, he was actually out and about being Jimmy," Trent nodded, his mind following the pattern more and more as knowledge formed clearer pictures in his mind. "Still, why did Jimmy kill these guys? Seems a little extreme."

"I thought that too. Which is why, before I asked you to come here, I actually managed to get hold of Carl's old psychiatrist. She's retired now, of course, but she remembers the case well. She wanted to publish it in some kind of journal, said it was her biggest challenge, but we'd never allowed her to. Well, she was still interested in the whole thing. Her job had been her life, so when I asked her some questions about this she was happy to answer. Her theory is that Jimmy had never developed properly. He'd been a kid, then nothing, then an adult. His mind wasn't rational, it had been raced to adulthood to keep up with its 'host body', as she put it. That meant he wasn't quite... well, he was a little deranged."

"He said he wanted to protect Carl. That's what he yelled when he ran at me," Trent said quietly, trying to fight off the tears that wanted to fill his eyes at the loss of his best friend.

"That's all he ever wanted, in his twisted way," Grant nodded. "So that's about it. One more death we can blame Petroni for."

"No one breathes a word of this, ever. It dies with us, Grant," Trent said firmly, letting the tears slowly run down his face now and filing whatever embarrassment he may feel under the heading of 'screw it'.

"Glad we're on the same page," Grant nodded as he firmly shook Trent's hand. "Go take a few days off. We'll want you to speak at the funeral."

"Sure, I'll speak. And what they'll hear is that Carl Duggan was the best damn cop I ever worked with. That's how they'll remember him."

"Damn straight they will."

"You know what really gets me about this? Petroni's never gonna know. He just gets to waltz around his mansion in Washington, not giving a shit about the lives he's destroyed."

"That's the way it is," Grant sighed. "Don't beat yourself up over it."

"I hate this damn City," Trent sighed as he slammed the door behind him.

Epilogue One;
Snake Eyes

D ice sat in the office above his casino, staring at the monitor screens that gave him a view of the casino floor. All those idiots just throwing their money away. They might as well just line up at the door and hand it straight to him. None of them ever left with more than they'd had in their pockets when they arrived. The lucky ones got out straight, but even they were few and far between. Dice had a permanent sneer fixed to his face, just as he always did when staring at his monitors. It was almost sexual, and he had in fact gone as far as to masturbate to the moving images on more than one occasion. Leaning over his desk, Dice poured himself a second glass of scotch, letting it fall over the ice cubes and splash up the sides of the glass. With a satisfied sigh he sat back in his chair, only to feel something cold and metal pressed into the back of skull.

"If you want money then you should know I don't keep any here," Dice said nervously. "But if you let me call someone, I can have some bags brought up for you—"

"I'm not interested in your money, Mr. Dice," came a cold, softly-spoken voice.

At this point Dice saw a hand reach onto his desk and place two red dies in front of him. On the back of the hand near the thumb, Dice saw a Hebrew symbol tattooed in black against the white flesh. He couldn't read the symbol, but he now knew exactly who it was that had entered his office.

"Look... Pope... whatever you want, we can—"

"Roll the dice," Pope instructed.

"What?"

"We're going to play a game. Your fate is going to be decided by your namesake," Pope explained.

"I don't... I don't understand..."

"Whatever number you roll, that is how many times I am going to pull this trigger with my gun aimed at your skull. The best you could hope for is snake eyes... that's what you call two number ones, yes? That way your head might still be cohesive enough for you to enjoy an open casket."

"Pope, look... whoever has hired you... whatever reason you're here—"

"I am here for Felicity DuBois."

"I can pay you double whatever she gave you."

"She hasn't paid me a cent. I love her."

"You... then you should know that I looked after her, and her sister..."

"…Amber."

"Yes. Yes, Amber! She was safe with me, she would have never—"

"She left you and ran into the arms of a murderous pimp because she was terrified of you," Pope informed him as he pressed the barrel of his gun even more firmly into the back of Dice's head. "All the beatings she had suffered at your hands, all the bruises she had been forced to cover... the rapes she had tried to make herself forget... she ran because of you. There are many responsible for her death, and you are a very black link in that chain, Mr. Dice."

"What can I say to change this? What can I do to—"

"Roll the dice," Pope repeated.

Dice's hand shook violently as he reached for two small items of red plastic. His fingers trembled so much that it was almost impossible for him to lift the tiny, weightless things, but eventually he managed it. With a slight flick of his wrists he tossed the die onto the desk, letting them bump together and then roll to a stop. On both die, a single white dot was now faced upwards.

"Snake eyes," Pope commented. "Aren't you lucky?"

Epilogue Two;
What's there to Do In D.C?

Charles Pope entered his hotel and closed the door behind him. The large, luxurious room contained a king-sized four-posted bed and a large window outside of which he could see the Washington Monument. He had hoped it might be possible to also see the Lincoln Memorial, but one was better than nothing. From the half empty champagne glasses and discarded food trays it was apparent that the maid had yet to arrive for the morning, but Pope had no problem with that. Seeing its aftermath reminded him of the previous evening, which brought a soft smile to his face and a warmth to his chest. This feeling was only increased when he heard the sound of someone taking a shower in the en-suite bathroom.

Taking a seat on the edge of the bed, Carl took the television remote and turned on the large plasma screen that was fixed to the opposite wall. The news came on as the picture hummed into life, revealing a female newscaster holding a microphone, a small crowd behind her.

"...still reeling from the news of the apparent assassination of Senator Carlito Petroni, who was found dead in his own home this morning. No leads are held regarding the suspect at this time but claims over the past few days have increased regarding the Senator's alleged involvement with organised crime. Whilst sympathies have been expressed regarding his sudden death, his more vocal opponents have not hesitated to point out that any involvement with such activities could have given the Senator a long list of enemies capable of..."

Pope switched off the television, satisfied that he had heard enough. He noticed that a newspaper was resting on the dessert trolley, which he reached for and sat back in the bed to read. The champagne glass on the bedside table was stained on the rim with dark-red lipstick, causing Pope to smile once again as he noticed it. He opened the newspaper and found himself staring at a list of names, quoting those who had died in the service of America in the past month; firemen, soldiers, police officers. When Pope saw the one name he recognised, he closed his eyes and uttered a quiet prayer. He knew the officer in question would have hated him for that, but he still thought it was necessary. Let him be angry, at least he was at peace. The noise of the shower came to a stop, and Pope heard a voice call out, "Sweetheart, is that you?"

"It's me, I just got back," Pope replied, at which point Felicity DuBois entered the room, her slender figure wrapped in a short towel.

"Where did you go last night? I thought I felt you getting out of bed."

"I just had some unfinished business to take care of," Pope smiled.

"I know how you hate loose ends," she smiled, sitting next to him on the bed and holding herself close to him. "So did you do what you wanted to do?"

"Of course," Pope replied, kissing her softly. "She can truly rest now."

"I love you. You know that, right?"

"I do,"

"So can we leave Washington? It's kind of a bore."

"I'll arrange some flights. Where would you like to go?"

"I don't know. Where can we go?" Felicity smiled.

"We can go anywhere," Pope smiled in return. "Anywhere at all."

About Your Author

Lex H Jones is a British cross-genre author, horror fan and rock music enthusiast who lives in Sheffield, North England. He has written articles for premier horror websites the 'Gingernuts of Horror' and the 'Horrifically Horrifying Horror Blog' on various subjects covering books, films, videogames and music.

Lex's first published novel was "Nick and Abe", a literary fantasy about God and the Devil spending a year on earth as mortal men. Lex also has a growing number of short horror stories published in collections alongside such authors as Graham Masterton, Clive Barker and Adam Neville. He is currently working on both his 'Harkins' book series, the first of which 'The Final Casebook of Mortimer Grimm' is due for release Winter 2019, and also a trilogy of children's weird fiction books

centred around the reimagining of H.P. Lovecraft's mythology.
When not working on his own writing Lex also contributes to the proofing and editing process for other authors.

His official Facebook page is:
www.facebook.com/LexHJones

Amazon author page :
https://www.amazon.co.uk/Lex-H-Jones/e/B008HSH9BA

Twitter: @LexHJones

Other HellBound Books Titles
Available at: www.hellboundbookspublishing.com

Made in Britain

There is something quite special about this fine

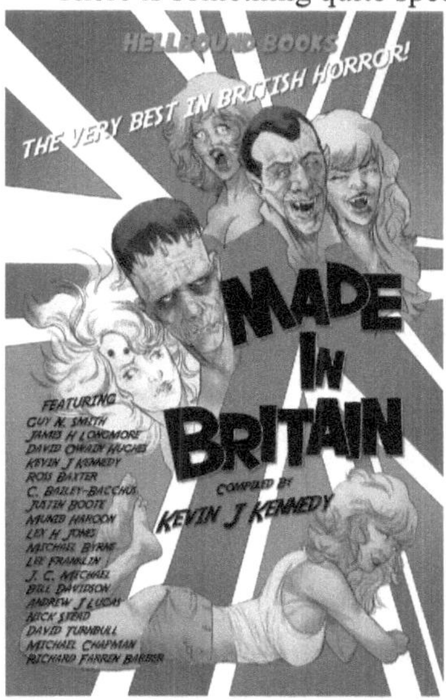

collection of tales of terror from the Sceptered Isle, each and every one crafted in the dead of the night by twisted, fevered minds, who have brought crawling and slithering to life the darkest denizens of the blackest shadows to terrify those brave souls amongst you who are brave enough to read...

For your delectation, Dear Reader, we have assembled together between these illustrious covers an array of the finest British authors writing today:

Guy N. Smith, James H Longmore, David Owain Hughes, Kevin J Kennedy, Ross Baxter, C. Bailey-Bacchus, Justin Boote, Munib Haroon, Lex H Jones, Michael Byrne, Lee Franklin, J. C. Michael, Bill Davidson, Andrew J Lucas, Nick Stead, David Turnbull, Michael Chapman, Richard Farren Barber

ROAD KILL: TEXAS HORROR BY TEXAS WRITERS - VOL 3

Everything is bigger in Texas - including the horror!

A Piney woods meth dealer clones Adolph Hitler. A nightmare exorcist meets an inexorable fined. An eyeball collector gets collected. The apparition of a lynching victim tracks down his executioners. A Texas lawman is undone by shades of his past. A Baphomet recruits converts as a local summer camp. The tales of the baker's dozen who appear in this anthology demonstrate why everything is scarier in Texas...
Including tales of terror

from
Jeremy Hepler
Madison Estes
Bret McCormick
James H Longmore
ER Bills
Shawna Borman

And many more...

I'll Come Back to Get You

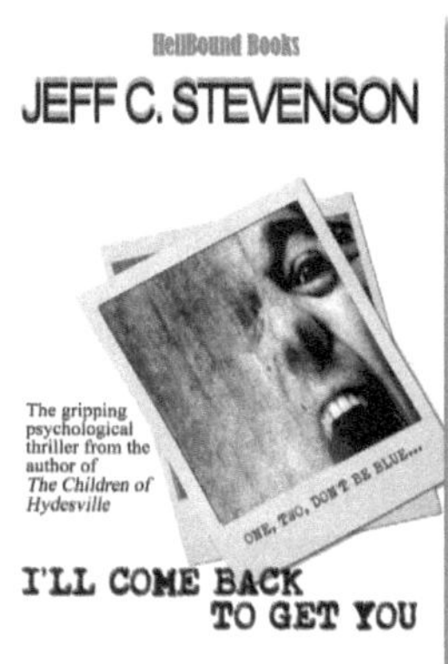

In the midst of a Manhattan heat wave, Adel Daniels' husband doesn't return home from work. A few days later, she receives a Polaroid of him; on the bottom of the photograph are the words I'll Come Back to Get You, on the back is written their six-year-old son's name - is he the ransom, or the kidnapper's next target?

Assistant Chief Detective Steve Willards heads up the task force assigned to the case, along with FBI Profiler Gail Skillman. They quickly learn that every person involved has a secret, and the truth is only as reliable as memory.

A week later, Penny Spencer's husband Graham, doesn't return from work and she receives a Polaroid of her husband - on the bottom of the photo is written, One, Two, Don't Be Blue, I'll Come Back to Get You; their son's name is written on the back.

Before Willards and Skillman can unravel the motivation of the twisted kidnapper, one person is murdered, a third adult is taken, and one of the children is abducted.

But, it isn't until an assault is made on the FBI profiler that the final pieces fall into place; but even then it may be too late for those who have read the words - I'll Come Back to Get You.

Mother Legs

A giant, telepathic spider befriends a small boy, seeing the world through his eyes, with murderous intent... When Blake Turner's addict mother disappears in rural Canada, he assumes she's simply relapsed. But, when his search for her uncovers evidence of a terrifying monster and the sinister conspiracy to hide its existence, he must decide just how far he is willing to go to protect his loved ones. With only a depressed park ranger and a local reporter to aid him, Blake delves deeper into the mystery to discover what the creature is, and why it wants to start a family.

Schlock! Horror!

An anthology of short stories based upon/inspired by and in loving homage to all of those great gorefest movies and books of the

1980's (not necessarily base in that era, although some do ride that wave of nostalgia!), the golden age when horror well and truly came kicking, screaming and spraying blood, gore & body parts out from the shadows... This exemplary 80's themed/inspired tales of terror has been adjudicated and compiled by one Mr Bret McCormick, himself a writer, producer and director of many a schlock classic, including *Bio-Tech Warrior*, *Time Tracers*, *The Abomination, Ozone: The Attack of the Redneck Mutants* and the inimitable *Repligator*.

Featuring stories from: Todd Sullivan, Timothy C Hobbs, Mark Thomas, Andrew Post, James B. Pepe, Thomas Vaughn, Edward Karpp, Jaap Boekestein, Lisa Alfano, L. C. Holt, John Adam Gosham, Brandon Cracraft, M. Earl Smith, Sarah Cannavo, James Gardner, Bret McCormick, and James H. Longmore.

An Unholy Trinity
3 TERRIFYING NOVELLAS, 3 SUPERLATIVE AUTHORS,
1 BIG, FAT, JUICY BOOK!

ENÛMA ELIŠ (When on High) – Terry Grimwood. The Babylonian Creation story is a tale of monsters and cataclysmic wars. An epic saga dominated by the gods Tiamat and Mardak, bitter rivals who battle for supremacy over the unformed universe. It is a story replete with Minotaurs and scorpion men, dragons and monstrous blood-sucking demons.
A myth, a fantasy...
But when a traumatized ex-soldier rescues a young woman, washed up and barely alive on the shore of a sleepy English seaside town, the fragile borders between myth and reality begin to crumble and gods and their legions wake from their long-slumber.

THE REMNANT - C. Bailey-Bacchus
When fifteen-year-old Bianca Baker is blinded by rage and hatred, her inner demons take control and turn an ordinary school trip into a horrific tragedy. Witnesses to her violent act, succumb to Bianca's aggression and agree to say events were a terrible accident. Sixteen years later, those involved find the past clawing its way from the shadows to haunt them, and this time there is no way it will stay buried.

ALICE IN HORRORLAND - Vanessa Hawkins
Alice is an 11 year old orphan living within the veins of industrial England. When she meets a mysterious gentleman with the power to turn into a white rabbit, she finds herself tumbling down a

manhole into Horrorland.
Here the creatures are strange and uncanny, lost in a revolution of madness. Drug addicted Caterpillars, grinning cats and homicidal Mad Hatters gambol around Alice like blood-drunk
mosquitoes. However, at the center of it all is the Queen of Hearts: said to have given up her own a long time ago…
Horrorland used to be so wonderful… Can Alice make it so again?

Lex H. Jones

**A HellBound Books LLC
Publication**

http://www.hellboundbookspublishing.com

Printed in the United States of America

354

9 781948 318600